TO BLUFF A BRIDE

BRIDGER BROTHERS
BOOK TWO

KATE CONDIE

Copyright © 2024 by Kate Condie

Cover design 2023 by Winter Designs

All rights reserved.

No part of this book may be reproduced in any form or by any electronic or mechanical means, including information storage and retrieval systems, without written permission from the author, except for the use of brief quotations in a book review.

CHAPTER 1

*T*itus burst through the front door and dropped a sack on the table. The table wobbled on uneven legs, a travesty in a carpenter's home. Ellen glanced at the bundle, swallowing her shock. She was supposed to have the house to herself during the day. Her one sanctuary from this marriage she'd gotten herself into. Yet here Titus was, stealing her hours, her solace.

"Pack what you need. We're going west." He pressed both hands onto the table, his tone calm, as if he'd just told her his folks expected them for dinner.

Ellen cocked her ear toward him, waiting for more information. Or, really, any information.

"I won at cards."

So, naturally, they were going west. Ellen curled her toes in her shoes, the only expression of frustration her husband couldn't see. Titus rarely won at cards, but he did so just often enough to get drunk and play again.

He flipped open the sack to reveal two pairs of boots. "I have a wagon, filled with supplies, and I've been told to pack an extra pair of shoes. It's a bit of a walk."

He snickered at his own joke and ambled down the hallway to their bedroom.

Ellen lifted a lady's boot from the table. It was used, but of fine quality. *West?* Her throat constricted. That had been her first husband's plan, and all it had gotten him was a bed six feet underground. She would be too glad to never travel by covered wagon again. But Titus was slamming drawers in the bedroom and, during their brief marriage, Ellen had yet to change his mind once it was made up.

It didn't matter what Ellen wanted. Her husband wanted to go west, so Ellen would be going too. Like the clothes Titus was pulling out of the drawers, she was just another item to be packed for the move.

"When do we leave?" Ellen tried to keep her voice light so it wouldn't betray her emotions, emotions she didn't even have a name for.

"Tomorrow."

Ellen's heart stuttered. "But the piece you're working on for the Andersons." The family of Ellen's closest friend had paid Titus for a wardrobe. It would be a gift to their eldest daughter upon her wedding day, which was fast approaching. Ellen had convinced them to allow Titus to do the work, rather than the more popular carpenter who had a store off Main Street. If Titus was ever going to get out of the business of coffins, he had to make a name for himself.

Titus laughed. "They can come take what they want once we're gone." He stopped rifling through his top drawer and leveled Ellen with a look. "You'll not go running your mouth to that friend of yours."

That friend was Demi Anderson. Titus knew her name; he just refused to acknowledge it. Heaven forbid Ellen had any comforts outside of Titus and his family.

"I have to tell her goodbye. Surely word has gotten out that you have a wagon and plan to move west."

"This town ain't gonna miss me." He turned to the trunk he was packing, pressing down the fabric contents with both hands. "You better put a few things in before this trunk is full. There ain't much room left in the wagon."

Ellen opened her mouth to ask if he truly intended to leave behind everything that didn't fit in that trunk when a knock sounded, followed by the front door opening. Titus' brother, Cyrus, entered. He pinned Ellen with his usual disconcerting gaze. "My brother around?"

"In here," Titus called. Cyrus came toward them, and Ellen pressed herself against the wall as he moved past. He didn't touch her. He never had. A contradiction to the way he looked at her with those inky eyes.

She'd never dared voice her discomfort with Cyrus. While Titus was set to making coffins, Cyrus, the eldest, had inherited the family wheelwright business. In a town like this, where folks gathered to jump off onto the Oregon Trail, wheels were snatched up like bread from an oven and devoured as quickly. Sometimes folks weren't even five days west before they needed a spare.

"Heard you were headed west."

"Care to join?" Titus' offer was like a spider on bare skin. She couldn't imagine sharing a wagon with Cyrus, sharing the ground beneath that same wagon night after night.

Cyrus chuckled in that usual way that caused Titus' cheek to twitch. "Now, why would *I* go west? Can't say I even understand *your* reason."

"I'm tired of making coffins."

Ellen's heart pinched at Titus' words. He was a hard man, but he rarely spoke of the hurt he had experienced when Cyrus had ejected him from the wheelwright shop. Their father hadn't objected, said the business was Cyrus' now and Cyrus could do as he pleased. Well, it pleased Cyrus to cut Titus out of the business the same week Ellen married him.

"So you'll set up shop and be a wheelwright somewhere west?"

"Seems a good enough plan."

Ellen made herself busy in the kitchen, pulling preserves from the shelves and setting them in a crate. She hoped Titus would at least allow food. It was far more important than clothing, for someone along the trail was bound to perish and the clothing of the dead could be tailored to fit any body. Food on the other hand...on the trail here, she'd seen people come to blows over a single cut of fresh venison.

"Pop ain't goin' to like it," Cyrus continued.

"It don't much matter what Pop wants. *You're* under his thumb, not me."

Ellen froze, not willing to make a peep in the kitchen. Even the gentle click of glass on wood felt too big just now.

"Under his thumb." Cyrus repeated Titus' words with a slow drawl. His voice was lower than usual and Ellen waited. This moment had been brewing since their marriage less than one year ago. Titus soothed his pain by feeling superior. There was no father to command Titus in *his* work. He was his own master, and boy if he didn't remind himself often, and vocally.

But right now, Titus said nothing. Ellen didn't even dare swallow the fear lodged in her throat. Both Titus and Cyrus were large men, much like their father. A brawl within the walls of this house would mean more than one broken item. Perhaps it didn't matter, seeing as how they would be leaving these worldly possessions behind.

Cyrus' voice came again, softer and condescending. "You should go. Make a life your wife can be proud of."

Ellen winced. Ever since she'd met him, Cyrus had used her as a pawn in the unspoken feud between the brothers. He strode down the hall and through the kitchen, stopping with his hand on the handle of the front door. Locked on Titus, his gaze was murderous, but when it drifted over to Ellen, it softened. He sighed and shook his head as though something had been lost forever. He pulled the door open and stepped through. It banged against the wall so hard that it closed itself.

Ellen let out a shuddering breath and pressed a honey-colored curl out of her face. She listened, but heard only silence down the hall. She preferred the sound of Titus' frantic packing. At least then he'd had heart.

Did this mean they were still going? She didn't know why not. If anything, this argument should be pushing Titus to go. His logic was sound. There was bound to be work for him on the trek. There were settlements along the Oregon Trail. They didn't have to go all the way to Oregon. They could set up anywhere, at an army post even.

Ellen went into the room to find Titus on the bed, his back slumped and a balled-up shirt in his hands.

She placed a featherlight hand on his shoulder. "It's a good idea to go west. Cyrus is just going to miss you."

Titus gave a hard laugh and stood. "He's going to miss me like a scorpion under his boot."

Titus wasn't inferior to Cyrus. It was merely birth order that saw Cyrus inherit the business when their father had a fall and couldn't manage it anymore.

Titus took Ellen's hand. "I still have you."

Ellen's heart warmed as Titus pulled her into his arms. His chest rumbled as he spoke. "He always wanted you. Now I'm taking you away, and he can't stand it."

Her heart sank. Titus' words hadn't been the declaration of fondness she'd always hoped for. They were continued anger at his brother. Perhaps if they went west, they could get out from Cyrus' shadow. Make a life without the weight of his family pressing him flat. Titus could be the man he'd been before they'd married. The sweet one who had courted her and won her affections and painted a future she'd wanted. Perhaps there was some of that far from this town. All they had to do was get away from Cyrus.

CHAPTER 2

Their third day on the trail, Benjamin rose before the sun. He and Pa had the wagons ready and were due to be at the front of the line. The company rotated this privilege, and even just two days in, he was thrilled at the prospect of breathing clear air. Folks were still moving quickly, their animals hale and healthy. Over the next few months, folks would slow down. Their stock would tire, the meat on their bones growing wiry.

The group had gained a few new wagons just before they'd left. He'd even heard that one wagon had been traded for a game of cards. He shook his head at the fool who would trade his future for a pair of queens. It was possible the new folks were even more foolish. Who would brave the journey west with only a day's notice?

By late afternoon, they stopped at their first river crossing. As the first in the line, Ben's family was crossed and settled before the majority of the wagons had even touched the water. Ben and his brother, Sam, returned to the river on their horses, assisting with the crossing. Most of the women were wading across with the aid of a rope strung between two trees on either side of the river, but the children were small enough to climb up and share his saddle.

Women and children. Ben shook his head. No woman should be crossing these plains without a man at her side and a band on her finger. This trail was still too dangerous. Ma would disagree. Since none of her boys were married, her only hope for grandchildren was unmarried females. Everyone knew women were scarce the further west they went. Ma had even tried to convince Pa to wait until her boys were all married. Pa had quashed that dream, using Ben as an example. "If Ben ain't found a wife by now, he ain't going to find one."

Ben had bristled. It wasn't for lack of trying. He'd had a sweetheart back home, Jane Connor, whom he'd known since they were young. And yet, when he'd proposed, she'd rejected him. Who could blame her? What woman wanted to toil her way across the plains of the west with a family of rowdy sons, only to arrive on bare land with no roof over her head?

He'd been a fool to ask, and she far wiser for refusing him.

But the west was full of possibilities. Free land and plenty of it. They would have to work for it, but once they carved out their part, they could live in peace. Ben could build himself a place where he wouldn't share walls with all his brothers. He would find himself a wife eventually, once he had time for such things as courting and perhaps an extra dose of patience for small talk. His lip curled at the thought. Perhaps he would simply hire a maid and not bother with courtship at all.

The last wagon dipped its wheels in the water. The occupants, a man and a woman, sat closely on the spring seat. From the contrast in their looks, he guessed they were husband and wife, not brother and sister. Her honey curls framed eyes wide with fear while his dark brows dipped into a scowl.

Ben urged his mount closer and spoke to the gentleman. "She shouldn't be there. You're going to need all the room you can get while you lead this team across." The man's fists were clenched around the reins and his elbows flew as he tried his best to control the panicking oxen. He wasn't practiced leading this team and Ben's heart thumped once in fear.

"They said no stopping." His lips were pale as he focused on the water in front of him.

Not only was his companion on the seat, but she was on the wrong side of the rig. If she fell out, the current would crush her against the wagon or she would be swept underneath. This man had ignored the trail guide's instructions. Anger flared in Ben's belly.

Ben rode his horse in front of the team, forcing them to a stop. The man finally looked up with a scowl.

Ben spoke slowly. "Your wife shouldn't be on the seat."

The man glanced at his companion and, with a jerk of his head, told her to get off. Ben blew a hot breath through his nose. The rope strung across the water to be used by those crossing on foot was downstream, on the other side of the wagon.

Her eyes were still wide as tea saucers, and she glanced between her husband and the raging river. Was she meant to swim to the rope?

"Sir." Ben spoke through clenched teeth. "May I escort her to the other side on my mount?"

The man merely grumbled.

Ben drew his mount closer and reached a gloved hand out. She took it and he hauled her from the wagon, seating her in front of him. Her skirts billowed around them, the bottom hem darkening as it sucked water from below. He imagined the fabric wet and as heavy as a boulder. Had she tried to swim without the assistance of the rope, she would have gone right to the bottom. She should remove her petticoats next time, leave all that fabric in the wagon. Or better yet, leave the frills in Independence. Lace had no place out west.

Without another look, her husband snapped the reins. The oxen started again and he continued slapping the reins, urging them faster. A bit too fast, but better too fast than too slow.

As the wagon bounced past them, he saw one trunk unsecured, as though it had been placed there while they had waited for their turn to cross. It bounced once, twice, and out of the wagon, then bobbed on the surface of the water. The woman reached out, but Ben kept hold of her waist.

"It's gone." He watched it float, contradicting his claim, but there was no saving it. Even now it was filling with water and would soon be too heavy to haul up. By the time they reached it, there would be nothing to do but kick it downstream.

He led his horse past the trunk and up the bank on the other side. He stopped his horse and she slid down, her boots hitting the ground with a muted thud. She turned her pretty eyes on him and pressed those unruly curls from her face. He expected a scolding for not allowing her to fetch her trunk.

Instead, she dipped her head. "Thank you."

"You're welcome." He watched her make her way toward the circle of wagons and her husband.

Ben shook his arms, sore from the back and forth of helping folks cross all day, but she'd been the last. He could find his family now. A hot meal would be waiting.

His brother Sam rode near, his dog Boomer keeping close to the horse's feet. "Careless." He spat at her retreating wagon.

Ben nodded. His and Sam's horses moved faster than the

wagons, and as they made their way to camp, they passed the couple's wagon. The wife spoke to her husband in a soft voice, like the one their mother used when he and his brothers were young boys and had harmed themselves with their own reckless behavior. "At least it wasn't the one with our food."

He shook his head. A woman comforting a grown man. Those folks had no business going west.

CHAPTER 3

Four days on the trail and Ellen could still recall the cries of the woman whose husband had lost their wagon to Titus in a game of cards. Ellen had squeezed her eyes tight, willing her tears back inside. It wasn't her place to weep when she wasn't the one losing everything, no matter how her eyelids burned.

Only fourteen months ago, her first husband had dragged her west. They'd only made it to Missouri before he'd died. Now another husband was intent on taking her farther west. The idea that she was going again still made her so angry she wanted to spit. Titus' countenance had grown more sour with each passing day. The river crossing yesterday had been humiliating. Worse, they'd lost their trunk of clothes. So, in addition to feeding and watering the stock, gathering wood to make a fire and prepare dinner, Ellen also needed to figure a way to launder their clothes while they wore them.

How could she complain at the loss of one trunk when she and Titus had essentially taken an entire wagon from that poor family?

In a way, she too was at the mercy of her husband. If

Cyrus hadn't claimed ownership of Titus' home and everything inside, Ellen might have offered it to the family. As it was, that family had been left with nothing. Ellen had yet to fall asleep without thinking of the woman's face.

On her darkest nights, she'd wondered what Titus had wagered to win the wagon. Perhaps the house, the one thing Titus had gotten from his parents—save the rifle his pa gave Titus the day they set off on the trail. Or had Titus risked losing something else? She didn't dare ask for fear the answer would crush her very soul.

As the day wore on, thick clouds rolled in and a strong wind kicked dirt and debris into her eyes. After some time, the wagons slowed, and when they stopped altogether, Ellen risked a glance toward the front. Their trail guide was speaking to folks as he rode his horse along the line. He gestured to the sky on the other side of the wagons and Ellen followed the point of his finger.

The clouds that had been sitting low all day were moving, shrinking toward the center like water down a drain. A funnel cloud weaved and danced its way from the gray sky, down to touch the earth.

Fear froze her limbs, but others must have seen it too, because shouts and screams erupted all around her. The cries swirled in the wind, making it impossible to tell where they originated.

A strong wind buffeted Ellen and she stumbled several steps sideways. The wagon in front of them rocked as Ellen stared at it in wonder. She looked at her own wagon, firmly on the ground, but still she stepped away, unwilling to allow herself to be crushed if the wind blew their way. As though encouraging her to give their wagon ample space, another gust pelted Ellen's face with sand and rocks. She cursed and wiped her watering eyes.

She put her back to the wind and saw Titus speaking with

the trail master. Titus returned and promptly unhitched the oxen from the wagon. Ellen helped, the howling wind making it impossible for Titus to give her any instructions, even if he had a mind to. The usually calm animals pranced on hooves that were no doubt unused to such lightness or such fear.

Their neighbors had all crawled under their wagons and were covering their heads. Ellen eyed her wagon with wariness, still unconvinced it would provide shelter and not death. As she contemplated the safest place, she caught sight of Titus rounding the corner of the wagon. The wind hummed in her ears as she followed him and climbed up next to him on the tailgate.

"Titus!" she screamed. Though she was directly to his right, she wasn't sure if he could hear her over the howling wind that tore her hair from its pins.

He passed her the small trunk that held their savings. She took it and climbed back down, backing away from the wagon. Titus was still rooting in their supplies.

The glint of metal shone in his hands and Ellen knew what it was. Titus may not have gotten the wheelwright business, but he'd gotten his father's prize rifle.

Titus tugged at the barrel, the muzzle pointed right at his middle, but the day's shifting must have trapped the gun. Ellen cast around, watching wagons tilt, sure theirs was going to tip with Titus still inside. She reached up and touched his leg. "Titus!" she called, but he shook her off.

She turned, lifting the small trunk from the ground. Her skirt tangled in her legs and she fell to the earth. The trunk hit the ground at an angle and the clasp broke. The force of the collision caused the lid to bounce open, and all the paper money inside twisted up and out of reach.

Still flat on her stomach, Ellen righted the lid with a snap and shifted, searching for Titus. A crack split the air and

Titus was blown backward, off the wagon, landing on his back on the grass beside Ellen. Before she could move toward him, a dark spot appeared on his chest, spreading outward. Ellen blinked in confusion, watching it grow, clutching their meager savings, unable to do more than flatten herself against the earth and pray the twister didn't have a mind to force her into its mayhem.

As she prayed, she didn't even have the capacity to consider the fact that she'd just become a widow. Again.

The storm had been quick, taking less time than it took to brush down a horse. Yet the destruction it left behind was staggering. Ben stumbled to his feet. His folks' wagon was gone. He spun and found it lying on its side, its contents pouring out. Ma was going to be furious to have lost a sack of flour.

But Ma wasn't there clicking her tongue. She wasn't anywhere. He walked around the overturned wagon and found Pa, flat on his back, his head bare and his hat nowhere in sight.

Ben ran to him and skidded to a stop. Blood painted the earth below Pa. Ben watched Pa's chest, waiting for the familiar rise and fall, but it wasn't there.

"Ben!" Someone shouted his name, and the call was followed by a deep bark. Sam.

Sam appeared at Ben's side, falling to his knees and laying an ear against Pa's chest, coming up with hollow eyes. Ben touched his shoulder, unable to offer anything more when his insides felt like they'd been scooped out.

"Have you seen Ma?" Ben asked. Boomer took off running, and Sam rose to watch where the dog went. On a ridge in the distance, Ben caught sight of his brother Will along with his companion, Fenna. Ben put his fingers to his mouth, gave a sharp whistle, and waved his arm. Fenna saw and tugged Will's shirt, pointing toward Ben. They started running. Ben sighed. Help was coming. Except, doctor or not, there was nothing Will could do for Pa.

Behind him, Sam cried, "Mama!" and jogged over to another form lying on the ground.

He joined Sam at Mama's side. She was alive, but blood leaked from the corner of her mouth.

"Mama, you're hurt." Her head was in Sam's lap, but Ben wanted to lift her from the ground, to take her somewhere safe, to get her help.

"Will!" Sam called.

Ben turned to see not Will, but his three other brothers running over. If they were running, that meant they weren't injured, yet that truth merely registered like a check on a paper list. He didn't have the heart to rejoice in what they had, not when they'd lost so much.

"Will!" Ben called again, unsure if his voice would carry.

Mama took Ben's hand, and he turned his attention to her. "Your father?"

Ben's throat was too tight to reply. He only shook his head.

She closed her eyes and seemed to sink deeper into the earth. Then she opened them again. "Are all my boys well?"

Ben nodded, unable to take his eyes from the blood that pooled in a wrinkle, the one she'd earned after so many years of smiling.

She nodded and closed her eyes again. The twins, Nate and Alex, still knelt by Pa's body, but Will and Fenna were headed this way.

Ma looked up, tears in her eyes. "I want to talk to my boys."

Her boys. Folks were always sighing over her having six

sons, grieving that she'd never had any daughters. Ma always set them straight. He had never felt regret from her. And now she had something to say.

Ben tried to look at only her eyes, but the blood registered out of focus, striking in its bold color. "They'll come." Not only was her face contorted in pain, but it was as white as her wagon's canvas bonnet.

Will arrived and Ben stood, making room for him at her head. Will pulled a hanky from his pocket, wiped the blood from Ma's mouth, then tucked the cloth into her hand. Ben should have done that, but his mind seemed to be bouncing everywhere all at once.

A whimper came from behind and Ben whirled to find Fenna, shoulders slumped inward, her face in her hands. He strode over and slung an arm around Fenna's shoulders, but he didn't have anything else to give her.

Just then his cousin appeared and took over, leading Fenna away with whispered words. The kind that were shared between women and spoke of sorrow as well as strength, words that Ben didn't have.

The twins rose from Pa's side, their postures matching even if their faces never had. With slumped shoulders, they made their way over and knelt next to Mama.

She gave them all a wan smile, five of her six boys all crowded near her. Ben straightened, using his height to look over the prairie. Though he'd been with the twins just a moment ago, his youngest brother, Chet, was nowhere in sight.

"You boys go back home."

Ben turned back to his ma. *Back?* There was nothing to go back to. They'd sold everything to buy four wagons and enough supplies to fill them.

"Ma," Ben started, but her fingers gripped his wrist with such force that he stopped.

"Your pa filled your head with notions. But he's gone now. Don't go for his benefit."

"There's nothing to go back to."

She winced, perhaps at the pain, perhaps at the truth, then looked around at each face. "Decide together. Do you want to keep going?"

Sam met Ben's eyes. Sam had wanted to go every bit as much as their pa did. Ben looked at Nate and Alex. They nodded. Will was busy, his fingers prodding Mama's extremities. He'd never had to come. He was the one brother who might have made something of himself back home.

Ben pressed Ma's palm. "We want to keep going."

Ma's lip quivered and she nodded, ever the bravest soldier of them all. "You'll do well if you stick together. Will you grant your mother one last wish?"

Last wish? Ben's body revolted, begging him to run away. She winced as Will touched her side, so he forced himself to stay, to nod at her request.

It was Sam who spoke. "Anything." His voice cracked, something Ben hadn't heard since Sam became a man.

Ma smiled at Sam. "You can't go west without a woman." She coughed again into Will's hanky. "You'll turn into ruffians and I'll not have it." Her voice held a note of authority, one practiced over years of keeping six rambunctious boys in line.

Her lively eyes flashed to Ben. The oldest. "You find yourself a wife." She scanned all her sons. "You should all find wives." Back to Ben. "But you're in charge now. Promise me."

Ben nodded, unable to deny her this wish, not with blood on her lips.

She lay her head down, the muscles in her neck relaxed. "Whoever you marry will be the matriarch of the family. Choose well, my son." She patted his hand, then moved her attention to Nate.

Ben pulled Will to the side. "Is there anything to be done?"

Chet appeared around the side of the wagon, his face grim and determined. He knelt by Ma as Ben focused again on Will's answer.

Will shook his head, his tears spilling in earnest now. "She's punctured a lung."

Ben embraced his brother, tight, like Will could hold him to this cruel earth. When he looked back at his mother, she was patting Chet's hands. Chet was barely eighteen and his father was gone, his mother on her way. Ben almost wished he'd heard her words to the rest of them, wished someone were there with a pencil in hand, ready to write them down. Her last words to her children. Her sons.

He scanned the prairie once more, this time looking at nothing in particular. Merely taking in the wreckage. Theirs wasn't the only family gathered around a loved one. Alive or dead, there were many whose lives would never be the same.

CHAPTER 4

*E*llen sat at her husband's side, staring out at the long grass. It barely moved now. The wind was gone, had donned the mask of a repentant child who knows they've misbehaved. The new calm felt wrong when the prairie was peppered with destruction. Her wagon hadn't tipped, but others had, and their things were scattered like chicken feed in the dirt.

Titus lay there, a victim of his own pride. Perhaps it was his pain and the need to fill the void of a parent's love. The wind hadn't carried him away, making it clear that the way Ellen had held on to the ground had offered only the appearance of control. If the wind had had a mind to take her away, it would have done so no matter her grip.

"Can we help you bury him, ma'am?"

Ellen glanced up. It was a pair of men, one of them the man who had helped her cross the river. He was easily distinguishable, even without his horse, in his same faded red shirt that looked like a dusty old brick. His hat was set low on his brow and his mouth turned down in a frown. Only, this time, she guessed it wasn't disapproval that soured his expression.

"Did you lose anyone?" she asked.

The man who'd given her a ride pursed his lips. The other one nodded. "We've buried our own. Some haven't even a spade to dig, not anymore."

Ellen glanced at her wagon, some twenty yards away from where Titus had been deposited. "I might have one." She pressed her hands into the ground, feeling the clumps of grass beneath her palms. Low and strong, holding tight to the earth. She wanted to do the same. To go home and find a bit of earth and cling to it, never wanting for anything more. Except she had no home to return to. No husband to buy a patch of earth.

The man in the red shirt reached out to help her up. There was dirt in every crease of his knuckles, and it looked like the hand of an elderly man. She looked at his face—young. Burying the dead had weathered his hands. She hoped it hadn't weathered his heart.

"What's your name?" He was one of the familiar faces in the company, and this would be the second time she'd accepted his assistance. She ought to know his name.

"I'm Ben. This is my brother, Alex."

Alex tipped his chin. He didn't wear a hat, and though his straw-colored hair didn't match Ben's dark coloring, she could see the resemblance in their nose and strong jaw.

She slipped her fingers into his, warm and strong, and for a moment she wished she could lose herself in that hand, curl up in his calloused palm and stay where it was safe. "I'm Ellen."

She shook her skirts, but what was the point? Surely her every crease was lined in grime just as the man's hands were covered. Instead, she gestured to the wagon.

Alex gave her a grim smile. "Pleased to meet you, ma'am."

He put a foot on the step and hauled himself into her wagon. "Where would your spade be?"

She hadn't used the spade yet, was still discovering just what was inside the wagon they were driving.

She shrugged. "It ain't our wagon."

He stopped and looked back at Ellen. "I mean, we were driving it, but someone else packed it." The man glanced down her frame, no doubt expecting a woman a sight fancier than her to have afforded going west without dealing with any of the trouble of packing. Then, as though it didn't truly matter, he turned and began rifling through the wagon.

She turned to Ben. "Will we head back to Independence?"

He stared east, his chest rising and falling with a deep breath. "I suppose most will want to do so. We may as well and allow those who are continuing west with us to resupply."

East. Back. Ellen wouldn't be safe no matter where she went. Titus may have burned her best bridge. She'd been embarrassed enough to leave town, knowing her husband had swindled Demi Anderson's family. But to return and beg their assistance? It would be humiliating. Not to mention Demi's father was not the type to stand up to Cyrus. They would offer little to no protection, even if they were willing.

They might even have seen Ellen's persuasion to allow Titus the wardrobe job as part of a plot to swindle them. Who would believe she had no knowledge of going west? Folks prepared for months to go west. Nobody went with only a day to spare. Nobody went without saying goodbye to those they loved.

"What about you men? East or west?"

"West. There's nothing for us anywhere else."

Me neither, Ellen thought.

Ben walked back to Titus, spade in hand. He paused and

turned back to Ellen, his eyes flicking down to her boots and back to her face. "This man has been shot."

Ellen nodded solemnly. "He tried pulling the rifle out of the wagon." She shook her head, the memory as faint as a dream. It should be burned into her mind, but instead she remembered more the wind and how it had nearly lifted her off her belly.

"He shot himself?"

"Not on purpose. The gun was caught."

Ben shook his head and drew a deep breath, his shoulders rising and falling, before he hefted his spade and jammed it into the earth. She watched him turn scoops of earth, revealing darker dirt underneath.

The other brother appeared out of her wagon with a shovel in hand. "Mind if we borrow this? I'll be sure it gets returned."

Ellen shrugged. "Take all you want. It's staying here. I can't drive a team. Even if I could, I've no livestock to pull it." The animals had fled during the storm. She'd be walking back to Independence with only the gear she could carry. At least they weren't farther on the trail.

The man glanced between her and the wagon. "We can help you drive it, supposing we can find your animals."

"Alex." Ben's voice came as a warning.

Alex leaned around Ellen to look at his brother and shrugged. "There's no use leaving it all here. Sam's bound to find enough animals to bring the remaining wagons back." He focused on Ellen once more. "Any distinguishing marks?"

Ellen didn't know the oxen. They'd come with the wagon. "Brown." She'd closed her eyes, remembering. She'd ridden or walked behind those beasts for four days. "One has a white boot on just one foot. Another has a black streak in its tail."

"When Sam returns, I'll bring them over and let you have a look."

Ellen nodded. "Thank you."

Alex set off with a spade over each shoulder. She didn't much care if he returned it. She should gift it to these brothers for their service.

Ben stopped and faced Ellen. "D'you have a sheet to bury him in?"

Ellen nodded and retrieved one from the wagon, along with a needle and thread.

Ben lifted Titus onto the sheet. Titus still wore a leather pouch on his belt. It would have coins and his compass. Ellen recalled how their money had flown away—only the coins were left. Precious money she ought to keep close. She knelt at his side and unbuckled his belt, tugging it free. The pouch and his knife stayed on the belt and she set it all in a pile next to her. She would have to give the belt another hole, one that would allow it to be fitted small enough for her waist. She folded the sheet around him and set to work sewing the ends shut.

Ben had dug a hole that was barely deep enough to cover the top of his boots, but it was long enough to fit Titus. He slid Titus into the hole and stood, looking at Ellen. He gestured to the hole now occupied by Titus. "Anything you want to say?"

She straightened and shook her head. Then she looked out over the disaster. "Is there anything I can do to help?" It was incredible how unaffected the land was. Sure, around them were tipped wagons and debris. But, beyond the wreckage, there was peace. A yellow aster even winked at her.

Ben's voice was hoarse. "There's always something to do if you're willing to look."

Ellen watched him shift the dirt on top of Titus, the pits

of his shirt dark from sweat. There was a slick down the center of his back too. She pulled a skin of water from the wagon and handed it to him.

He stopped working, sniffing and wiping his forehead. He took a long drink from the skin, his neck moving with each swallow. A man like that had little to fear. He could point his wagon in any direction and carve out a life for himself.

"What do I do?" The words slipped out. They were quiet, but he must have heard her, for he stopped and pinned her with a pair of dark eyes.

"Go back to whatever you left."

A home that Cyrus had commandeered. A friend who surely felt betrayed and might refuse to look upon Ellen's face. Just as the last time she'd been widowed, she didn't have the funds to take a train all the way home. Even if she could, they wouldn't want another mouth to feed.

"There's nothing left."

Ben handed the water skin back to Ellen. Along with the skin, he gave her an appraising look. "Find another husband."

Ellen narrowed her eyes. As if finding a decent husband was as easy as snapping one's fingers. Titus hadn't exactly been her idea of decent, but far worse men existed. An image of Cyrus popped into her mind and her insides writhed.

Ben went back to work and Ellen went in the opposite direction to do the same. Going from wagon to wagon, she offered help. Sometimes that meant sitting for a bit with the children while a mother sat alone in tears. Other times, she returned to her wagon and pulled apples from the barrel, offering it to those who had lost everything except the clothes they wore.

Night had fallen when Alex returned with her spade. He was dirtier than before and she smiled at the way his bright teeth showed through his dirt-streaked face.

"You have a minute to come see the livestock Sam found?"

Ellen nodded. She'd been contemplating whether to sleep on the ground without a husband to protect her or tuck herself away in her wagon. She'd like to have thought today had been traumatic enough for everyone, but evil never rested. Just as there were good people in this band, there were sure to be bad ones too.

She followed Alex as he weaved through a few wagons until he stopped. There was a small fire and the smell of burnt biscuits. The young man tending the fire stood and tipped his hat at Ellen. "Good evening, ma'am."

She smiled. "Good evening." She looked at the pot to see a few blackened biscuits. "Have you already burned all the dough, or shall I help you cook another batch?"

He smiled, a sad, crooked thing lifting one cheek. "I'd be mighty obliged for a bit of help."

Ellen glanced at Alex, who nodded. She drew nearer to the boy, a man really, maybe only a year or two younger than her, and found the burned biscuits were good and stuck to the pot. "Were you hoping to save these, or can we toss 'em for the birds?"

"To the birds is fine with me." He scratched at the back of his head, then pulled the brim of his hat lower.

Ellen nodded and pushed her sleeves past her elbows. "A bit of water…?"

"Chet," he finished for her.

"Chet." She gave the young man a small smile. "If you please."

Once she had a few biscuits above some coals instead of flames, she stood and brushed flour off her hands. Or maybe it was dust. She'd be hard pressed to tell the difference in the dark. "D'you think Alex is still around to show me the animals?"

"I'll take you," came a voice, deeper than Chet's. Ben's tall form appeared around the wagon. He was as filthy as Alex, but without the contrasting smile. He was a guard, and she was an intruder to his camp.

She gave him a silent nod and fell into step at his side. "Just you four brothers?"

Ben's strides were long, and Ellen found herself nearly jogging to keep up. "Six. One is a doctor. He's out tending to the wounded. And we have two women."

Ellen perked up at that. "A doctor? There was a young girl I saw to earlier today. Her ankle was swollen."

Ben held up a hand. "He's the only doctor in the company. He'll do what he can for whoever he can."

Ellen swallowed her joy. Of course, he was doing his best. He was only one man and there had to be over one hundred folks in their group. "I'm sure those he's seen to have been mighty glad to have him here."

Ben didn't answer, but she hadn't really asked a question. Soon they reached a wagon with several horses and oxen tethered to it. Another brother looked up at Ben's approach. He resembled Ben very much, except his face was narrower and he didn't have a scowl line between his brows.

Ben said, "This lady wants to see if you've got one of hers."

The brother glanced over the horses, mules, and oxen. "Take a look, ma'am."

Ellen smiled at him. "Thank you for rounding these up." She glanced at Ben. "You boys sure are kind to help out."

The new brother laughed. "Ben doesn't help to be kind. It's just that nobody can do anything as well as him."

Ben grunted and headed off, back to the fire. Ellen remembered the biscuits and hoped Chet was watching them before they burned. She turned to the man. "I'm good with faces, but I'd like a name to go with it."

He smiled. "I'm Sam. That there is Ben, he's the oldest. Chet is the terrible cook. Thing is, he's better'n the rest of us, with Fenna and Molly off helping Will with the injured. Alex is somewhere, and Nate is setting up camp."

Ellen's mind spun at the tally of names. If she were part of a family like this one, she would have nothing to fear at losing her husband. She turned and saw a socked oxen and stared at it. How could she be sure? There were probably plenty of animals with one sock.

Sam came to stand beside her. "That one yours?"

Ellen pursed her lips. "I can't be sure."

"You better take him, else he might not be here come sunrise. I'm going to look for more in the morning, but folks will be getting desperate soon enough. After a trial like this, folks tend to be a bit closer to God. But give 'em a night to think on it and they'll remember their faults right quick."

Sam unwrapped the animal's harness from the wagon and held it out for Ellen. She took it with a gulp, never being much the one to handle the beasts. It had always been Titus, and even he hadn't been too keen on it.

Sam watched her with a critical eye. "You need a bit of help getting him back to your wagon?"

"I'll be fine," Ellen lied. These boys were doing enough for everyone, had done enough for her already.

She led the ox past their fire, stopping only to tell Chet to remove the biscuits. He was leaning against their wagon, his eyes closed.

"How are they doing?"

He jumped at her words and used the iron hook to remove the pot. When he opened the lid, Ellen could smell the freshly baked biscuits. Her stomach rumbled as she weaved through the wagons.

Every face she passed was solemn. She didn't know a single family who hadn't been affected. Whether they'd lost something as replaceable as the bonnet for their wagon, or much more, nobody smiled tonight.

She shouldn't smile either. She'd lost her husband, had helped bury him, yet instead of hollow, she felt light. Like she'd just set down a basket of wet laundry and was stretching her back at the eased burden. She frowned. Two husbands gone, but this time she hadn't even felt shock or grief. Just disappointment that this was her life.

When she reached her wagon, Alex was there, harnessing an ox to her wagon. This one was black.

"Alex," she said, "that one's not mine."

He spun to face her. "I know. It's one of ours. I was just going to bring your wagon closer. It's not right for a woman to be alone at night."

Ellen watched him, trying to note any hint of ill intentions. "You boys have done plenty. You can't save all the widows."

He gave a thoughtful chuckle. "I don't mind tryin'."

He harnessed her ox and led both beasts and her wagon in a wide arc around the camp. Eventually they stopped her wagon near enough to Chet's small fire. The coals were dying down and Chet was nowhere in sight.

Alex unharnessed the oxen and fettered their ankles so they could graze but not wander too far. Ellen climbed into the back of her wagon, doing her best to shift everything to make room for a bed. Near these brothers was safer, but safety was a loose term this far from civilization. Without a husband, she would never be safe again.

CHAPTER 5

When they reached the outskirts of Independence, many wagons continued straight into town, while a few circled up like this was any other camp. Ellen stalled as long as she could, but soon Ben looked up at her. "You go on ahead. I'll bring your wagon by tomorrow when we've unloaded our supplies."

Ellen glanced at the one barrel he'd already removed. Where were they going to put the things they'd stored with her? Were they going to buy another wagon before they started west again?

Ben rose, wiping his hands with a rag. "Go on. I'm sure you're anxious to see your family." He nodded toward the town. Ben's voice was calm, and Ellen wanted to grab hold of it and squeeze the courage out so she could drink it down.

Part of her wished to lay the truth before him, but he couldn't help her, and she'd seen how he took on everyone's burdens. She wasn't cruel enough to lay another one on him.

Even now, at her hesitation, he narrowed his eyes and stepped closer.

Ellen cleared her throat and nodded, mustering the

courage to face her fate. "I'm next door to the wheelwright shop."

Ben nodded. He knew. Everyone knew. A few folks from the company had come to offer condolences, and more than one had mentioned they'd see her in town when they resupplied. Cyrus ran the largest wheelwright in Independence. No small feat, and with that accomplishment came an automatic power within the town. Folks admired his success, and those who didn't feared him. Both of those things boiled down to something that resembled respect and loyalty.

She turned and, with a lonely ache, she walked away from this family that had done so much for her these past few days. They'd not only brought her back; they'd filled her heart with a camaraderie she'd never known.

They would do well in Oregon, each of them looking out for the other. She frowned. Why hadn't she and her siblings been that way? Why hadn't they cared more for each other and less about their individual survival? She might never have come this far west if she'd been less selfish, less willing to leave them behind.

The buildings in Independence grew larger as she drew near. Each dry step twisted Ellen's stomach with anxiety. As she entered the town, buildings enclosed her on either side. Compared to the open prairie they'd come from, the tall storefronts leaned in like the bars of a jail cell.

Over the last few days, she'd recklessly lived in the moment, pushing off thinking about what it would be like to return to the Moren family as a widow. Telling them about their son wouldn't even be the most difficult part. Living with them would.

As she ventured further in, it was obvious the twister had touched here too. Some of the buildings were torn to shreds while others stood unharmed, as though not even the wind had touched the flaking paint.

She lifted onto her toes and stretched her neck, trying to see past the buildings to which ones had been destroyed. She'd never expected the same storm would hit the town. Somehow, it comforted her to know their wagon party wasn't the only ones the good Lord had targeted. She had heard so many claims these last few days about their journey being cursed, she'd started to believe it for herself.

The bakery was gone, as was part of a saloon. Further down, the bank had been destroyed too. Were the families dead as well? She'd only been in town a little over a year, but it hurt her heart to think of them all gone.

When she rounded the corner onto her street, her eyes searched first for Demi Anderson's house. It stood hale and hearty. Next, she looked for her own. It too stood, as did Cyrus' shop next door. The sight of her own home brought no comfort; only frustration that her vacant house remained. It could have been destroyed and nobody would have missed it.

She passed the shop and was almost to her own door when a noise came from behind, followed by Cyrus' voice.

"Ellen," he breathed.

She flinched, her shoulders lifting to her ears. With a gulp, she turned to face the first of Titus' family.

His eyes were wild, scanning the space around her as though his brother would appear at any moment. They returned to her with expectation. "Titus?"

Ellen shook her head, dropping her gaze to Cyrus' boots.

She risked a glance up. Cyrus ran a hand over his face, his expression so broken she could forget for a moment all the bad blood that lay between him and his brother. "I should have let him stay at the shop. He didn't have to go west to find a life. He had one here."

If he had been anyone else, Ellen would have reached out to him in comfort, but Cyrus still unnerved her. If anything, her recent change in circumstances meant she must tread even lighter.

"Your folks?"

Cyrus' eyes were red and the stillness there told her they'd been red before she arrived. "Gone. The twister broke their house over their heads."

Ellen's breaths grew short. She was ashamed at how little she cared for this man in front of her, who had lost everyone he loved. All she could think was that they were supposed to care for her. Now all she had was Cyrus.

He must have come to the same conclusion because he stepped forward, too close. Ellen stepped back, meeting his eyes. "I'm sorry about your folks."

He gave a grim nod. His eyes darted around her again, this time without hope of seeing anyone in his family. "Did you lose everything?"

Ellen looked at her empty hands. "No. A family helped me drive the wagon back. They're going to drop it by once they've removed their own supplies from the bed."

"Ellen!" A cry came from behind.

Ellen spun to see Demi racing down her porch steps, and in a heartbeat she was in her friend's arms.

Ellen clung to Demi, her rose oil scent so comforting Ellen's eyes filled with tears.

"I'm so glad you're alive," Demi spoke into Ellen's hair.

Ellen nodded. "I was glad to see your house standing. Is everyone well?"

Demi released Ellen and nodded. Then Demi glanced behind Ellen, her face falling. "Did he tell you about Mr. and Mrs. Moren? I'm so sorry." She caught Ellen's hands and pressed them. "Is Titus inside?"

Ellen shook her head. "Titus is dead."

Demi's mouth fell open. She blinked away her shock and said, "Oh, Ellen."

She pulled Ellen in again, but there was no desperation left. Now that she knew Demi and hers were well, Ellen itched to get out of Cyrus' sight. The heat of his gaze still seared her back, and she doubted it would go away until she was on the other side of a heavy door.

Demi stepped back, her hands patting Ellen's arms and shoulders. "You're filthy." She wrapped an arm around her shoulders and led her back toward her house. "Let's get you some hot food and a bath. Mother will be so pleased to see you."

Ellen cast a quick glance at Cyrus, who remained glued to the spot where she'd gutted him with news of his brother. Sadness had done nothing to dim his foreboding presence.

Ellen spent the rest of the day being spoiled by the Anderson family. Demi's father owned several buildings in town, and though they lived on the same street as Ellen, they lived a different life. One with plenty of food and a huge brass tub where Ellen soaked all the way to her ears. Once she was clean, she slipped into in a simple chambray dress from Demi's closet. Just as the smells of dinner were filling the house, there was a knock at the door.

Demi and Ellen paused their conversation to listen to who would be on the other side. Someone opened the door. "Hello, Mr. Moren," came Mrs. Anderson's voice.

"Is Ellen here?"

"Why, yes. Won't you come in?"

Ellen gulped and rose to standing just as Cyrus entered the sitting room. He removed his hat. "It be supper time, Ellen. I thought you should come home."

"Oh, Cyrus. She is welcome here for the meal. As are you."

"No, thank you, ma'am." Cyrus had eyes only for Ellen.

She nodded to her friend, whose expression was unreadable. Ellen walked to Mrs. Anderson. "Thank you so much for your hospitality today." She glanced at Demi. "I'll return the dress tomorrow."

"Nonsense." Demi rose. "Mother, she lost everything on the trail."

Mrs. Anderson's face softened. "Oh, darling. You keep it. I'm sure we can find you a few other items."

Ellen shook her head. "No need. I can sort it out." Untrue. She had nothing to her name save the wagon she'd inherited. The image of that family watching her and Titus driving away with everything flashed into her mind again. "That family. The one whose wagon I have?"

Demi shook her head. "I haven't seen them."

Cyrus' voice was hard. "They left, back to wherever they came from."

"Oh." With that mention, Ellen couldn't help but think of the other things Titus had stolen, his craftsmanship of the wardrobe for Demi's sister. She straightened her back and faced Mrs. Anderson. "I'm so sorry Titus never finished the wardrobe for Petra."

Mrs. Anderson waved her hand in the air. "Oh, my dear, it's of no matter. I—"

"Ellen," Cyrus said, her name a warning.

Ellen's cheeks warmed at Cyrus' brusque interruption. "Well, I must be off. Thank you again." She glanced at both women as she made her exit. Her heart hammered at the prospect of leaving with Cyrus, but Mr. Anderson had never been the type to stand up to anyone, Cyrus least of all.

She followed Cyrus across the street and down a few doors to her house. He pressed inside and Ellen followed him.

Her brows drew together as she looked around. Dirty dishes littered the counters and a stained shirt was draped over a kitchen chair. "Have you rented the space?"

Cyrus collapsed into the chair. He dropped a meaty hand on the table, leaning back with his knees wide.

Ellen glanced into the kitchen and found a clean cup and water in a pitcher. Pouring a glass, she brought it over to Cyrus. He wrapped his hand around the cup. With his other hand, he took Ellen's wrist, pulling her close so she stood between his knees. With one long pull he drained the cup and set it on the table.

"Cyrus," Ellen warned, stepping backward.

But he stood, one hand still clamped around her wrist. "Ellen, we've both lost so much." His voice was weak, but his hold on her strong, as was his towering height. He spoke of loss, but his charade didn't fool her. He was in charge, and he was dangerous.

He lifted a hand and brushed a loose curl from her face. Ellen couldn't help the impulse to shy away from his touch.

Cyrus either didn't notice or didn't care. He continued, "I should have taken care of him. I should have let him do what he wished at the shop."

Ellen had only ever heard Titus' version of events, where Cyrus was the bad wolf and Titus the innocent lamb.

"You did what you thought was best," she said. The truth of the matter was of little consequence to her. All that mattered now was putting distance between her and Cyrus.

He took her face in his big hands and with his thumbs he stroked her dry cheeks. Then, with a swiftness that shocked her, he pressed his lips to hers.

Ellen skittered back and wiped her mouth with the back of her hand. The misery of his earlier words vanished, and Cyrus' eyes tracked her movement with steely determination.

Ellen took another step away from him. "Cyrus, you are grieving. This is not proper."

"You should have been mine. Titus hid you from me."

Her gaze flitted around in search of rescue. A dirty dish caught her eye. "Who has been living here?" She glanced toward the back door. Were her chickens still there, or had Cyrus moved them to his parents' place?

"I have. I couldn't stand to lose you." Suddenly the misery he'd shown earlier took on a new meaning. Had he been miserable even before he lost his family?

Ellen wiped again at her mouth, remembering his kiss. It hadn't been a reaction to his grief. It had been the claiming of something he'd wanted.

"I love you." His voice cracked as he reached a hand out.

She swallowed, unwilling to be what he wanted. He was right—Titus had hidden her from Cyrus. She remembered those days, lighter and filled with courting and secrets. She could almost hear Titus' voice, the hardness that entered it whenever he spoke of Cyrus. *He ruins everything he touches.*

Cyrus stood, determination in his eyes.

Ellen backed up until she hit the counter. She gripped its edge. "I've just lost Titus. We've both lost him. We need to grieve." She used 'we,' hoping he would see Ellen as a person like himself instead of an object, a toy of Titus' that Cyrus wished to possess.

A knock sounded at the door and Ellen gave a shuddering whimper.

Cyrus took two long strides and yanked the door open. "What?"

The voice on the other side was understandably shaky. "I hoped to speak with you about a spare wheel."

"Tomorrow." Cyrus' words were harsh, but they gave Ellen a moment to compose herself.

She lifted the iron poker that went to the stove and held it between her and Cyrus.

He closed the door and turned. Ellen steeled her voice.

"I'll tidy this place up. You should not stay here tonight, or any night while I am still here."

Cyrus lifted his chin.

"I am not ready to accept suitors." As if what Cyrus wanted was to court her.

His eyes narrowed, but then the expression disappeared, leaving Ellen to wonder what it was she'd just seen. She'd opposed him. The question was what would he do about it. In this town, nobody challenged Cyrus.

"I want breakfast in the morning."

Ellen blinked, surprised at his sudden change of direction.

"All my meals. I'll not be taking them at the café, not now that you're here, living in my house." He gestured to the walls and the ceiling.

"Yours?"

"Everything that was my brother's is mine now." His mouth lifted at the corners and his gaze drifted from Ellen's face, slowly down to her toes. When he'd sated his thirst, he left, leaving Ellen alone in the mess of a house.

Her breathing quickened. He was right. This house and everything in it was his now. Even the wagon Ben would be bringing by tomorrow would belong to Cyrus.

Ellen sank to the floor and dropped her face into her hands. What a mess she was in. Again. This was the same as the last time she'd lost a husband. When would she learn that a marriage didn't solve anything? It only brought a host of new problems.

Morning had passed and Ellen had yet to think of a satisfactory plan for her future. The best she had come up with was to sneak off to Demi's place and hide there, not just from Cyrus, but from Demi's parents as well, until she could scrounge up enough money to buy a train fare someplace else.

Now, Cyrus was sitting at her table, eating the lunch she'd prepared, and she understood why nobody dared cross him. He was frightening and all too influential in this town. Those he couldn't influence… she rubbed at the purple marks on her wrist from when he'd grabbed her yesterday.

A knock sounded and she glanced at Cyrus, whose intense focus on his food told her he had no intention of rising.

Ellen went to open it, giving Cyrus a wide berth just in case he got the idea to grab her again. She had no desire to earn a matching set of bruises on her other wrist. She pulled the door open, relieved to have another witness, no matter who it was.

But the moment she saw his face, that brawny jaw and towering height, she wished she'd ignored the knock.

Ben.

She leaned into the frame, closing the door as much as she could behind her. "Take the wagon and go." If only he could do the same with her.

Ben blinked at her, his brows drawn as his gaze flicked to the interior of the house. "Is everything…"

"Take it." Ellen moved to close the door, but it stopped with a lurch, and she looked up to see Cyrus' thick fingers curled around it.

He tugged it open. "Can we help you?"

Ben glanced from Ellen to Cyrus. "I just came to return Mrs. Moren's ox and wagon."

She wanted to step over the threshold and go back to those days before she'd returned to Independence, before Cyrus had laid claim on her.

Cyrus looked down at her. "You were telling him to go?"

Heat rolled off Cyrus in shimmering waves, and Ellen swallowed the lie coming easily amid her fear. "I asked him to sell it. There are plenty of folks at the camp who will buy it and everything inside. I do not need it."

"That wagon belongs to me."

Ellen cut her gaze to Ben. He stared at Cyrus with narrowed eyes. In a moment, his face transformed, his expression becoming light, indifferent. "I can sell it if you want. Or I can leave it here."

Cyrus' face relaxed, the muscles in the side of his jaw sliding in like the uncocking of a trigger. "Leave it here. Any interested parties can come see me. My shop is next door. Ellen is my responsibility and, upon the death of my brother, that wagon belongs to me. You'll bring any business to my door, not this one."

Ellen couldn't hold herself back and she turned to see what Ben would say. He placed his hat on his head. "I believe I can manage that." His gaze didn't fall to Ellen once as he nodded and turned away from her. If a man like Ben bowed so quickly and completely to Cyrus, what hope had she to stand strong in defense of herself?

CHAPTER 6

*B*en's chest was coiled tighter than a spring as he walked down the dusty road, Ellen's house at his back. That man was her brother-in-law, yet Ben only had to glance at the way he stood too close to Ellen to know he had other things in mind than helping her grieve her lost husband.

He cursed himself for not asking Ellen about her family as they'd returned to Independence. He'd assumed she had a life to return to. If that was true, why was she cowering in the doorway beneath the thick arm of an openly jealous and hostile brother-in-law?

He crossed a road and slipped into a nearby café. He found a seat near a window and watched Ellen's door, but it did nothing to ease the concern threatening to choke him, not when he couldn't see inside that house.

Eventually, the brother-in-law exited alone. One coil of that spring unwound at the thought of those two separated. But that man had answered the door; it was his home, and surely he meant to return to it. If he meant Ellen harm, who would there be to protect her?

Some time later, Sam entered the café, his face relaxing when he spotted Ben.

"Been looking for you." He took the seat across from Ben, and Ben shifted so he could still see Ellen's door. "I have news of a guide."

Ben's gaze flicked toward Sam, then back out the window.

Sam helped himself to Ben's drink and set it back on the table with a soft sigh. "There's a man in our party who is already fit to be our guide. D'you know Fox, the man who is taking those brides west?"

"Yes." They'd all heard of it. Some of the women had been scandalized, complaining that the company was nothing short of a bride ship.

"Well apparently he's better even than Wilson."

"Why hasn't he volunteered?"

"I figure it's because he's got all those women to care for. Perhaps if we offer to help..."

Ben cut a look to Sam. "He doesn't want a bunch of bachelors helping his brides."

Sam scoffed. "We ain't going to be vultures or anything. Just do what we did for Ellen—keep close and help where needed."

Close. Needed. Ben continued staring at Ellen's door. Perhaps their time on the trail had given him a false sense of duty. He'd helped her across the prairie, but he had no business meddling now that she was at her destination.

Sam glanced over his shoulder, following Ben's line of sight. "What are you staring at?"

Just then, Ellen exited her house in a faded blue dress. Maybe she'd been wearing it before; only all he'd seen was blackness as she'd stood under the man's shadow.

"Ellen?" Sam turned back. "You're watching her house?"

"She's got a brother-in-law."

"I would suppose so, since we buried her husband."

Ben leveled Sam with a glare. "I don't trust him."

Sam looked out the window once more as they both watched Ellen cross the street and out of sight.

"Why don't you trust him?"

"His intentions aren't clear. I think he means Ellen harm."

"Harm?" Sam pressed his palms on the table. "Why?"

Ben shook his head. He didn't know. Logic told him the man was hostile because he didn't want a new man sniffing around his brother's widow. It was too soon for her to be receiving suitors anyhow. But his gut disagreed, and he wouldn't be able to settle it until he knew for sure.

Sam's voice leaked into his thoughts. "Are you wishing you'd asked for her hand while we were still on the trail?"

Ben glared at his brother. "I don't mean to marry the girl—"

"Woman," Sam corrected.

Ben narrowed his eyes. "I only mean I don't like leaving her in a situation that isn't safe."

"I'll marry her." Sam's voice was nearly a laugh.

Ben ground his teeth and waited for a wave of irritation to pass. His brother was too flighty. "I believe you would."

"She's got the face of an angel and Lord knows she can cook. She's not the type to dissolve into tears, neither. I didn't once see her cry over her dead husband."

Ben couldn't deny noticing the same thing. He'd been impressed, but he was unwilling just now to agree with Sam. "Perhaps she's heartless."

Sam gave a conciliatory frown. "If that's the case, she's better suited to you."

A flash of blue caught Ben's eye. Ellen walked past their window. Her gown was unfamiliar, and he remembered their clothes had been lost in the river. Was she wearing someone else's clothes? Did that man, Cyrus, have a wife of his own?

That thought uncoiled one more row of the too-tight spring in his chest.

Sam was right; Ellen was beautiful. A girl like that needed a strong man to protect her from the lawless men in this country. If her brother-in-law was merely ensuring Ellen's safety, Ben doubted there was another man in town better equipped.

"She ain't wearin' black. D'you think we need to let a wife grieve, or is that a tradition that gets lost the farther west we go?"

Ben stood and moved toward the exit, pushing through the door. A bell sounded his exit, and he jogged to catch up to Ellen.

"Mrs. Moren."

She stopped, her face lighting up. "Ben." Her smile fell as her gaze flashed across the street to Cyrus' shop. "What can I do for you?" She gestured for Ben to follow her as she rounded the corner of the building.

Ben followed, his mind racing as he tried to find the words.

She was waiting around the corner, her arms crossed.

Ben swallowed. "I just wondered if I could escort you to your destination."

She pursed her lips in something like amusement and cocked an eyebrow. "Haven't you got plenty to do, like finding a buyer for my wagon?"

"I think you mean Cyrus' wagon."

Her face lost its humor. "Yes."

"That dress. Does it belong to Cyrus' wife?"

"Wha—" Ellen looked down. "No. Cyrus isn't married."

Unmarried. His fears returned, as tight as the time he'd been pressed between a horse and its stall. "Do you want to go west with us?" The words were out of his mouth before he'd even really thought them. He balled his hand into a fist, wanting to press it to his lips, cursing them for running like a mountain spring.

She reeled back, taking a step and nearly walking off the boardwalk. Ben caught her wrist, his fingers touching the bare flesh at the base of her palm.

She jerked her hand away and rubbed at her wrist. Embarrassment welled up at his forwardness in touching her like that. He dropped his gaze to her hands. Where she'd rubbed, there were purple blotches. Without thought, he stepped closer and took her elbow, lifting her wrist so he could see the markings.

"Who did this to you?"

She pulled her arm away and tugged the sleeve down to hide the marks, but it was too late.

"Who?" he pressed, watching her face. He knew the answer, and a ringing started in his head.

"It's not what you think."

Ben had to focus on his breathing. Deep breaths, in and out.

"He didn't mean... It's nothing."

Ben swallowed. *Nothing* meant such treatment was acceptable to her, and that cut deeper than any excuse she could have given. "Come with us."

When he met her gaze again, her eyes were cool with calculation.

"Word is you boys are looking for wives to take west."

"Who...?" Ben shook his head. It didn't matter who had given her information. "We're looking for a cook, and Sam seems to approve of your cooking."

"Sam." She said his name with affection and the side of her mouth lifted in a smile.

His gaze raked over her expression, memorizing it, interpreting it. Did the mention of Sam make her rueful, or was it fondness he saw? "Yes, he thinks you'd make a fine cook. We aren't looking for wives, just a bit of help with the female work."

"Female work."

Why was she repeating everything he said? Ben clamped his lips, refusing to speak again until she said more than him.

She stared back and his resolve nearly broke. He wanted so badly for her to accept. It felt like his heart was trying to beg her in Morse code. Finally, she spoke. "The longer I stay in that house, the fewer options I have."

Ben's brow furrowed, trying to decipher the meaning behind her words. He had an idea, but he wanted certainty. Did Cyrus intend to marry Ellen himself? Ben couldn't blame him. The feelings that had come over him were new, but whatever they were, Ben had never wanted to possess a woman so badly.

A few days without a mother on this earth and already he was turning into the very heathen she'd feared. "I want you to have options."

Ellen shot a glance around the corner and Ben wondered if her destination had merely been out of sight from Cyrus' shop. "If you want me to go, you need to get me out of this town. Now."

It was Ben's turn to reel backward. "Now? Surely—"

"He'll not let me leave, not when he's waited so long."

Ben's brows drew together. "Waited?"

Ellen shook her head and lowered her voice. "How many are in your camp?"

"Ten or so wagons."

Ellen chewed her lip. "He'll come lookin' for me."

Ben stepped around the corner to look at Cyrus' shop.

Ellen caught his cuff and tugged him back. "He'll know it's you I've gone with. He suspected something was between us."

"Why are you afraid of him?" There were obvious reasons

—his size and his power over her—but he wanted the ones that only Ellen knew.

She chewed her lip, and he could almost see the lies forming in her mind.

Ben hooked his thumb on his belt. "The truth. I'm not sticking my neck out for a skirt who isn't honest with me." A lie. He would do anything for her just now. The image of those bruises were seared behind his eyelids.

"I don't want to lie, it's just…" She chewed her lip again, then released it, leaving it glossy in the afternoon sunlight. "I have no proof. It's just a feeling. If you won't take me on a feeling, I understand. I'll keep heading to my friend's house and see if she'll let me hide for a few days until…"

"What?" Ben was desperate to hear her plan. What would she do if she didn't go west? If it was a good enough plan, maybe he could take back his impulsive offer for her to come along with them.

"I don't know." She sighed. "I have a friend, but I'm not even sure Demi's family will take me in. Her father… few dare cross Cyrus."

Ben's chest swelled. "I'm not afraid of him."

Ellen chuckled, and Ben glared at her inappropriate response to the situation.

"I'm sorry." She reached a hand up as she collected herself again. "It's just…you are right." Her tone was incredulous. "I've never seen anyone so relaxed around Cyrus, not even Titus."

Titus. He'd never heard her speak her husband's name. "Your husband."

Ellen nodded, all laughter gone from her now. If speaking of him sobered her, perhaps she wasn't as heartless as he'd suggested.

Sam rounded the corner and skidded to a halt before he knocked into Ben.

"Ellen." Sam smiled. "What a surprise seeing you here." His gaze shifted and his tone lost its jest. "Ben, I paid the tab on your drink."

Ellen smiled at Sam, and the way it reached her eyes made the spring in Ben's chest coil tight once more. "Good afternoon, Sam. Your brother was just making me a proposition, says you vouched for my cooking."

He could feel Sam's eyes on him, but Ben studied Ellen. Did she harbor an attachment to Sam? Should Sam marry her in town and take her west not as their chef, but as his wife? A marriage to another man would surely protect her from Cyrus. Would earn her a spot in one of their wagons and save him the trouble of tending to her wagon. All logical reasons, yet Ben couldn't force himself to give voice to the idea.

Sam's voice was playful. "Mighty fine cooking. I'm afraid to go to camp and see what charred food Chet and Molly will be serving."

Ellen crossed her arms. "I'm just waiting to see what your brother here has decided."

Ben's gaze snapped to Ellen's face.

The side of her mouth lifted. "Will you take a dishonest cook?"

Ben glared. The silence stretched, turning the dry air heavy. Sam shuffled toward the street. "I'll just go get the horses."

Ben didn't take his gaze from Ellen.

She held his gaze, meeting his determination. "I've said all I can say. It's your turn to decide if you're taking me out to your wagons or leaving me here."

"Leaving—" The word denoted abandonment. "I'm not *leaving* you anywhere. You aren't my responsibility."

"Then you shouldn't feel any guilt about your decision."

Oh, he felt guilt. Plenty of it. How had burying this

woman's husband brought him here, negotiating with her about honesty and considering her status as a wife for one of his brothers? "Why didn't you cry over your husband's death?"

Ellen's stern mask broke and shock was plain in her wide eyes. She recovered almost as quickly and sighed. "I suppose I wasn't sad to see him gone."

"Why?"

Ellen's mouth opened and a small scoff sounded in the back of her throat. "I didn't love him."

"Why?"

She glared at him now. "*You* are not a gentleman."

"No gentlemen out here. Only cowboys. Tell me why you married a man you didn't love."

"Foolishness and desperation." She flung the words at him in anger, but her eyes widened as though shocked at having revealed too much.

Unintended honesty was exactly what he'd been waiting for. He nodded. "Let's see if Sam has found the horses."

As they made their way west, out of town, Ellen rode his horse as he and Sam led the horses by their reins.

Ben spoke, anything to distract him from the figure sitting high on his horse behind him. "If Fox can take us west, why didn't he volunteer four days ago?"

"He can take us west. His pa is a famous guide."

"Famous?" The word conjured an actor on a stage, not a trail guide.

"He founded half the trails we'll be driving through, and Fox was with him, a boy, but he's grown now and capable. Everyone in town is saying so."

Ben rolled his shoulder, a weak attempt to loosen the tightness growing there. He would need to speak with Fox, get an idea of the man's motivations.

When they arrived at camp, the circled wagons pricked at

51

his chest with their familiarity, the families blending, enjoying one another's company and comfort. Yet it brought him no joy to see the ease they had with one another. This place already felt a little like home, and yet they had wasted supplies, time, and energy, only to be back where they started.

Sam rode ahead and presented Ellen with such fanfare that Chet asked outright if he'd married her. Ellen's neck flushed and she kept her eyes down as she climbed from the horse. Ben stood close in case she needed assistance, but she didn't meet his gaze.

Molly sidled close and said, "I'm glad you're back. We're celebrating tonight."

Ben paused. "Celebrating?"

Molly took Ellen's hands, her eyes glimmering. "You missed quite a bit while you were gone." Her gaze raked up and down the poor girl's frame. "But it looks as though you've had a bit of fun yourself."

He'd hardly call it fun. "No trouble here, I hope?"

Molly cut a gaze at Ben, then just as quickly returned it to Ellen. "Will and Fenna are married." She looked right at Ben. "Tell me you two are as well."

"Married?" Ellen breathed.

An image flashed into his vision, of himself holding Ellen's hands, of hearing her say those words to him. If he and Ellen were married—

"Two years ago." Molly spoke the words with a flourish. "Oh, Ellen, it's so romantic."

Across the clearing a head of copper hair glinted in the sun. *Fox.*

"Excuse me." Jogging to catch up to the man, Ben called after Fox, who stopped with a curious expression.

Ben stuck his hand out. "I'm Ben Bridger. We met once before."

Fox took it, eying Ben warily. "I remember."

"Folks in town said you might be able to take us west." Ben gulped. He'd flung the words, and only once they were spoken did he realize how nervous he was about Fox's reply. How desperate. What if the man refused? What if he charged a sum too great for Ben's family to pay?

"I ain't a guide."

Ben blinked away his hope. Had Sam been fed faulty information? "I heard you grew up taking the trail." That was as good as any guide in Ben's mind.

Fox drew in a slow breath. "I ain't a guide."

Ben tamped down the frustration that threatened to surface. All the rest must be true, or Fox would be denying those facts as well. "Do you know anyone who might do the job?"

Fox held Ben's gaze, then nodded once. "He's over in Dundee."

The hope grew once more, crowding out the frustration. "Do you know how we might contact him?"

"I had planned to send him a letter on the morrow."

"Why not tonight?"

Fox glanced to his left and Ben tried to follow his gaze, but Fox spoke. "I can't be detained past dark. You might remember I'm responsible for several women."

Ben eyed the sun. It had barely begun its descent. "Just a trip to the post office? I can deliver the letter if you'll write it. I'm sure a request would hold more clout coming from a friend."

"He ain't my friend. Just a guide I know."

"Of course." Ben was suddenly glad Fox hadn't agreed to guide them. The cagey way he spoke didn't exactly instill confidence. There were plenty of folks who could perform the job of watching brides, but few who could lead a company west. There had to be some other reason for his unwillingness.

Fox gestured with his head. "Follow me. I'll write a note."

Ben did. Though he wasn't inclined for marriage himself, he couldn't help but survey the women in Fox's camp as they weaved through the many tents. A few of the females were quite pretty. What desperation could have placed them here, heading west, risking life and limb to marry strangers?

He had only to recall the bruises on Ellen's wrist to answer his question. Desperation was limitless. He was sure each of the women possessed a story and a darned good reason for going west.

Ben stood awkwardly, tapping his boot on the ground while Fox scrawled out a note on the tailgate of a wagon.

Soon Fox brandished the folded paper at Ben. He pointed to the writing on the outside. "Tell them to send it with the Pony Express. We ain't got time to waste." He reached into his pocket.

Ben held up a hand. "I'll pay. I just hope this works. How many weeks you think we've got to get back on the trail?"

Fox's mouth pressed flat and that was answer enough for Ben. The anxiety that had built as they traveled back to Independence surfaced once again. They were losing precious time, and the mountains were only going to grow colder with each day spent searching for a guide. "Thank you."

Ben found his horse still saddled. Sam was nearby, so Ben told him where he was headed before riding off, back to the city, back to the town where he knew trouble was brewing. He hoped Cyrus had not yet noticed Ellen's disappearance. He tugged his hat low just in case. It might be a good idea to change clothing, but Ben wouldn't mind feeling the flesh of that man's face under his knuckles.

CHAPTER 7

A celebration was held with music and what little food could be scrounged up in camp with only a day's notice. Molly tried to convince Ellen to join the festivities, but Ellen's gaze remained on the town of Independence in the distance, wondering what Ben was doing and when he'd be back. She hated to think of him in town once Cyrus discovered she was missing.

Ellen found a seat at the end of one of the Bridgers' wagons that faced east. She watched the partygoers. None of them had come away from that twister unscathed by its violence, yet there they were, smiling and dancing. It gave her hope for her future, that no matter what life had given her, something bright and joyous might still come along. A distraction like the festivities tonight, or maybe something else. Something more permanent.

Sam came around the wagon with a tin cup. He lifted it and she took his offering and sipped. A warm barley drink. If she closed her eyes, she could almost pretend they were on the trail somewhere, not back on the edge of Independence where they'd started.

As much as she grieved for these folks who had lost something in that storm, she couldn't help but feel grateful for what it had taken from her—her shackles. She wasn't safe, far from it. But without a husband, the future held endless possibilities. When she had been in that house with Cyrus, she'd felt like she was looking through a spyglass; everything else was blacked out except one distant spot she couldn't see well enough to know if it was good. Not all of her options were positive, but she was filled with hope at having options at all.

Sam settled against the wagon, his shoulders level with Ellen's knees. "He'll be back." He gave her a reassuring pat on the toe of her boot.

Ellen locked her gaze on the darkening sky, waiting to see a figure and praying it would be Ben and not Cyrus who came for her.

Ellen didn't know Ben nor what he was capable of. She could only think of what Cyrus was doing. Was he looking for her? Had he questioned Demi's family? It had been a poor idea to try and hide at Demi's place. That was surely the first place Cyrus would look.

Ellen glanced at Sam. "Are all you boys looking for wives, or just Ben?"

Sam stepped back to get a better view of her, as though Ellen had just made an uncouth offer of marriage to him. "We're not…" But his voice was weak.

"Molly told me."

Sam heaved a sigh. "Our ma told us to find wives. Some of us are more willing than others."

"Ben?"

Sam barked a laugh. "The least willing."

Ellen nodded. "There are women in town, ones who need husbands."

"Why aren't they married?" His voice was tentative, suspicious.

Ellen chuckled. "My friend Demi has strict parents." Ellen didn't mention the scars that marred the left side of her friend's face because, deep down, Ellen believed it was her parents who prevented Demi from marrying, not Demi's appearance.

"They don't want to see her married? I thought that was every mother's wish."

"It might be her mother's, but her pa is not about to give his daughter over to anyone he doesn't believe deserves her."

Sam leaned back against the wagon and crossed his boots at the ankles. "Sounds like a man I can respect."

Ellen frowned. Men knew so little about what it was to be a woman. How little choice they had in every decision. An accident had disfigured Demi's face when she was young. Ellen knew of one suitor that had tried for Demi, but Mr. Anderson had deemed him unsuitable and that was it. Demi hadn't fought her father, at least not that Ellen knew about. Ironically, Demi wasn't *allowed* to marry, while Ellen had tried marriage enough times to know she was through with the institution.

After a certain age, a girl became a burden to her family. She'd seen fathers give their daughters to men much older on the simple basis of friendship, as though a young second wife was something earned after years of loyal friendship.

When Ellen had reached the age of marriage, she'd taken matters into her hands and found herself a good man. But her first husband's dreams had killed him as surely as Titus' had.

These thoughts fled from her mind the moment she saw a rider. Ellen gripped the closest thing—the sleeve of Sam's shirt. "Ben sent *me* on his horse." She'd seen it earlier, set to grazing near the cattle. Surely a rider meant it wasn't Ben.

Sam's voice was calm, "We have more than one horse, Ellen." He stepped forward calling out, "Olly!"

The rider slowed and lifted a hand to his mouth. "Tree."

Sam holstered his gun. Ellen hadn't even seen him pull it out. He patted her boot again. "It's Ben."

"Olly Tree?"

Sam smiled. "Chet coined the phrase when our mama read from the Bible. It's as good a test as any."

Ben's horse galloped to their wagon, kicking up dust. He climbed down and wrapped the reins around an exposed wagon rib. "Your brother is questioning the whole town. It's only a matter of time before he comes looking."

Sam came to his brother's side. "He doesn't know *me*. Doesn't know how many brothers there ought to be. Let me take her—we'll camp in the hills."

A flash of distrust crossed Ben's face. "You'll not be safe alone."

"And if he comes?" Sam's voice was strong. A challenge. Ellen stared at these men, immensely interested at how there was room in one family for more than one strong brother.

"She's ours now." Ben's tone was bold, but it lacked foundation.

There might have been a time when such language would have made Ellen bristle. Instead, she looked around at this band of brothers and knew they protected their own. "Can't we just leave, start on the trail?"

Ben shook his head. "We need a group. Otherwise, we're fodder for bandits and Indians alike."

Sam turned to her, his face softer than Ben's. "Plus, once a few families join us, they can help protect us from your brother."

"He's not my brother." Ellen muttered. It didn't matter for the situation, but every time they said that, Ellen's insides protested like a pit of snakes. Cyrus didn't want to be her brother. He never had. That was why he was scouring the town for her.

"Sure isn't." Ben's voice was low, almost a growl. He offered Ellen his arm. "Will you walk with me?"

She braced a hand on his shoulder as she climbed down from the wagon. She pressed her empty cup into Sam's hands and gave him a small smile. Then she took Ben's arm and let him lead her in a loop around the corral of wagons.

They'd almost gone a full pass before Ellen gave up waiting for him to speak his mind. "You're missing your brother's wedding celebration."

Ben stared forward, his eyes not even sliding to watch the party. "He's saying you're his affianced. Claims his brother entrusted you to him before he left."

Ellen's boots skidded to a halt on the dirt. "That's false!" Her throat grew tight with rage, and she sputtered before finding words. "How could Titus have known he was going to die? What man sets off on a wagon knowing his death is at the end?" She took a slow breath, trying to calm her irritation. It did nothing, so she continued to rant. "Even if he did, Titus would never have *entrusted* me to Cyrus."

The word was vile on her tongue. Even worse was the reason Titus wouldn't have entrusted her to Cyrus. "He would have killed me with his own hands rather than see me wed to his brother." Anything that hurt Cyrus gave pleasure to Titus. She was certain that would remain true even in death.

Ben watched her face like he'd done earlier when he asked about why she didn't grieve Titus. Then his focus cleared, and he said, "There are many things I would do to ensure you didn't marry him."

He stared hard at the ground ahead of them and rolled his shoulder as though it pained him. Then he nodded, softly, like he'd been having an internal conversion and the two sides had just reached an agreement.

Lifting his face to hers, he spoke. "Here's how I see it. You can either pick one of my brothers to marry, or you can take your chances with Cyrus coming out. I might be able to speak with the parson on short notice and get him to marry you on a whisper. We can pray Cyrus doesn't get wind of the arrangement before it's complete."

She'd never heard Ben say so much in one breath. The number of words spoken should have been shock enough, but they were nothing compared to what he was suggesting. "Marry your brothers?"

"Just one." Ben's mouth twitched in what might have been a smile.

Ellen blinked, her mind flashing images of what life would be like if she agreed to marry a Bridger brother. Fenna as her sister, Molly her cousin, and the protection of all these men, her family, just as they were Molly's. But she'd tried this twice before, running from the unknown into a marriage, and both times it had failed her.

She wasn't a fool. She recognized that this family was different from both Harry and Titus' families. And yet a rod straightened along her back. She would be a fool to try the same thing a third time and expect a different result. Wasn't that the definition of madness?

Marriage didn't solve anything. It only created new problems. She wasn't willing to bring down this family she'd grown to respect.

She shook her head. "I'm not looking for a husband."

"You might not have been *looking*, but you've found yourself in a tight spot. I'm sure Sam would marry you."

"I don't want to marry Sam." Ellen's tone was hard, but she immediately regretted it. Sam didn't deserve such a hostile rejection. Yet she wasn't sure how to explain herself to Ben.

There was no man, no matter how kind, who could fix the past. Nor could he promise a future. If her marriage to Titus had taught her anything, it was that she was better off alone, that she was more capable than she'd thought, and that hasty decisions made in desperation never played out well.

"He'll see to it that you're cared for. And safe." Ben's voice was tight, like it pained him to speak.

"Safe," she whispered, a word that was as likely as a mythical unicorn pulling one of these wagons all the way to Oregon. Ben was a strong man, with every ability to choose whatever life he wanted and take it with both hands, shaping it into whatever he wanted. He would never understand a woman's plight, how she could not muscle her way out of a tight spot. But there was one thing he might understand. "What about love?"

Ben's gaze lifted, and he stared at the disappearing horizon while his chest rose and fell. Perhaps he was thinking of his parents and the love they'd shared. "I suppose he could do that too."

During the few days she'd spent with the Bridgers, they'd been grieving the loss of their parents. Many stories had been shared over the fire and, from what Ellen had heard, his folks' marriage had been a love match, both of them defying their families to be with one another.

It was romantic, but nobody spoke of how years later, they'd decided to brave danger and come west. Whatever life they had found hadn't been enough. They'd sought the west, sought a place of their own, just as Titus had. And their dreams had stolen their lives. Just as Harry's had.

As her mind turned back to Cyrus and the issue at hand, she knew Ben was right. Cyrus wasn't going to leave her alone just because she was out of sight. But though he held sway in that town, no amount of threats or bullying could dissipate a marriage in the sight of God.

She watched Ben's profile. So at ease, just like he'd been with Cyrus earlier. He was still the only person who hadn't cowed to Cyrus' temper.

"What of you?" She hadn't missed the fact that he'd offered his brothers as husbands, and not himself.

Ben's brow tightened and the corners of his mouth tugged down into a frown as he turned to face her again. "Me?"

"Yes. Do you have a plan for a wife?" Her heart began a quickstep in her chest as an idea unfurled.

Ben almost laughed. "Sam would be a much better husband than myself."

Ellen raised her chin. "I don't mean to marry you."

He pierced her with an unnerving stare that told her he was reading something in her eyes. What did he see there?

She gulped, afraid if she waited too long, she'd lose her courage. "I don't want to stand in the way if you *do* intend to marry."

"Stand in my way?"

Ellen huffed. Of course, Ben was confused. "If Cyrus comes—"

"*When* he comes."

Ellen acknowledged his words with a half nod. "You could *claim* marriage."

Claim. He mouthed the word.

"*Say* we got married. We don't actually have to do it. Then, once we get on the trail, we can separate."

Ben rubbed his jaw thoughtfully. Ellen tried to keep hope from rising in her chest, but like a weed, it grew quicker and taller than all the planted, intentional thoughts.

He frowned. "He's been looking all over town. Someone would have either seen you go into the church or out of it.

Word would have gotten around." He shook his head. "The plan's no good."

And the weed was ripped from the earth. Only now could she see the flowers she'd planted—they were stunted and thirsty from growing alongside the hearty weeds of hope. "You're right that word would get around quickly enough." Ellen chewed her lip, then lifted her gaze, her eyes wide with excitement. "We could go to the church, speak to the parson and exit with clasped hands." She shrugged one shoulder. "It might work." Ellen ignored the fear at the back of her mind. If it didn't work, she'll have delivered herself into Cyrus' hands.

Ben held her gaze, so unwavering and certain. Then he gave a single nod. "There's enough daylight left. I'll saddle you a horse."

A laugh bubbled from Ellen's mouth, stilted and half crazed. Thoughts bounced around her head like fleas on a coyote and that fearful one took its turn in the front. "Are you sure it would be safe to go into town? What if he sees us on our way in?"

"My brothers can accompany us. They are strong enough to hold him off until we speak with the parson."

Ellen shook her head. "I cannot believe you're agreeing."

Ben took her hand, his calluses rough on her palm, and led her toward the horses. "Neither can I."

CHAPTER 8

Ben kept his horse close to Ellen's. His three brothers fanned out behind them on the darkening road, Sam in the back, the twins on either side. Will stayed at camp with his new bride, oblivious to the location and intent of his four brothers. It might have been a decent idea to clue him in, seeing as how Will would be patching them up if anything went awry. But Will had had enough stolen from him after he'd lost Fenna. Ben wasn't about to take any more.

The moment they neared the first building of the town, Ellen dipped her head down, her bonnet blocking her face. It wasn't until her profile was impossible to see that he realized he'd barely taken his eyes off her. He kept waiting for her to look at him with horror on her face, to pull back on the reins and turn her horse around. But she held steady to the course, and if she was convinced this was her only way to safety, Ben wasn't going to be the one to cower.

The further they got into town, the more folks noticed them. It was impossible to tell what they saw. A group of folks wouldn't have caused such a fuss, so he had to assume it was Ellen they recognized in some form. Her dress, or the point of her chin which barely showed beneath her bonnet.

As he tried to survey their group from an outsider's point of view, her chin quivered. He reached a hand over, placing it on her thigh, just above her knee. Inappropriate, but she didn't move to push him away.

When they arrived at the church, Ben dismounted and helped Ellen do the same. He kept his arm around her waist just in case more than her chin was growing weak. Strangely, the gesture served to comfort him too. Ever since he'd left her in that house with that brute, Ben's body had begged him to draw her close and to never let her get away again. It might have been easier if she'd married one of his brothers, but since she'd refused, he was glad she'd had this idea. One that kept her safe and kept her close until she was out of Cyrus' reach.

He glanced back at his three brothers, then nodded and led the way through the chapel doors. The parson looked up and rose with a smile. Though it was practically nightfall, the parson squinted like a mole in sunlight.

"Father, it is me, Ellen Moren."

"Mrs. Moren." He walked toward her with hands outstretched.

Ben released her, but he did so with a glance toward the unsecured doors. His brothers leaned against them, a formidable barrier, but Ben wasn't certain how big of a foe they would be facing.

"Father." Ellen took the parson's outstretched hands. Then she turned back to Ben. "We are here to ask a great favor."

The father tilted his head, waiting patiently for Ellen to explain herself.

She glanced up at Ben. There it was—the fear he'd expected from her on the ride here.

He stepped forward. "This young lady needs your protection."

The parson's brows drew together as he glanced between her and Ben.

"Father," Ellen pleaded. "He has agreed to help me find a home out west, but if Cyrus thinks me unmarried, he will insist upon my marrying *him*."

The parson's shaky voice was slow, only this was not some sermon to be slept through and Ben couldn't help but wish he would be a bit quicker to understand. "You mean to marry this man?"

Ben shook his head. "Father, we hoped you might allow us to give the impression that Ellen and myself were married just now. We will be on our way and out of your town before anyone discovers the truth."

"Lie?"

"No," Ben replied sharply. He had only to remember the scoldings of his own childhood ecclesiastical leader to know they could not word their request that way. "I only wish for you to keep this young lady's confidence and not speak of what has just occurred."

A shout came from beyond the door.

Ellen caught Ben's hand, her eyes tight with worry. She turned to the parson. "Please, Father."

He too seemed concerned with whatever was going on outside his church. His face shifted from worried to angry. He met Ellen's eyes and gave her a stiff nod. "Cyrus Moren is a brute. If you wish to leave him behind, I'll not stop you. I will protect your secret."

The thin man slipped between herself and Ben and marched down the aisle, hollering, "Who dares defile the house of the Lord?"

Sam's boots shuffled as the door behind him bucked.

At the parson's signal, the three brothers stepped away

from the doors. They immediately flew open and a grubby man fell through. Just beyond him, a horse skidded to a halt and Cyrus slid down, marching straight towards the open doors, his steps eating the stairs to the porch.

The parson spoke to the man still on the ground. "Carlsbad, I suggest you go home and tend to your new baby."

The man had the sense to look bashful as he crawled to his feet and exited the church.

Ben and Ellen followed the parson, and when he stopped, Ben continued forward, pulling a hesitant Ellen along until she stood among four Bridger men.

Cyrus glared at Ellen. "I've been searching for you."

Ben glanced over to see her smile was more a grimace of terror. If he was a gambling man, he would have bet Ellen had feared Cyrus long before her husband's death. Ben took a step to the side, breaking Cyrus' view of Ellen. "I'm glad you found us. You'll be relieved to know Ellen is no longer your concern." Ben extended his hand to Ellen. "Come, wife."

Ellen dutifully slipped her own hand into his and Ben looked down at it, so small cradled against his own. The marks Cyrus had given her barely showed beneath the cuff of her dress. Anger beat in his chest, but this was no time for a brawl. All that mattered was getting Ellen to safety. Ben made to leave the church, stepping closer to Cyrus and his murderous glare. As he started down the church steps, he did his best to keep Ellen as far behind him as he could while also keeping a tight grip on her hand.

The parson began another lecture, this time directed toward Cyrus. Finally, the two men's eye contact was broken. Rather than take the stairs, Ben jumped down from the porch and turned to help Ellen. When his hands gripped her waist, he felt the heat of Cyrus' gaze on him. Or perhaps they were on Ellen, and now that she was Ben's responsibility, he felt the threat in his own bones.

He pulled her down and snaked an arm around her middle, tucking her tight to his side. The feel of her against him was familiar. The day he'd arrived in Independence, he'd been unsure about going west, but walking those streets, negotiating for the supplies they would need for their journey... something had settled inside him. The unknown becoming routine. Ellen at his side felt much the same.

With much pushing and elbows, the Bridger men carved a way through the small mob and came out to empty posts where the horses should have been. Of course, the men had scattered the animals. It was likely the first thing they had done while waiting for a message to Cyrus to be delivered.

Sam found Ben's ear. "I'll find the animals. Just get her out of sight."

Ben groaned at their foolishness. Sam would have made this woman a fine husband, and she'd turned it down for want of love. He gave a rueful shake of his head and quickened his pace. With Ellen still pinned so close to his side, she had no choice but to keep pace with him.

They'd only passed two buildings when Sam rode up behind them. He slid off the horse and offered the reins to Ben, his eyes darting around. "You two go. I'll find the others."

Ben wasn't sure if he meant the horses or the twins, but he took the reins and gestured for Ellen to climb up.

Ellen, however, stepped around Ben and stopped in front of Sam. She looked up at him for a moment before saying, "Thank you."

Then she turned and, without looking at Ben, climbed into the saddle.

Ben took a few steps, but Sam called his name.

He turned and Sam looked from side to side before stepping closer. "Ain't you gonna ride with her?"

Ben's head reared. "No."

Sam leaned closer still. "It's supposed to be your wedding night."

Ben glanced around the streets—not empty—but he doubted folks were out trying to disprove a wedding they didn't yet know had occurred.

Ellen leaned down so her head was in the conversation as well. "We didn't go through all that only for our bluff to be called in the first hour."

Ben let out a drawn breath and turned, placing one hand on the horn and the other on the back of the saddle. Ellen sat between his arms, his to protect, at least for now.

Ellen shifted forward, making space in a saddle made for one.

Ben swung his leg over and adjusted the reins, trying his best to ignore the warm and pleasantly petite form in front of him.

When he glanced at Sam, his brother wore a wide grin, and Ben wondered if Sam hadn't already found several horses and this was all some ploy to get Ben closer to Ellen. It worked, for the moment the horse started forward, Ellen's back bumped against his chest. He rested one hand on his thigh and the other held the reins, his arm brushing against Ellen's shoulder with every shift of the horse's gait.

Eventually, his brothers appeared behind them, leading Ellen's riderless horse, but they hung back as though giving them privacy. Keeping up the ruse forced Ben to ride so close to Ellen he could smell the lavender soap she'd used on her hair.

Once they reached camp, the twins broke off to return the mount they had borrowed as Sam followed Ben back to their family's wagons.

Ben was acutely aware of all the strangers and acquaintances in camp, all of whom would also need to believe this ruse. All it took was one person to walk into town and flap their lips and the act was over.

Ben dismounted first and reached up to offer Ellen assistance in coming down. With his hands still on her waist, he leaned in to whisper in her ear, "I can't decide if we've solved our problem or poked the bear."

Another waft of lavender came in with a deep breath. How easy it would be to keep hold of her, to snake his hand around her back and tuck her into the crook of his arm as they joined the others.

He couldn't. Whatever closeness he felt for her now was a result of the closeness of the ride they'd shared and a small saddle. Touching her had been inappropriate an hour ago, and it remained so now.

He released her and turned to Sam. "We'll have a watch tonight. Sam, you take first shift."

Ellen touched his arm. "I can take a shift. This is my problem, after all."

Ben looked at her hand on his arm, wondering if she felt the same pull to be close in proximity. "So long as they think you're my wife, it's my problem too. And this is my family. We watch each other's backs."

"I know."

His gaze snapped to her. What did she know? Did she know he wanted to climb back on that horse and keep her safe between his arms? Or to tuck her away in a wagon and stand guard with a rifle in hand until the sun rose?

She tugged at the tie under her chin and removed her bonnet. She ran a hand over her mussed hair and looked up, meeting his eyes. "Thank you, Ben. Very much."

Ben's gaze faltered before he turned and walked away. Ellen watched him, strong and confident. He was different from Titus and his brother. They were large men, strong too, but they commanded fear while Ben earned respect.

She and Sam followed Ben into the corral of wagons and the party within. Ben weaved his way to Will, and she watched as his lips moved near Will's ear. Ben sliced a hand through the air, a heated gesture. Ellen's gaze bounced to Will to see if he would retaliate. Would she once more be the reason for an argument between brothers? But instead of anger, Will's eye grew wide and shifted to land on her.

Molly appeared, blocking Ellen's chance to read Will's lips. "You've married him." Her expression was so smug, Ellen couldn't help but laugh.

She drew Molly closer. "It was only an act. The parson agreed to keep our secret."

Molly's brows dipped. "You aren't married?"

Ellen shook her head, immensely pleased with their ploy.

But Molly's expression was the opposite. "Why *not* marry him? He's honest and handsome, he took care of you when you needed him..."

All Ellen wanted was safety. She placed a gentle hand on Molly's arm. "I'm not ready for another husband."

Molly's face softened. "Of course."

Shame pricked in Ellen's belly at Molly's guilt. Titus wasn't a topic that brought Ellen grief, and Molly shouldn't feel any guilt at having brought him up.

Molly crossed her arms. "I don't suppose you're going to dance with your new *husband*."

Ellen skewed Molly with a look. "Have you met the man? Besides, he's not my husband."

"And your brother isn't going to check up on you?"

Ellen opened her mouth to answer, but she was surrounded with the evidence. Sure, Ben's family would lie for her, but the rest of these folks didn't give a lick about what happened to Ellen. Worse, some of them had resided in town long enough that they might still share loyalties with Cyrus.

"You just leave Ben to me." With a smirk, Molly strode away, and Ellen lifted a hand in a half-hearted attempt to stop Molly from meddling.

She watched Ben, the side of his face lit by the large fire in the center. Molly approached him, and Ellen allowed herself to appreciate the cut of his jaw as he listened to his lovely cousin. His expression was serious, his brow low across his eyes and his mouth turned down in a frown.

Without warning, he looked at her. She blinked, but it was too late to wipe the hope from her face and feign indifference.

He strode to her, glancing around as he did so. When he stopped, he was too near, at least closer than a bachelor should be standing to an unmarried woman. "Molly thinks we should keep up the ruse in camp too."

Ellen nodded, her throat suddenly dry as images of what this ruse would entail flashed in her mind. Her hand in his. Their bodies close. His lips at her ear. She swallowed, but her voice still came out in a squeak. "She said as much to me."

Ben offered her a hand and Ellen was reminded of how he had done the same the day he'd buried Titus. She slipped her fingers into his warm and callused ones, not daring to meet his gaze. She knew what she'd find—that same stern expression that said everything he had too much decency to speak aloud. She was a trouble and a bother and she'd suggested a plan that hadn't been properly thought through. And he had too much chivalry to decline.

Once they were near the fire, Ellen knew her face was visible to everyone who cared to look. She tried to don the joy of a new bride, but it was difficult when she was afraid to look upon the face of her would-be husband.

Ben lifted his arms in a surprising show of a learned dancer. Ellen took her own position and as Ben moved through the steps, she stared at the buttons on his shirt, the collar, even the stubble on his neck. The attraction was there. It wouldn't need to be feigned, but she possessed none of the comfort that should accompany a marriage. In a real marriage, any awkwardness would be dispelled tonight once they had a chance to be alone in their tent. But she and Ben wouldn't have that experience. How was she supposed to pretend to be in love with a man she could barely face?

She hadn't wanted a husband, but it seemed that fate was intent on seeing her hitched to a man one way or another.

CHAPTER 9

*B*en made a small fire near the foot of his wagon. He warmed his hands by the weak flame and listened to Ellen's movements inside. By the sound of her shifting, she was struggling to get comfortable even though they'd emptied enough of the items from the wagon to give her ample room to lie down. Eventually, she stilled.

He longed to climb in and check to see if she was covered, to see her brow relaxed, to watch the rise and fall of each safe breath. But he was on watch, a perfect excuse not to be in that wagon with her if anyone in the company cared to wonder. He glared in the direction of the city, toward the man who resided within. Cyrus would not get Ellen. Ben stared into the dancing flames and hoped their ruse would be enough.

He hadn't even asked her plans for going west. What was she going to do when she got there? Would she remain his responsibility one way or another? He cursed himself for agreeing to such a hastily devised plan.

His mama's voice rang in his ear, not the bit about finding a wife, but the other part. The part where she feared they'd become heathens. He didn't entirely disagree. There was a softness the women in his life brought. But they had Fenna and Molly now. Surely the pair of women would do a fine job taming the Bridger men.

But thinking of the two women in his party only caused his stomach to clench. He was the head of this family and that was no small responsibility. If they'd been at home on the farm, it would have been hard enough, but out here, where death could find them in their beds, what chance did Ben have of protecting those in his sphere?

And now he'd promised protection to another.

Sam joined him at the fire, using a stick to scratch mud from the sides of his boots. "What are you going to do when folks learn of your marriage?" He pointed his stick at the wagon where Ellen slept. "You going to sleep in that wagon with her? How long are you going to continue this lie?"

Ben bristled at Sam's tone. "What was I supposed to do?"

Sam leaned back and met Ben's glare. "Marry her for real."

Ben scoffed. "She doesn't want me."

"Did you ask her?"

"I told her to marry you. She doesn't seem keen on marriage, and what little I know of her late husband, I understand why."

"You ain't like him."

"No, I've got my own set of flaws a woman won't want."

That quieted Sam. Finally.

CHAPTER 10

*E*llen rose in the morning after a restful sleep. She had forgotten her troubles so thoroughly that it took her several moments of blinking at the crates and blankets around her before she recalled the sham wedding last night. She crawled to the foot of the wagon and stuck her head out from the canvas. Chilly outside the cocoon of the wagon, the morning air bit at her flesh and Ellen retreated in search of her shawl.

She dressed and was tucking her shawl into her belt when Ben approached, a barrel on his shoulder.

He glanced up at her, his mouth set in a grim line. He set the barrel down near the small fire with such ease, Ellen wondered if the thing was empty. He brushed his hands together and walked over. His long legs gave his gait a lope, and she couldn't help but admire his powerful frame.

If she was going to stick with anyone to keep her from Cyrus, she could not have picked a better man. He reached the foot of the wagon and lifted his arms, twitching his fingers in a gesture that signaled for her to come closer. She did, and he caught her waist in both hands and lifted her down. Her hands naturally fell to his shoulders, his muscles rolling beneath her palms as he lowered her to the ground.

"How'd you sleep?" His question might have been considerate, but his tone was anything but kind. It was gruff like the stubble that covered his chin, softening the sharp cut of his jaw, but she knew if she touched it, she'd get pricked.

"Very well."

He gestured for her to sit on the barrel and stood on the other side of the fire warming his hands.

She perched on the makeshift seat and, as soon as she was still, Ben spoke. "Ellen, what is your plan?"

She blinked. She had no plan. She had no wagon. It would have been much better if they'd decided to play house before they'd given all her supplies to Cyrus. Ben had agreed to protect her from Cyrus, but he hadn't promised to feed or shelter her.

"Maybe we can get my wagon from Cyrus."

Ben barked a harsh laugh. "Doubtful."

He might be correct, but his curt deduction of reality cut. "It's mine. It's all I have left from my marriage. Cyrus took the house and he's the reason I couldn't live in peace. He's the reason we're in this mess."

Her face burned with anger and the unfairness of being a woman in the west. Back home, she'd have her family. Perhaps she could still beg funds from Ben to send her east. At least there she'd have had a bit of time to sort out her affairs before finding another husband.

Another husband.

Her insides beat against her ribs like a child throwing a tantrum. She was done with husbands. They only took and what did they ever leave her with? Was it fair to blame them for everything? She hadn't gone far in school, but she remembered common denominators. In this case, she was it.

Perhaps it was her husbands who had right to curse her name.

She looked up to Ben, who studied her. When he didn't say anything, she asked, "What?"

Ben shrugged. "It might be worth a try." He moved closer. "If we get a few folks from the company to come with us and really make a fuss, Cyrus might sell it to us at a fair price."

There he went again, agreeing to her outrageous plans. Even he must not have realized her destitution.

Ellen cringed, remembering their paper money twisting away during the storm. She also recalled the broken trunk with what little gold they had—still in the wagon. Everything was in Cyrus' possession now. She should have thought to take it when she left the house. But Ellen had never been allowed to handle money. "I don't have any money to buy it. At any price."

Ben nodded. "I believe that will work in our favor."

Ellen could picture the scene they would make, traipsing into town and pounding on Cyrus' door. Folks would gather, they would hear what Ben asked and they would hear how Ellen had nothing.

At least a few of them had sided with Titus when Cyrus had ejected him from the shop. They wouldn't stand by while Cyrus took everything of Titus' and left his widow with nothing.

She shrugged. "We ought to at least try."

Once the morning chores were through, Ben and Ellen stood at one another's side and waited for those from the company who would join them into town.

Many of them were coming along just for the entertainment, and Ellen couldn't blame them. If this weren't her life, she might be able to appreciate the drama of it all. As it was, she regretted eating breakfast as the hash sat in her stomach like a ball of lead.

Ben's hand brushed against her knuckles and he wove his fingers through hers, rubbing against that sensitive valley between each finger. The spot that was never touched except by a lover. She glanced up at him, worry no doubt etched into every line. He nodded once and turned forward again. So serious. She glanced at their hands. A ruse, and yet the contact lent her a sort of solid comfort that she gobbled up like a chicken just out of the coop.

She glanced around at his brothers, who knew the truth, and beyond them at the company, who didn't. She wasn't even sure if the company knew a marriage had transpired. Ben's brothers had spread the word about today's goal. They must have also shared the details of the wedding.

She still wore Demi's pale chambray dress. Perhaps when they went into town, she could collect her old dress from Demi's house and wash this one to return it. There was no clothing left in her and Titus' home, but perhaps a bit of fabric remained and she could use it to make herself a piecemeal dress.

They moved through town, and the closer they got to Cyrus' shop, the tighter Ellen gripped Ben's hand, until she had to let go because her muscles protested. Ben tugged her closer and weaved her arm through his, resting her cramped hand on his forearm.

Demi rushed out of her home and ignored the throng of people to approach Ellen and throw her arms around Ellen's neck. "I'm so glad you're alright. Cyrus came here, so worried. He thought you were in danger."

Ellen stifled a scoff and returned the embrace. "I'm sorry I couldn't tell you."

They broke apart and Demi's gaze slid to Ben, curiosity plain on her face.

"Demi, this is my husband, Ben." She cut off as her mind searched frantically for his surname. She knew it, had used it in reference to his family, but it had vanished, hidden in some dark recess of her mind. She closed her eyes against her reckless plans, praying that this wouldn't be the one that proved to be a mistake.

They'd been foolish not to share the wagon last night. Folks were bound to notice. But when the time came to end their ruse, it would work in their favor if folks knew they had been sleeping separately. So they walked like nimble cats atop a fence, hoping they weren't forced to pick a side sooner than they were ready.

Ben reached out a hand. "Ben Bridger. Pleased to meet you."

Ellen closed her eyes in frustration. *Bridger*. He was *Ben* and his last name was *Bridger*. She chanted the name, cementing it in her mind. It would do nobody any good if she allowed the stress of their situation to drive away her senses.

To be fair, she hadn't yet put his name together in her mind. He was Ben and he was one of the Bridger brothers. It wasn't as though she was some young schoolgirl ignoring her lesson to scrawl their names beside one another on her slate. The thought conjured up an image of his name drawn in a swirling hand.

Ben Bridger. She loved the alliteration, the flow of it and when she turned back to Demi, she couldn't stop the name from rolling in her head like a herd of wild mustangs traversing the hills outside Independence. All grace and thundering hooves that threatened to drive away all coherent thoughts.

Demi blushed as she took Ben's hand, turning her face in such a way as to hide her scars, a habitual move Ellen had seen her make countless times before. Ellen hated that Demi had to feel insecure over something she couldn't change.

Ben shook Demi's hand and looked at Ellen. Heat flashed

up her neck and she couldn't stop her spreading smile. She felt like a youth once more, blushing at the merest hint of attention from a handsome man. She certainly played the part of an enamored wife. She could hardly force her gaze away from him and back to Demi. "Demi, are your folks inside? We need as many souls as we can find to act as witnesses."

Demi's brows lowered. "Witnesses?"

"Cyrus has my wagon and he's cross with us for marrying. He won't give it up willingly."

Demi turned her head, surveying the crowd for the first time. "Is that why all these people are here?"

Ellen nodded.

Demi sunk into herself, ever afraid of confrontation. "Cyrus isn't going to like it."

"No, he is not. But I have a right to my things. Titus wouldn't have wanted me left destitute."

Demi glanced up at Ben and leaned in closer to Ellen, lowering her voice. "You're hardly destitute."

What did Demi know about Ben? Aside from him being physically appealing, who was to say he wasn't just as destitute as she? "Yes, well, I haven't a scrap of clothing other than that dress I left in your house yesterday. And for Ben to take one more person across the plains, he needs more of everything. I don't see what use Cyrus has of it. If he sells it, he's not going to give me the money."

Demi still frowned and Ellen could tell she wasn't convinced. "Go get your folks. I won't ask your father to cross him, only witness."

Demi nodded slowly and turned, walking up the steps to her front door.

Ellen turned back to Ben. "This is a bad idea."

He wrapped an arm around her and leaned in to whisper in her ear. "We're desperate."

Ellen gulped and threw back her shoulders, which wasn't easy with Ben's arm draped over them. He chuckled and a bit of her anxiety eased. She looked up at him with his rueful expression. "I've never seen you smile."

His grin fell and he glanced up at something behind her.

Ellen turned to see Demi Anderson's family standing on their porch. Even Demi's beautiful, affianced sister Petra stood in the line, her head high. The family made no move to come down the stairs, but they were close enough that they would witness whatever happened from their step.

Ben and Ellen led the procession on to Cyrus' shop.

They didn't have to knock. Their party had drawn enough attention that Cyrus stood in the doorway with his arms crossed. He held a large mallet in his hand and glared daggers at both Ben and Ellen.

"What are you doing at my door?"

Ben stepped forward, blocking Ellen's view. "We came for Ellen's things. Her clothes and her ox and wagon."

Cyrus' face flushed crimson. "Those things belong to me."

Ben made a show of turning and looking Ellen from head to toe. Then he turned back to Cyrus and donned a jovial voice. "I don't know that you'll fit her dresses."

Ben knew she had no clothing inside, but perhaps Cyrus didn't. A laugh rumbled through the crowd.

Cyrus shifted and glared at the onlookers. "You came with a mob because you know they aren't hers. They were my brother's and when he died, they became mine. Any man in your company would agree."

Ellen stepped forward, gripping the back of Ben's jacket. Maybe to hold her back from scratching Cyrus' eyes, maybe because merely touching him lent her a bit of his power. "He would have wanted me to have them. That wagon was meant to take me to Oregon. It still can. That's what he would want."

Cyrus glared at her. She'd never experienced such hostility from him. She'd seen it directed at others, but he'd always been soft or pitying with her, and always too attentive.

"He would have wanted you to marry me."

Ellen choked on a laugh. "You know that isn't true. He would want me cared for and I will be. I only need my things so I can start my life with the comforts *Titus* provided."

His expression hardened. Despite Cyrus' attempts to destroy Titus financially, Titus had given her a life without Cyrus' help. She understood now how Cyrus had hoped to bring Titus low. She'd tried to deny it, but the timing of Cyrus ejecting Titus from the shop was no coincidence. Titus had something Cyrus wanted and for a moment Ellen wondered if it was possible that Cyrus had planned on Titus' death.

His glacial stare didn't warm. "Annul your marriage and you can live in the house."

Ellen scoffed and went to argue, but Ben cut a hand through the air, stopping it just shy of Ellen's waist. "We want her clothes, her ox, and her wagon. They are hers. As she said, her husband would not have wanted his widow to be left with nothing." Ben looked around and murmured agreement rippled through the crowd.

Cyrus eyed them too, his eyes widening at something behind them, something Ellen would have had to turn around to see. She didn't dare take her attention away from her opponent.

"Fine," he barked. He gave her one last lingering glare, then turned and stalked back into his shop. Her heart thundered in her chest, not yet convinced the threat was over.

Ben tucked her into his side and pressed her close in the briefest embrace. "You did well. We ought to move quickly before he changes his mind."

Ben set off for the house and Ellen followed. She packed as haphazardly as Titus had the day he'd announced their departure. Perhaps the only reason Ellen hadn't shared his urgency was that she didn't yet share Titus' desperation to put space between herself and Cyrus. Now she felt it all too keenly.

CHAPTER 11

*E*llen led Ben around the side of the house to where the ox was being kept. Her chickens scuttled toward her. When they caught sight of Ben, they became a mess of squawking and feathers that only settled when Ellen tucked the last one safely under the stairs. The ox's bridle hung over the fence post and Ellen passed it to Ben.

He nodded, stern and silent as he opened the gate and entered the pen.

Ellen glanced around the space, feeling oddly sad to leave the only home she'd ever had. The chickens were still clucking and, through the stair slate, Ellen could see the head of her favorite one, Goldie, a yellow-speckled female who often laid blue eggs. She glanced at Cyrus' shop, wondering if he would notice a chicken missing. They hadn't been on Ben's list of items.

Before she talked herself out of it, she moved forward and reached under the stairs, gripping the chicken by its leg and pulling it out. The others panicked as Goldie's wings flapped. Ellen winced, squinting against the feathers and dust being kicked into her face. A black chicken came out with Goldie, so Ellen stuck both the hens under her arm and walked briskly back to the wagon. She fairly threw the birds inside, then climbed in after them.

Pulling a folded quilt from a crate, she made a bit of a nest between two barrels and the chickens gladly took refuge in the nook. She turned and surveyed the wagon. Everything was still tied down from when Ben had delivered it. With a nod, she glanced out the back, hoping to see Sam with a second ox to help pull the wagon.

Instead of Sam, she caught sight of Cyrus stalking toward her. She rushed to climb out, not wanting to be stuck in here with him, especially with two stolen chickens inside.

But she wasn't quick enough, and by the time she weaved through the stacks of supplies, Cyrus stood at the foot of the wagon. He reached across the side and gripped her waist, tugging her out. Her shins hit the buckboard on the way down, burning with the ache of helplessness. He set her roughly on the ground and Ellen let out a cough.

He yanked on her upper arm, the movement causing her neck to crack like a whip. "How could you do this?"

Ellen glanced toward the house, but Ben was mostly likely still coaxing the ox from its pen.

"The wagon is mine." She tried to wrench free of Cyrus' hold, but he held her arm as easily as if it were one of the ropes he used in his shop's pulley system.

"I don't care about the wagon. *You* should've been mine." His glance flicked to her lips and back to her eyes.

Ellen stepped back, keeping what little distance she could with his grip on her arm. But Cyrus matched her movement. His legs were long, and every step he took stretched longer than hers. Another step and another, until the wagon was at her back, the sturdy wood anything but comforting. He took a final step, his boots only a hair's breadth away from her own feet.

"I tried to accept your vows to God." His voice cracked, and Ellen couldn't tell whether he wanted pity or fear.

As foolhardy as her and Ben's decision had been, she knew now that God might be the only being powerful enough to defeat Cyrus.

He reached forward and brushed the lace trim on her bodice. "I cannot accept it." His gaze flashed up to hers. "I can convince Pastor Ellis to annul the marriage. *He'll do it.*" There was a hardness to that last line. Ellen feared for Pastor Ellis' safety.

"I'll not annul my marriage." She brushed his hand away, resenting the liberties he took in touching her at all, but he caught her fingers and held them to his chest.

He looked longingly into her eyes. "I'll not stand by and watch you marry another, not again."

Ellen pulled at her hand. "You might not care for promises made to the Lord, but I do." Ellen sent a silent prayer heavenward, asking forgiveness for her lies, for the sacrilege of bringing Him into them.

Finally, Cyrus released her, and she sagged against the wagon.

Ben appeared around the side of the house with a rope in hand. He dropped the harness in the mud and, with murderous eyes, rushed toward them. Ellen stepped around Cyrus and met Ben. He didn't slow so she put her hands out and pressed them against his chest. "He was just wishing us well."

Ben kept his eyes on his opponent. "I'll bet he was."

Ben's words held a terrifying bleakness, but he'd stopped stalking toward his opponent. For a moment Ellen regretted the way Ben stood up to Cyrus, like he wasn't the most dangerous man in this city.

Without Ben attempting to approach Cyrus, Ellen's hands on his chest felt too intimate. She let them fall, but Ben was still poised like a beast ready to pounce. His hands were balled at his sides. She caught one of them in both of hers, stroking calloused knuckles, begging him to look at her.

He did, but what she saw there was not what she expected. Anger, even irritation might have made sense. She'd brought him and his family a world of inconvenience. Instead, his eyes raked her frame, and when they landed on her face again, they were soft. "You're unharmed?"

She thought of her shins and how they would be painted violet when she removed her stockings tonight. "I'm unharmed."

Ben slid his free arm around her, hugging their bodies together and resting his chin on the top of her head. "Don't come near my wife again. If you have something to say, say it to me."

Ellen remembered Cyrus saying something similar to Ben when he'd brought the wagon to the house. This time, instead of filling her with dread, those words filled her with security. Though her future was as unsettled as ever, unreasonable or not, it was also brighter than ever.

Ben stood as a guardian over her rather than ruler. She watched him, his attention fixed on Cyrus. His strong jaw flexed as he tried to assert his dominance from afar. He had every reason to command her every move, but he hadn't. At least not yet.

She would do well to remember how a man could change. Especially a man like Ben, who was used to being powerful and dominant. How would he handle the day when there was someone bigger and stronger than he? Would he take it out on the weak in his life the way Titus had whenever Cyrus had injured his pride?

She knew from her time with Titus how a man could pretend, like an actor on a stage. It didn't matter what she thought of Ben, how safe she felt around him and his family.

He still had the ability to wipe it all away when acting like a gentleman became inconvenient.

By the sound of gravel, Ellen knew Cyrus was leaving. Ben's hold on her loosened and Ellen drew in one final breath of Ben's spiced smell before stepping backward.

"Why didn't you call for me?" His softness had vanished, replaced with hardness. Ellen pulled on her sleeves. In an instant, his comforting, solid presence had vanished, and she was back in her old life where she was responsible for Cyrus' actions.

"I didn't think to call for you." She truly hadn't. For so long, the discomfort that accompanied Cyrus was something she could never reveal. Titus would either have blamed her or he would have brawled with his brother and ended up worse off for it. Neither of those ways had prevented Cyrus from being in her life. She wasn't being brave. She'd just never had someone she could truly rely on.

She still didn't. That much was clear in the set of Ben's brow as he stared at her. "Let's get back to camp." Ben glanced behind her. "Sam isn't here with the other animals. Your ox can't pull the wagon alone."

Ellen nodded. Ben's practical words helped settle her emotions. He didn't need to be kind. This arrangement was for convenience only. Ben didn't have feelings for her, and she hadn't any for him.

"Ellen!" A voice came from behind. Ellen spun to find Demi rushing around the side of the wagon. Ellen went to her friend and the two embraced. Demi pressed her forehead to Ellen's. "Now that that's over, you must come inside." She glanced at Ben and leaned closer. "We have so much to discuss." Demi stretched her neck to see behind Ellen and inched close again, her voice low. "First, where'd you find him?" She leaned back again and gave Ellen an impressed smirk.

Ellen tried to smile. It was time to don the mask of a newlywed. "On the trail. His family is from North Carolina."

Demi's eyes widened. "So far?"

Ellen glanced at Demi's house, grateful the porch was empty. Demi's family was kind, but Ellen hated that she'd had to ask a favor from them. They willingly gave to Ellen, but she had only ever had gratitude to give them in return. "How is Petra? Is she very upset that Titus didn't finish the piece for her wedding before we left?"

"We sent it over to Atkinsons to finish. Petra doesn't even care that it won't be ready in time for the wedding."

Ellen nodded, relieved that there was no ill-feeling between them, but she wondered if there was more to Petra's indifference. The fact that the Andersons had found a man deemed worthy to marry their daughter was nigh on a miracle. But Petra had never been besotted with the match, merely going along with plans made for her. If Demi were the bride, she would have been devoting her every hour to ensuring the wedding went forward as planned.

Ellen cupped her friend's cheek. "It will be your turn soon enough."

Demi shook off Ellen's hand and straightened her shoulders. "Not likely. For now, I would like to meet your husband."

Ellen cast a look over her shoulder at Ben, who was tightening the rope on a crate. She leaned closer. "Demi, come west with us."

Demi balked and stepped back.

"Everyone wants a wife out west. There will be plenty of men who won't mind your scars."

Even as she said the words, she felt heartless. Demi tried her best to hide her scars, but shy of covering the left side of her face, it was impossible. Ellen had learned not to acknowledge them, to pretend they didn't exist. But this was

Demi's chance, and Ellen wasn't going to waste it by being gentle.

Ellen caught Demi's arm and led her to the bench on their porch. They settled and Ellen looked her friend in the eye. "It isn't the scars that prevent you from marrying. It's your parents. Come with me. Now that I have my wagon, I have food and shelter for the both of us."

Demi's dazed look hardened. "The wagon you are already sharing with your husband?"

Ellen chewed her lip and searched Demi's face, trying to decide. In the end, she tossed her head and let the words flow out like a waterfall. "He's not my husband. I'm just trying to make a life for myself, and you and I both know Cyrus never would have allowed it. Ben has his own wagon and this one is mine. Come with me." Her words were thick with a desperation she hadn't realized she possessed. Perhaps it was merely that she would like a friend, someone who had known her before. Perhaps she trusted Ben less than she thought.

Demi's eyes danced around the scene in front of them. Ellen could almost hear her mind digesting Ellen's lie and what opportunity lay before them. Her throat bobbed, and for a moment Ellen thought she'd convinced her friend. But then the front door opened and Petra stepped out.

Ellen straightened, guilt washing over her at the underhanded way she'd just tried to steal away Petra's sister mere weeks before her wedding.

Petra leaned against the doorframe. "Ellen, you were always so quiet. I never expected such excitement from you." Her tone was impressed.

Ellen forced a smile. "Good morning, Petra."

Petra tossed her head, her attention catching on Ben as he drew near, her gaze raking down his long frame. She lifted a coy eyebrow at Ellen.

Ellen couldn't comment before Ben arrived, leaning against the post. "Will you be safe here until Sam arrives?"

She nodded, but Ben stayed put, curling and uncurling his fingers.

Ellen didn't blame him. How far away from this street would they have to be for him to feel truly secure? "Would you rather we step inside?"

Ben nodded and glanced over his shoulder.

"Who's Sam?" Petra's voice held none of her usual merriment. Instead, it sounded lifeless.

Ellen's gaze shot to the girl. As much as the Andersons had snuffed Demi into never marrying, it was just as possible Petra's marriage was a grass fire, consuming everything in its wake and leaving no room for argument.

Ellen ushered the two sisters toward the front door. "We'll wait inside."

What a trio they were. One prohibited from marriage, the other pressured into it, and the third widowed twice with no desire to try again.

CHAPTER 12

Ben gave a sigh of relief when Ellen's friend's front door blocked his view of her. Being alone with Ellen served only to teach him how wrong he'd been to make an offer of marriage to Jane Connor. All this pretending with Ellen had him realizing how little affection he had granted Jane. He hardly knew how to treat a woman. It seemed his time with Jane had been so vapid, so brief, it served more as an excuse not to pursue any other women than to truly further his understanding of the opposite sex.

He blew a frustrated breath through his lips. None of it mattered now.

The only thing he should be worrying about was finding a guide to take them west. Acquiring Ellen's wagon only mattered if she was going to be allowed to use it.

He considered once more the idea of going to Colorado, or anywhere that wasn't Oregon. To let the seasons and the snow determine how far west they went.

Before he'd finished checking the balance of the wagon, Sam arrived with an ox.

"Took you long enough." Ben glared at his brother.

Sam just smiled. "I stopped by the post office. There was a letter for Fox." He patted his breast pocket.

Ben clapped his brother on the shoulder. "Let's get it to Fox and see if our prayers have been answered."

Once the oxen were hitched, Ben strode up the porch steps and rapped on the door. He swallowed, feeling every bit like a gentleman come courting. He even removed his hat and ran a dusty hand through his unruly hair.

The other girl, the one Ellen wasn't friends with, answered. She leaned against the frame and crossed her arms. "When are y'all leaving?"

She watched him with an ease that spoke of self-confidence, but he sensed an indifference in her. He knew well the way a woman looked at him when she wanted his affection. This woman didn't care for it, not the way she had pretended when he'd first approached them on the porch. He had the brief suspicion that her earlier attitude was as much an act as what he and Ellen were performing.

"Soon as we can, ma'am."

Ellen and her friend came to the door, each holding the handle of a trunk. They placed it on the floor between them. Ellen eyed the sister, then shifted that hard stare on Ben.

He gulped, feeling like a man caught staring at another man's wife, and placed his hat back on. "Ready?"

Ellen nodded and turned, embracing her friend. The two held each other so tight, for a moment Ben wondered if Ellen would reject their plan and stay put.

It seemed a decent plan, better than the crude one they'd slapped together in one conversation. Surely, she would be better off going anywhere rather than going west. She didn't have to stay on the same street as Cyrus. Nor did she have to stay in the same town. There was a whole country where she could get away from that man. She didn't need to take the most dangerous trail in the United States. To fake marriage to a man who already had enough weighing him down.

She looked up and caught his gaze, like she had a sense when it came to him. Her eyes bounced between his, and she pressed a hand to his chest as she stepped through the doorway. He put his arm around her, unsure why she felt the need to make a spectacle of their relationship. He and Jane had hardly touched this way, and never in front of others. Ellen's friends shouldn't expect it, and yet he must follow her lead.

Just as he decided a firm embrace would do, she weaved out of his arms and breezed past him. "Can you take that trunk?"

He glanced up at the two sisters before lifting the trunk from the ground and following Ellen, unsure of what exactly they'd just communicated to her friends. He shook his head. Lies were like the web of a spider, delicate, sticky things with a pattern that was easy to create but impossible to untangle. He just hoped he didn't get wound so tightly he would arrive in Oregon hollow on the inside.

As he approached the wagon, Sam helped him load Ellen's trunk into the back. Sam waved him away. "I'll tie it down. You help her."

Ben swallowed but knew Sam was right. Both he and Ellen had roles to play, and it seemed so long as they were touching one another in any way, their ruse would be believed. If he had any inclination that she would have taken his physical affection as anything else, such actions would have been inappropriate. As it was, he knew she didn't want him, and that served to both make him comfortable and to allow him to be as convincing as possible.

He went around the side and helped Ellen up into the seat. He turned to Sam. "I'll walk."

Sam laughed and slapped Ben on the back. "You can't rob the citizens of their victory. It was the folks from town that caught Cyrus' eye." He hefted the trunk from the ground. "I suspect he didn't want to tarnish his reputation, not even for a pretty girl like Ellen." Sam winked at Ellen, and Ben longed to shove his brother out of sight.

Instead, he climbed into the wagon, the shocks bouncing as he took his seat on the bench. The shifting caused Ellen's shoulder to brush against his, but she righted herself quickly enough. He risked a glance at her. Tendrils of her curly hair had escaped from her pins, giving her an exhausted appearance, but her dark eyes were bright, clashing with his deduction. She sat with her back ramrod straight.

Ben chuckled softly. "I'm up here for the town's benefit. We may as well give them a show."

Ellen turned to him with those big, dark eyes. "What do you want me to do, climb into your lap?"

Sam, who stood on the ground on Ellen's side, chuckled. When Ben shot him a glare, he gestured toward the back. "Ellen's trunk is loaded." He started walking back to camp. He would make it there before the wagon and Ben was glad to see him go.

Ben snapped the reins and the oxen started pulling, slow as ever. When they'd passed Cyrus' shop, Ben said, "I don't need you in my lap. Just try not to look as though I'm taking you hostage."

Ellen shook out her shoulders and folded her hands in her lap. She picked at her nails for a bit then looked up at Ben. The oxen were well behaved, but just now he would have liked a decent excuse not to meet Ellen's gaze.

"Perhaps we can make a camp away from the others." She leaned close. "We won't have to pretend if we aren't around others."

Ben shook his head. "The group is a protection more than anything. Your brother ain't the only danger around these parts."

Ellen nodded, but her mouth fell into a thoughtful frown.

This woman was a puzzle. She'd practically burrowed into his arms at her friend's house, only to turn around and plot ways to prevent them from pretending. "You know, we can be a more… discreet couple. Nobody expects Fenna and Will to spend the day in each other's arms."

Ellen slowly turned to him. "*They* have no need to convince anyone."

Ben shrugged. "If it pains you to pretend—"

Ellen faced forward, her brows lowered in a glare. Then she begrudgingly took his arm and leaned her head on his shoulder. "There. Are you pleased?"

Ben sighed. Was it always this way with women, the feeling that he was having an entirely different conversation than she was having? He'd merely meant to assuage any expectations and, somehow, she'd heard a demand for more.

The wagon bounced and her head lifted and fell against his shoulder in an action that could not have been comfortable. Instead of surrendering her hold, Ellen held him tighter, pressing her head more firmly on his shoulder as though determination could overrule discomfort.

Ben smiled, content to let any onlookers assume it was joy at his recent nuptials that had him glowing with pride.

When they reached the camp, Ellen released her hold, setting her hands in her lap once more while Ben climbed down. He glanced back up to see her looking at him with expectant eyebrows.

He glanced around to ensure they were still alone. "What?"

"Help me down, please."

Of course. He'd helped Fenna and Molly down countless times. Yet, as he reached up, he couldn't deny the feel of his hands around her waist was beginning to feel like routine, like comfort, like home. Awareness traveled up his arms and took hold of his lungs.

When her feet touched the ground, rather than lift her hands from where they lay on his shoulders, one stayed put and the other traveled up his neck and brushed at his chin.

Ellen scrunched her nose. "You have a bit of dust, Mr. Bridger."

He searched her face, finding traces of the fine dirt on her cheeks as well. He told himself to brush it away, to play along with her ruse, but he didn't want to take his hands off her, even for a moment. The instant that thought registered, he released her waist like it was a cast iron pot fresh from the coals.

He stepped back, scrubbing at his face. "I'll wash up before supper."

"I didn't mean..."

But Ben had already rounded the wagon, his legs all too willing to take him far away. At least some of his limbs obeyed in a timely manner. He climbed into the back of her wagon, unsure of his purpose. His family's wagons had been parked too closely to let Ellen's in. There was no way he planned to leave this on the outskirts of camp, even if it was mere feet from his own wagon. If anything, Ellen's wagon should be surrounded by Bridger wagons.

So he stood there, inside her wagon, unwilling to unload anything until he'd parked it where he wanted it. But he feared if he climbed out now, Ellen would be there watching him with that genuine expression.

A small noise came from the area near his feet. He scanned the ground, both searching for the sound and trying to identify it. He walked slowly, quietly and there! A second sound. Less like a coo and more like a scratch.

Ben squeezed between two crates, the wood scraping against his chest, when the squawk of a chicken became apparent, followed by the desperate flapping of a frightened bird. Ben changed his course, sliding back through the crates while wings beat at his boots.

Once he was free, he looked into the dark space where the chicken had been and saw nothing. He shook his head, certain Ellen had taken a chicken and failed to inform him. He rolled his shoulder, wondering if this would be one more reason for Cyrus to come after them. The guide Fox had written to couldn't get here soon enough.

The trunk she'd just obtained from her friend was on the floor by his feet. He lifted it, but there was no point in removing anything, not until he'd parked her wagon for the night. He made his way back out of the wagon. Ellen had gone. He circled the wagon once, then heard a laugh from afar. He followed the sound with his eyes and found Ellen and Molly, arm in arm, walking away from him. He released a breath of relief and set to work on the time-consuming task of unhitching and re-hitching animals to adjust the wagons so he could drive Ellen's inside the corral.

Sam approached with a light step. "Fox's man is coming. Should be here in two days."

Ben gave a huff of relief. "Good work."

Sam raised his hands. "It was all Fox. We're lucky he has connections."

Ben nodded, enjoying the weight of one less problem. All he'd seemed to do since that twister hit was take on more responsibilities. It was nice for one of those to be finished, like the seal placed on a barrel of beans. A help instead of a hindrance.

He'd just finished tucking Ellen's wagon inside the corral when Ellen appeared in that now-familiar blue dress. Ben watched her come his way and, just for a moment, allowed himself to admire her. Brave and beautiful. Her shoulders were straight and strong despite whatever she had endured.

He tried just for a moment to imagine what her life was. To live at the whims of her husband and then in fear of her brother-in-law. To be beautiful, but for that beauty to make her a bullseye men wanted a chance at.

She had food in her hands, as always, and a smile lifted the corner of his mouth at the easy way she had fallen back into his family's rhythm.

He climbed down from the wagon and met her in the clearing. She pressed the bowl into his hands, and he took it, allowing his fingers to brush over hers.

Her gaze bounced between their hands and his eyes, and his smile widened to think he'd affected her so. Neither of them wanted to be married, yet this game they played could be fun if they allowed it.

With the progress Fox had made acquiring a trail guide, there was little to do besides wait for that guide to come and pray he wouldn't require everyone to pay more than they could afford.

He scooped a spoonful of stew, but before he put it in his mouth, he said, "I met your chicken, but is there any money in that wagon?"

Ellen's throat bobbed as she glanced at the wagon, as though the look of it had the answer. "Should be some, unless Cyrus took it."

Ben nodded. That small chance was more than he expected. "I wonder what the guide will charge. We're in no position to barter."

"I hope he is a fair man and not taken to greed."

Ben's gaze ran along Ellen's frame—much shorter than him, with a waist that looked small enough to snap in two. Again, his thoughts strayed to Ellen's situation, intrigued by the fact that she must hope for many things that would inevitably contribute to her safety on the trail. But she had little power to take what she wanted. "Whatever you don't have, I can pay."

"Ben."

He lifted a hand, and she stopped. "We have enough, and we've already started this charade. I'm not giving up one day in."

Ellen gave him a coy look as she sucked her tooth. "Alright, Mr. Bridger, but if you do, I'll find a way to pay you back."

He lifted the bowl. "You've used plenty of stores on me." He shook his head. "No more."

"Fenna made that."

Ben leveled her with a stare. "I see you bringing food from your wagon. Just because you didn't this time... I mean it. Don't use anything extra on me."

She nodded and looked out over the camp. "I was going to walk. Want to join me?"

"Walk?"

The side of her mouth lifted in a grin. "It clears my head."

Ben scraped the last of the food from his bowl. Ellen reached out, but he pulled it from her reach. "I'll just clean this and we can be on our way."

Ellen searched his face, like if she looked hard enough, she would find a hidden truth. He held her gaze, daring her to find one. He had plenty, but he doubted she'd be looking in the right places.

CHAPTER 13

Ellen searched the wagon for her new trunk. It wasn't until she gave up that she found it on the ground on the other side of the wagon. The one item that had been unloaded. She opened it, lifting the straw hat Demi had gifted her. It would be more comfortable than the bonnet she'd been wearing on the trail. It didn't provide as much cover from the dust and sun, but while they were in camp, it would be sufficient.

There were no looking glasses in camp, but upon donning the piece of millinery, Ellen instantly felt more normal, like taking off a wet pair of boots when entering the house. It was both familiar and relieving. She glanced in the back of the wagon, considering the search for the money. She wouldn't even know where to begin, nor how much she'd find when she did locate it.

How was she going to find the funds to make life on the trail a success? She had everything she needed, but accidents happened. Food spoiled, clothing tore, animals died. She needed currency, some sort of trade that would provide her with a living.

She thought of the trading post in town, where most folks outfitted themselves for the trail. Of the gruff trapper, who would come into town with nothing but goods and leave with money in hand. As tough as she was, she was no trapper. She'd watched him interact with folks from afar. He bullied them into giving the prices he demanded, no doubt about it. Not only did Ellen have no tradable skills, she also didn't stand a chance at threatening anyone beyond the age of adolescence.

Ben returned, his steps light and his expression nearing a smile.

He offered his arm and Ellen took it, unsure why she'd invited him on a walk with her. She preferred to walk alone, but she planned to walk the perimeter of camp, and it would do their cause good for everyone to see them strolling in their free time.

Apparently, Ben didn't stroll. She had to take two steps to his one, and she was soon warm enough to remove her wrap.

Ben waited, watching her with a curious expression. "Is your head clear once more?"

She folded her wrap and hung it over her arm. "I'm not finished walking. Only warm."

Ben plucked the wrap from her arm and held it in his free hand while he offered her his other one. She took it, glancing at the wagons. Nobody looked to be watching them, but Ben was wise to pretend just in case.

"Do you often walk?"

"I used to go every afternoon."

Ben gave her an incredulous look. "*Every* afternoon?"

She lifted and dropped a shoulder. "If it wasn't too cold. I always get sleepy at that time."

"So rather than rest, you walk?"

When he said it that way, it made her sound daft. "Do *you* have time to sleep?"

Ben huffed, but the laugh didn't reach his lips. "As much as I have time for a stroll."

Ellen took her hand back. "I'm sorry to have inconvenienced you." She gestured toward the camp. "Please, continue your work without ceasing."

Ben laughed and snatched her hand once more, weaving his fingers through hers. Big as his hands were, it was like they were meant to be entwined with her own. "Life is not normal on the trail, nor at camp. Now is the perfect time to store up our energy to build farms when we arrive in Oregon."

Ellen tried to picture Oregon. She'd heard plenty about it, how green it would be. Except they would arrive in the fall when the leaves were turning. She would have to wait until spring to see the emerald folks spoke of. "How will you live the first winter? You'll have no crops to harvest."

"We'll buy supplies when we arrive."

"With money." Ellen didn't have to locate the box to know she didn't have much. She'd have to find work right away, a job with lodging included.

"Yes." Ben gave a soft chuckle. "We have a fair bit. Sold everything we owned back home and, with the land in Oregon being free, I don't see how we'll run out in the first year. It will be difficult, but I'm going to build a life for us."

Us. Ellen closed her eyes and for one moment pretended that *us* meant her and him, that their marriage was real, that she could trust Ben would keep his word, and that he held her hand because he wanted to be close to her, not because of the roles they were playing.

Then she opened them and everything that had always been true returned. Even Ben's fingers felt stiff in her own, the set of his jaw serious. Though... did he possess any other expression? "Will your family all stay close? Within walking distance?"

The ghost of a smile graced Ben's face, threatening to prove her wrong—he possessed other expressions—but one could hardly call it gleeful. Nevertheless, the knowledge that speaking of his family brought him something like joy felt like finding a patch of blackberries. It promised sweetness, but only if she was careful of the thorns.

Ben cleared his throat. "Close enough, but we want room to grow. I know folks who have farmed the same land for generations. If the plot is big enough, the children who want to farm can take parcels from the main plot. One day it will be my children I want to stay close to instead of my siblings."

"It makes me sad to think of you distant from your brothers."

Silence fell for a beat before Ben spoke. "Do you have siblings?"

Ellen nodded. "I'm in the middle. I never thought to stay close. They always left as soon as they could. I did the same, though I never expected to go so very far."

"How far is Independence from your home?"

Ellen drew in a long breath. "Far. Pennsylvania."

Ben looked at her through narrowed eyes, but the corners of his mouth lifted. "A Yankee?"

Ellen smiled back. "And a Reb." She shook her head as though she cared about such things. There was little time for caring about politics when consumed with survival.

Her efforts to survive had been used in vain, because here she was again, considering how she would afford to eat once she arrived at her destination. Winning her wagon back hadn't gifted her security; all it had really done was make her less of a burden on Ben. It guaranteed nothing. Somehow the sliver of independence the wagon had granted felt less like freedom and more like loneliness. She stopped the thought, refusing to allow herself to long for reliance on another man.

Ben cleared his throat. "On the side of my parents' wagon is a chicken coop."

Ellen blinked. How had she not noticed?

"You can put your chicken in there so it doesn't muck up your wagon or fly away."

"Chickens," Ellen corrected.

"Chickens?" He drew out the 's' in the word so it sounded more like a buzzing fly.

Ellen laughed. "I brought two. Why did they have a coop and no chickens?" It seemed silly when everyone was always focused on lightening the wagons and not bringing anything extra.

"The folks who sold it to them already had it on. Alex is quite good with snares. They figured they could use it to store birds, pheasants, maybe even a turkey."

"Fresh meat even on the days when there isn't time to hunt. Clever."

Ben smiled, but it didn't reach his eyes. "They were very clever."

Ellen didn't know what to say. They reached the wagon and Ellen touched the buckboard. "Thank you for allowing me to use it."

"They won't last, you know. The chickens."

Ellen picked at a sliver of wood that was lifting away from the board. "I thought to at least try. If needed, they can be a meal."

Ben nodded. "I have an errand in town. Thanks for the walk."

Ellen watched him go, the soft shuffling noises of her chickens her only companion. What would it be like to have her family around her, to know she belonged someplace? She turned her gaze west, wondering what all the fuss was about. She didn't have a better option, but Harry had, and Titus could have moved them anywhere. What was it about the west that called to so many, called loudly enough that they were willing to risk lives to get there? She would find out soon enough. She'd rather risk her life trying than live in Independence near Cyrus, or even return home to the sad circumstances of her birth.

CHAPTER 14

Ben returned to camp just as the sun was crawling toward the horizon, painting the sky orange and blue. He was beginning to feel like the rest of his life was going to be spent entering and exiting that forsaken town. Would this camp become their home for the next year? Them eating through their stores, finding labor in town? He wouldn't be able to rest until that guide arrived and he'd paid the man his deposit.

He led an ox for Ellen's wagon and a newly acquired mare to replace the one they'd lost in the storm. They might do fine with only two, but they had feed for three and the horses would be useful for a hunt and during river crossings. In any case, his pa had thought to bring three and Ben meant to heed his counsel for as long as he could. He knew the time would come when his father's voice no longer sounded in his head. He wasn't in any rush to chase it away.

As he drew nearer his wagon, he could make out a figure sitting on the buckboard—Ellen. She was framed by the drawn white edges of the canopy, barely visible in the dark. He squinted at her, trying to make out her position. Was she facing him or turned away? The closer he got, the clearer she was. Facing him, definitely. Was she watching for him?

He led his horse right to her and slid out of the saddle. He held the reins and took the remaining steps, stopping when he was just at her feet.

Her face was drawn, tired. "I see you found a mare."

Ben nodded and turned to lean against the wooden frame as he eyed the beast. "She's smaller than Red, but I figure she'll do better on the trail. Not eat so much and might even be content with a bit of prairie grass." Ben had learned plenty about how only the oxen were sure to survive on the pale prairie grasses for the entire journey. Mules and horses required a diet supplemented with feed, which meant less space for his family's food.

Ellen climbed down from the wagon and let the new mare sniff her hand. "It's nice to know strength isn't the only thing to be desired on the trail." With the horse now acquainted with her scent, Ellen ran a hand along the beast's nose.

Ben couldn't help but let his eyes rove over Ellen's petite frame. He couldn't imagine how different he would feel if he was unable to provide for himself. If he had to rely on the kindness of others. He was glad he'd been one of those Ellen could depend on, and he hoped he would remember this feeling during the times when her presence felt like one more burden on his already laden back.

A couple, their arms entwined, laughed as they rounded the corner. "Oh!" They stopped, perhaps a bit embarrassed to find they had an audience. "Is that Mr. and Mrs. Ben Bridger?"

"Yes, ma'am," Ben answered.

"You should be at your own party, lovebirds." They laughed and walked off.

Ben turned and looked up at Ellen. "Party?"

Ellen shrugged. "Molly insisted. Said folks needed a bit of light in their lives."

"They had *light* just last night. Does she think we'll be having a party every night with a new Bridger brother getting married every day for a week?"

Ellen laughed and the sound altered something inside Ben. How could she still laugh when she'd endured so much? He stared at her, considering.

"Do you want to go?"

"I couldn't very well attend *without* my husband."

The fading light meant he couldn't make out her expression through the shadows. "Sorry to have kept you waiting." Ben led the horses to their makeshift hitching post and removed the bit from Red's mouth, sliding on a halter and tying both animals to the post.

When he was through, he turned to find Ellen back up in the wagon. She waved her shawl at him in explanation. He walked right to the bed and offered her a hand down.

She took it and, with her other hand, braced herself on his shoulder as she jumped down. Her landing was harder than he expected, but she was small, so it was a higher leap for her than for him. "You should be careful about that. A broken ankle will do you no favors on the trail."

As they rounded the corner the firelight shone on her face, and she looked up at him with a curious smirk.

"What?" he asked, unable to look away. It seemed as though her every new expression was a treasure and he the greedy pirate who wanted to lock them away for himself.

"I can't tell if you are worried about me."

He adjusted his grip on her hand, weaving his fingers through hers the way he'd seen his pa do so many times with his ma. The warmth of her hand seeped into his palm. His hands were so callused he wouldn't have thought they could feel a simple touch so deeply.

His mind emptied and he had no reply. Thankfully, a cheer rang out as folks noticed their arrival. Citizens of their little community approached them with slaps on the back for Ben and kisses on the hand or cheek for Ellen.

One man lingered near Ellen. "Glad to see you away from the Moren men."

Ellen nodded and moved closer to Ben. He knew little of her husband, of the man he'd been. Titus' carelessness at the river crossing told Ben the man hadn't valued her life and likely had cared little for her comfort. It was no wonder she wasn't keen to marry again. Who would sign up to live at another's mercy?

As the crowd of well-wishers ceased, Fenna and Molly appeared with plates of food. Someone had set up a wooden dining table and chairs for them to sit and eat their meal. Ben helped Ellen into her seat, scooted it in, then took his own.

They ate and accepted congratulations from those who hadn't come by earlier. Ben couldn't forget that one man's comment about her being away from Titus and his brother.

He leaned in. "How long were you married?"

"Which time?"

Ben reeled. He must have looked comically stricken that Ellen chuckled.

"I was married twice. Widowed both times."

Ben clamped his mouth shut. He knew so little about this woman, and if a wagon master didn't arrive soon, they might be in for a lot longer of a ruse than he had planned. "We need to talk."

Ellen smiled at a passerby, keeping her lips still as she said, "Yes, we do."

There had been enough hints to them retiring for the night, but everyone knew their *marriage* had taken place the night before, so there shouldn't be the usual hubbub of the first night together. Nevertheless, folks would expect to see them retire with each other.

"I set up my tent near Molly's. After everyone has gone to bed, we can sneak you into her tent for the night."

Ellen nodded.

"Ready?"

Ellen's eyes widened. "You want to retire now? Folks won't be going to bed for hours yet."

"The longer we sit here, the more chances we have of saying something foolish. Your husband would know you'd been married before."

Ellen pressed her lips. "They cannot expect you to know everything. We've only just met. They know that."

Ben studied her. Had she *ever* been in love? He wasn't sure he had, but he had been able to watch as his brother Will fell in love with Fenna. They would spend hours out at the big oak tree talking and laughing.

"People in love learn as much as they can."

Ellen stood and a bit of color brightened her cheeks. "Folks will still make a fuss."

Ben offered his arm and leaned closer. "Perhaps leaving while the party is still rolling will discourage that. If we're sneaky enough, they might not even be able to tell which tent is ours."

In the end, they weren't able to sneak away. As soon as they started moving, folks formed a line behind them, clapping and banging cowbells in the usual shivaree nonsense. Ben stopped at Ellen's wagon and hefted the trunk she'd received earlier that day. But he couldn't stall any longer. The party was intent upon seeing them to their tent.

Ben stopped and gave everyone a hard stare. "Please, go enjoy the music and dancing. Good night."

A woman deeper in the crowd gave a hearty shout. "Kiss the bride!" The voice was familiar, and Ben had a strong suspicion that it belonged to Molly. Others joined and the crowd chanted in unison.

"Kiss. The. Bride."

Ben shook his head, but when he looked at Ellen to discuss how ridiculous this was, she was looking up at him with a worried expression.

Reasons for worry flashed through his mind. It was impossible to tell which she was most concerned about: Cyrus finding out they were unmarried or Ben kissing her. In the end, it didn't matter, because only one of those reasons was one that would endanger her future.

He set the trunk down and slid one arm around her, resting it at the small of her back. His other arm hovered, unsure what to do. It wasn't as though he had never kissed a woman. He knew where his hand should go, he should trace it up her arm then across her shoulder. He would cup the back of her head, letting the tips of his fingers bury themselves in her hair... Except she wasn't a woman he was pursuing. He didn't even like her. Well, that wasn't strictly true. The more time they spent together, the more he admired her strength.

The crowd still chanted, and Ben cleared his throat, shaking off his tentativeness. He placed his hand firmly on her upper arm. This wasn't romance. It was a lie, and he could sell it to these people.

As he brought her closer, he noticed how well they fit, as though the length of him was perfectly suited to her frame. If she leaned in, her head would fit in the hollow under his chin.

But she didn't lean in, not like that. Instead, she tilted her chin up. His imagination spun, and he realized she'd been a bride two other times. She didn't fear his kiss. No doubt it was the threat of being discovered that caused her to be stiff in his arms.

With the certainty that her anxiousness wasn't because of him but because they might not convince the crowd, he lifted one hand up and slid his fingers up her neck and into her hair. He pulled her closer, pressing her to him and dipping his face to hers.

Her breath hitched, and he smiled just before he pressed his lips to hers.

The kiss lasted only an instant before Ben pulled away. His lips were at once hot on her, then gone, as though she'd only dreamt the sensation and awoken with the dream still on her lips, stealing her breath. Ellen's legs had turned rubbery, and she gripped his jacket for support.

Ben released his hold, and Ellen's hands loosened, though she didn't yet possess the self- control to release him entirely. The crowd let out a cheer as Ben leaned down and plucked the lantern from her hand. With his other hand he parted the flaps of his tent. Slipping one foot inside, he hung the lantern on the peg and stepped out again, gesturing for Ellen to enter first.

She went down on her hands and knees and crawled inside, turning to wait for Ben. The tent was long and narrow, big enough for a full-grown man to sit up and lie down with about two feet of room along the side. An extra body would fit so long as they were sleeping close.

Ellen pressed cold fingers to her lips, feeling like a maid who'd never been kissed. Except she had been kissed, and far more thoroughly than that. Yet something in her was reaching out, begging for more. Titus' surely hadn't set her core to boiling the way it was now. Her neck to the tip of her ears were still aflame. Titus' attention had only ever been for his pleasure, and Ellen had experienced only tolerance with his every touch.

Had Harry's kisses been that way and she'd forgotten? She shook her head, certain a kiss had never done that to her. It must be the ruse, the fact that she'd given a piece of herself to Ben without loving him first. A shrill whistle cut the air and the crowd quieted. Ellen's thoughts stopped their frenzied attempts at understanding.

Ben's voice cut through the canvas tent as though it were only air. They would have a tough time finding privacy within its walls. "I'm not against clobbering any man who dares ruin our rest. Go enjoy the fire and leave us."

There were a few bawdy comments, but their voices grew softer.

Ben appeared through the flaps. First his hands with her trunk, then him. "Think I scared them off?"

"I hope so."

Ben shoved her trunk further inside. "Best to keep this in here."

Ellen's heart hammered in her chest. "I cannot dress in here with you." Her words were a whisper, but they held a frantic harshness Ellen couldn't control. She glanced at the walls of the tent, all too aware how easily her words could be heard if anyone had a mind to spy.

Ben faced her, misery written on his face. "We didn't think this through."

Ellen almost laughed, except he was right. "No, we didn't."

He shifted nearer and lowered his voice. "When the time comes, we're going to have a difficult time convincing these folks we *aren't* married."

Ellen sighed. "I don't care about my reputation. It's more important that Cyrus allow me to leave."

Ben looked relieved, then he moved and the lantern light

changed on his face, turning his expression to one of concern. "You didn't mind me kissing you?"

Warmth shot through Ellen once more. "It was necessary." No need to tell him that with one kiss he'd altered her definition of the word *passion*. That she now wondered if there was more to a marriage, something her previous marriages hadn't taught her.

She swallowed, unable to meet his eyes. Instead, she glanced around the tent and realized she was sitting on his bedroll. "Here, you should go to bed. No need for both of us to wait up. I'm the one who needs to sneak away."

She shifted slightly, but Ben didn't move, and there wasn't enough space in the tent for her to go anywhere if they didn't both move in a do-si-do.

He reached up and turned down the wick on the lantern. They were bathed in darkness and Ellen listened to her breathing while her eyes adjusted to the black.

A giggle came from outside the tent. The curious eyes and ears had yet to fully retreat.

Ben shifted and Ellen could just make out his shadow in the dark as he moved closer. His body brushed against her side and his lips found her ear. "It will be a while yet before they leave us be. We may as well both lie down."

Ellen's breath hitched. Just because the thought of sleeping beside this man didn't repulse her the way it did with Cyrus, didn't mean she had any intention of doing so.

But Ben's voice came again, his breath warming her ear and the skin just underneath. "I only mean we ought to be comfortable. And close. We have much to discuss, and it will be difficult to do so without them hearing."

"They'll know we're talking. What will they think of you?" She knew enough about what was expected of a man on a wedding night.

Ben laughed softly. "I don't care what they think, so long

as nobody goes tattling to Cyrus." He paused for a beat. "D'you think your pastor will keep his word?"

Ellen sighed. "So long as Cyrus doesn't have reason to ask him any direct questions. He may not be a friend to the Moren family, but I don't believe he'll lie either."

"I'm grateful he was a friend to you."

Ellen smiled, realizing that she was still lawfully a Moren. Pastor Ellis was a friend to at least one Moren. "Me too."

Ben pulled open the quilts and lay down in his bed. Ellen could still only see shadowy movements, but when Ben held the quilt open, she knew it was an invitation. She scooted closer and laid down, her heart beating like a thousand thundering hooves galloping a hasty retreat from the mess she'd created.

CHAPTER 15

Ellen settled in next to Ben and he flung the quilt over her. Then he lay flat on his back, wondering how he was going to speak with her when he could barely breathe.

She shifted, turning her head to face him. "I put the chickens in your folks' coop. It's a handy invention."

"Good." Ben squeezed his eyes tight, wishing he had more to say. They'd retired so they wouldn't give themselves away. But they would have to retire early every night unless he could summon the courage to get over their proximity and speak to her. They'd been this close before. They'd ridden that horse from the church back to camp. They'd been cloaked in darkness then, too. And he'd been just as able to smell her hair.

"I've been thinking about what I'm going to do in Oregon."

Ben waited, still silent.

"I'm a decent enough cook, and I'm hoping to have my chickens. I could sell eggs and perhaps work in a café."

Ben nodded. The men at her café would be proposing to her on the regular.

"Will you remarry?"

Ellen sighed, her warm breath reaching his chin. "I'm sure I will. I have to."

Ben's brows drew together. "You don't have to. I assumed you would *want to*, once your mourning period is over."

She huffed. "Ben, I'm not in mourning."

The way she'd said his name was breathy, and he imagined it might have been the way she would have said his name if that kiss had been real.

"Marriage hasn't worked out for me."

Her words were good. They brought his mind back inside this tent, to the purpose of their position. "I think it's worked out worse for them."

He'd only meant to tease her, but she didn't laugh, nor did she say anything for a long time.

"I'm sorry. Please tell me about your first husband."

She didn't and he waited, wondering if she was hurt or angry or asleep. It was impossible to tell in the dark tent.

"Harry. He was good."

Good. As though that was a ringing endorsement.

"How long were you two married?"

"Eight months."

Ben longed to ask about children. He had friends who'd had a baby less than a year after their wedding. It was a wonder Ellen had two husbands and no children. Given her circumstances, it was a blessing.

"He wanted to go west, but he got sick, along with a host of other folks in our company. We made it to Independence and no further."

"You didn't take the train to Independence?"

A rustling told him she shook her head. "Harry didn't have much money."

"What did you do?" He could only imagine arriving in a busy town like Independence, freshly widowed and poor.

"I married Titus."

Ben blinked. Had she even known the man? How had they even met? But imagining her with that man made Ben's ears grow hot, and he decided he didn't need to know. Plenty of husbands didn't want to hear the details of their wives' previous courtships.

"Tell me about your family."

A rustle, then her voice was facing the pitch in the tent instead of coming right at him. "It's my turn to hear from you."

"You've met my family."

"Yes, but I want to see them through your eyes."

Ben let out a long sigh. "Will is decent. Responsible, dependable. His marriage to Fenna might have been the only time he's surprised me." Will had always been their mama's pride. The fact that Will and Fenna had married against Ma's wish was staggering.

"Alex and Nate are—"

"No, they're not one person. You cannot lump them together like that."

"We always lump them together."

"Well, maybe you shouldn't."

Ben exhaled. "Nate's the oldest. He lords it over everyone, as if he were the actual oldest in the family and not just the oldest of the twins."

Ellen hummed, and he imagined the curve of her lips when she smiled in that dreamlike way.

"Alex doesn't like anyone, or at least he doesn't much talk to anyone besides Nate. He does well with the animals and, back when we had a house, always took his meals outside."

"Did your mama always get her dishes back?"

"I don't know."

Silence.

Ben cleared his throat. "Then there's Sam. You know Sam."

"I know all of them."

But he'd offered Sam as a husband, and she'd refused. She must have at least formed an opinion if she wasn't willing to marry him. It didn't have to be huge; just a small gesture was sometimes enough for a person to know someone wasn't right for them.

"Sam is a charmer. He took advantage of the Bridger name."

"How so?"

Ben thought of all the girls back home who had practically started a tradition of getting their first kiss from a Bridger. "With the ladies."

Ellen turned to face him, the position much too close since he was already facing her. "He doesn't seem the type. I hope he never took it too far..."

Her words lifted up at the end, making them a question, but Ben shifted sideways, only to brush against the canvas barrier. "I haven't asked."

"But your folks taught you well, all of you."

It was strange to hear her speak of them when she'd never met them. "What makes you so sure?"

"You helped me cross, helped others too."

"There are plenty of us to spare. Other folks had to get their camp set up."

Ellen hummed and, though she hadn't spoken, he knew she disagreed with him.

"Last, we have Chet. He has mastered the art of escaping chores."

Ellen laughed outright. "As little brothers are wont to do."

"Do you have a little brother?"

"Two. And a younger sister."

"Any older siblings?"

"Two older sisters."

The conversation continued until eventually the noises of the camp died down.

Ben sat up, listening hard for any more disturbance. "I think we can move you now."

Ellen moved to sit and whispered, "Okay." She scooted out from under the blanket, making room for him to get out as well. "Should I bring my trunk?"

"No, leave it here." She was still in her daytime clothing. "Just take what you need."

Ben didn't dare light the lantern while she rummaged through her things. Tomorrow she could have it ready before dark fell. They would find a rhythm.

He yawned and the fact that it was the first one he'd had tonight shocked him. Up later than the rest of the camp and not at all sleepy.

Ellen's silhouette was barely visible in the scant light, but soon she stopped searching and there was the thump of the trunk being closed.

"Ready?"

"Sure," she replied.

Ben poked his head out of the tent first, surveying the camp in the moonlight. It was quiet out here too. He ducked back inside. "Molly's tent is just there." He gestured to the right of the tent. "Can you go alone?"

"Of course." She sounded irritated, as though he'd offended her with his consideration.

She moved past him, pressing her way through the flaps with her bundle of clothing in her arms.

Ben followed behind, staying in the tent but watching to be sure she made it into Molly's tent.

Ellen hesitated for just a moment before stepping past the flaps and out of sight. He stared into the darkness for a beat, then ducked inside his own tent and sat on his heels. He turned to his empty bed and a strange loneliness cloaked him, like fog in the morning. Just there, but weightless.

CHAPTER 16

The next few days passed without fanfare. There was no sign of Cyrus, and Ben was glad to see Ellen settle in with Molly and Fenna. The more he watched, the more certain he was that Jane would never have fit in so nicely with the other women.

Ben should have appreciated the calm. The trail had been tough and all at the camp were glad for a bit of respite. Unfortunately, the calmness also spoke of the inability to find a trail guide. If Sam's guide didn't come today, Ben would have to start his search once more in earnest. They had little time to lose. Ben and Sam had been asking all around town, and he'd even considered hopping a train for a day to see if there was anyone in the next town over.

The best they could hope for was another party joining them and begging their guide to take on more wagons. The problem was, if another party didn't arrive soon, it would be too late in the year for such a large party. The animals wouldn't be able to find enough grazing and the company would move slower, the river crossings hardly able to be done in a day.

These thoughts plagued Ben as he rode from town back into camp. He spotted Ellen first, scrubbing a pot in the washtub. She looked up at his approach and gave him an easy smile. He didn't return it. Seeing her only brought uneasiness.

Where was Cyrus? Rather than feeling reassured that he'd given up, Ben had expected to see the man around every building and brush. Pretending with Ellen weighed heavy when he was already burdened by the fear they wouldn't leave town quickly enough. When they were ready to stop this game, what would the other folks think? Ellen said she didn't care what others thought, but Ben wondered what they would think of him. All day men would jostle him with their elbows and in the evening they would waggle knowing brows in his direction.

Made him wonder... was he taking advantage? If Ellen had a father, he would surely demand Ben marry her. He'd heard of such marriages, performed under threat of shotgun, and Ben had always assumed the man at the altar was spineless. Now he understood that not all situations were good or bad. Some were a muddy gray, and it wasn't easy to know what the right choice was.

He rode near and dismounted his horse, wrapping the reins around the temporary post that served as a hitch.

"Are those chickens portable?" Ben nodded toward the two hens tied to a wagon wheel.

"Yes." She watched him with curious eyes.

Ben removed his rifle from the saddle and stowed it in Ellen's wagon. His wagon until they revealed their secret and Ellen became a single woman again. When the time came, Ben doubted she would be single for long. Even here, men were on the hunt for wives. He could only imagine how that want grew as they moved west.

Ellen approached, drying her hands on the linen apron covering the front of her dress and draping past her knees. "Any luck in town?"

Ben shook his head. Fox had been expecting his friend today or tomorrow at the latest, but they'd received no word of him.

Ben went toward the chickens, sending them into chaotic attempts to fly away. He turned to Ellen. "They don't like me."

Ellen shrugged one shoulder. "They don't like men."

Ben harrumphed. He knelt at the wheel and worked each of the twine strings, making a simple loop and sliding them onto his wrist. The other end was tied to the chickens' ankles. Ben looked up at Ellen. "They let you tie those on?"

"Goldie likes me. The black one was more of a struggle." Ellen's eyes narrowed at the mentioned bird and Ben's eyes fell on a rogue black feather in her hair. He stood, handing her the line that attached to the golden bird, the one that liked her.

Ben took a few steps, waiting for the line to grow taut, then the black bird took a few steps closer. It pecked at the ground, picking up bugs and spitting out rocks.

Ben turned to Ellen. "This will be a slow walk." He offered his arm.

Ellen smiled and cocked her head, "Why, Mr. Bridger, I didn't think to be courted *after* our wedding."

Ben cut his eyes, searching for whomever Ellen was acting for. He didn't see anyone, but around here there was always someone.

"Just wanted a minute alone with you, my darling." The words bumped awkwardly off his tongue and his jaw twitched at the falsity.

Ellen took his arm. "Where are we off to?"

Ben glanced around the wide valley. There were hills in the far distance, too far to travel to, and the wide prairie before them spoke to the scene they would endure for the next few months. "Just around."

Once he started moving, the birds understood their relative freedom and moved quicker. Silence descended and Ben began thinking furiously for something to say. He'd hardly needed to ask for Jane to fill a silence. Just when he was about to comment on the dry landscape Ellen spoke, her voice splitting the quiet. "How are you doing? I mean with the loss of your parents?"

Ben's gaze shot to hers, his heart giving an eager thump. Part of him longed to speak of them and with someone who hadn't known them, someone his words wouldn't hurt. But this had nothing to do with their sham-marriage, and there was no need to burden her with his somber musings.

Ellen must have sensed his disapproval. She leaned in slightly, letting her shoulder press against his arm, but it only served to add weight to the way she was holding onto him— the way a wife held onto her husband. The way Mama used to hold onto Pa.

"I only ask because, well, that's the question most folks ask me."

"About my parents?"

"Well, they're always saying how good it is that we found each other just now, and how sad it is that all you boys have been left alone."

Ben worked his jaw. Folks had nothing better to do than gossip. Hopefully, when they got on the trail again, there would be enough toil to keep idle minds busy. "Will isn't alone."

"And neither are you. At least, that's what everyone thinks. Except you *are* alone and I wish you had someone real, someone you could talk to about all this."

"We aren't Adam, alone until Eve arrived. We don't need women. We're not *alone*." He spat the word and felt Ellen draw away from him. It was subtle, a straightening of the back, a tightening of the arm that was looped through his, as though she had to mindfully hold onto him instead of the natural way she'd been clinging to him before.

She fell silent and he stared at his black bird. What was it that made folks think a man couldn't live without a woman? Apparently, men all over the west were doing so. They were also richer than ever, finding gold in the ground and in the rivers. They didn't seem to be crumbling to a fine dust beneath the weight of womanlessness.

Yet Ma had wanted them to find women, him especially. He recalled the promise he'd made, a foolish one, but he couldn't have done any different, not when she was lying on the prairie grass, her life bleeding out of her.

He closed his eyes against the scene and changed the topic. "This bird needs a name."

Usually, he was opposed to naming an animal that was bound to be food, but he was hopeful that these birds would survive and allow Ellen a bit of independence in Oregon.

"I only bothered naming the ones that liked me."

"Well, this one likes me."

Ellen laughed. "No, it doesn't."

Ben held up his twine tether as though it proved his statement.

Ellen only laughed harder. "Go ahead, give her a name."

Ben studied the bird. "Nick."

Ellen reeled but came back to him, her hold once again comfortable. "You can't call her that."

"You said I could name her."

"Yes, well that's a boy's name and it's too human."

"Okay. Elf."

Ellen stopped walking and peered up at him.

Ben couldn't help but smile at her. "She's black, but she's got that red comb on her head and green in her tail feathers. Red, black, and green. Those are Christmas colors."

Ellen narrowed her eyes.

"And Elf isn't a human name."

Ellen looked at the bird, her eyes shifting from the red comb to the shimmering green feathers.

"Christmas," Ben said, holding back a laugh.

"Fine." Ellen tossed her head and a curl fell into her face.

Ben lifted his hand to tuck it away, but the twine between his wrist and Elf pulled and the chicken batted her wings. He let his hand drop as Ellen took care of the curl, tucking it back and securing it in her ribbon.

He cast around again, searching for something to say. "Did you always want to go to Oregon?" There were a few of their company bound for California. He had only just realized that once their ruse was complete, Ellen would have the freedom to take her wagon any place she wished. They would start the trail together and end it separately. She would have to learn to drive it, but they had months for her to learn.

"You know as well as I do that the west is too wild for a single woman." She sighed. "I'll find a husband quick enough."

She spoke of marriage with such calculation. It was no wonder she'd had two husbands during her surely no more than twenty years on this earth.

He sighed in pity. "Number three."

Ellen's attention snapped to him, anger in her eyes. He'd never seen this look on her face and he found himself strangely drawn to it. Perhaps he liked more his ability to create any sort of change to her tranquil demeanor.

"My first husband wasn't like Titus."

Ben swallowed, hearing his mother's rebuke in his mind. "I apologize. I spoke out of turn."

Ellen turned away and at once Ben missed her hot gaze.

"I'm glad to know he was different. I hate when I think of you married to Titus."

In his sincerity, he had given her more honesty than usual. But he still held back. In truth, he thought often of Ellen in that man's home, under his pitiful protection. His brother, Cyrus, had clearly gotten what little gallantry that family possessed, and he'd still planned to use it against Ellen.

"What of you?" Her voice was sharp once more. "Fenna said you might have been married. What happened?"

Ben glanced toward the camp, toward Fenna. That was a woman who talked, especially about Bridger men and the women connected to them. "It wasn't right."

Ellen scoffed. "That's hardly an answer."

"Well, nobody will expect you to know about my past conquests."

Ellen scoffed. *"Conquests.* Is that how you see women?"

Ben spluttered. "I didn't—"

Ellen pulled her arm free and shooed Goldie toward the camp.

Ben watched her go, too proud to call after her but regretting her departure all the same.

Her skirts swished with the movement of her hips. No wonder the men slapped his back and told him how lucky he was.

It only took a few long strides for him to catch her and match her angry steps. "Is it good if they think we've had a fight?" Elf flapped after him.

Ellen barely glanced up at him. "Right now, it's better if you don't speak at all."

He caught her hand. She pulled it free but stopped, glaring up at him.

Ben bit his lips to stop his smile. He'd enjoyed making her mad, and now it seemed he was accomplishing it without even trying. "We've barely learned anything about each other."

"What do you want to know?"

Her toe tapped against a piece of gravel in the dirt. "All the common things. Are your parents still in Pennsylvania?"

"My mama is dead, and my papa is always in his cups. He barely earns enough to feed the younger ones. I could never go back."

"That's why you're going west?"

"Do you see a better option for me?"

Ben shrugged. "Might've gone east again, found a husband there."

Ellen shook her head. "I'll have my pick of men this way." She nodded toward the sun setting in the west.

Ben followed her stare. "Not if you plan to marry on the trail. You'll have only a few choices."

"I'll figure it out."

"I don't doubt you will." Ben smiled. Might have been the first genuine smile he'd experienced since his parents' deaths. Perhaps there was more to what everyone said about a man needing a woman. It wasn't that women were necessary for living, but maybe they were necessary for joy.

"And you? Why didn't you just buy a bit of land back home? Why pull up stakes and go west?"

Ben shrugged. "It was my pa's idea, mostly. Now we've sold everything, there isn't much to do but follow through."

Ellen scoffed. "Seems we both need a better reason to make this trip. One of us might die on the way there."

"I ain't going back." Ben's heart thumped in his chest. The idea of going back nauseated him.

Ellen quirked a brow. "That doesn't sound like your pa's determination. It sounds like your own."

"There ain't nothing there but war and hatred."

"And the west promises peace and love?" Her mocking tone felt like a burr in his heel, and the same irritation she wore on her face rose up his back.

"It promises hard work, solitude, and ownership."

"More 'conquests'?"

He glared, not liking how she used his words against him. "As I hear it, you'll be the one with options to conquer. You'll have your pick of the men." He'd only meant it as a practical truth, but his tone held a shred of jealousy.

Ellen narrowed her eyes. Had she caught that tone? She heaved a sigh and Ben had to conceal one of his own.

"What is your plan for your family?" she asked. "You're head of the Bridgers now—it's a bit of responsibility."

Ben felt the weight settle on his shoulders, like the yoke they would lay on the oxen when it came time to move west. "Land. Farming. If the dirt's as good as they say, we'll do just fine."

"If it isn't?"

Ben narrowed his eyes. She was goading him. Perhaps the wrath of her sharp tongue wasn't worth the color in her cheeks. "Then we'll head to California."

"They're all looking for wives, you know. Your brothers."

"Yeah?" Ben hardly cared. He doubted any of them would be able to find a woman willing to marry them in two weeks' time, less likely one willing to go west.

"What if they don't want to go wherever you go?"

Ben opened his mouth, but he had no answer. He'd always pictured them all together, carving out a Bridger plot of land where their wives would socialize and their children would run and play together.

"A woman likes to be near her family." Her tone had shed some of that fury and was gentler now.

Ben cleared his throat. "If she marries a Bridger, she'll be a Bridger. We'll be her family."

Ellen glanced up at him, her eyes soft. "That's what I did. Look where it left me."

Ben's anger abated. Women were alone in this world. How often were they expected to leave their families behind to join their husbands? "Where is your first husband's family? Why did they not take you in?"

She shrugged. "They're back home near my folks."

"You didn't return to them?"

Ellen shook her head. "I thought about it, but when I wasn't carrying a child…"

Heat flooded Ben's cheeks. He hadn't meant to press about such a personal topic. But she wasn't angry with him this time.

That same softness hung in her eyes, and he took courage that it was a safe topic. "Did you want a child?"

Ellen grimaced. "No." She huffed. "But that's not entirely right. It's just that life is a whole lot easier alone."

Ben heard the contradiction and weighed whether to voice it. "Is a woman not better off with a companion the same way a man is?"

Ellen glared, and he knew he'd made the wrong call. "Is a wife the same to you as a child?"

"No…"

"A child is a dependent, not a companion. You're right, a woman *is* better off with a companion. Why do you think I married a man like Titus?"

"There was nobody better? I cannot imagine Titus was your best choice. Were you truly so desperate?"

Ellen's eyes held a fire Ben couldn't tame, not in a hundred months on the trail. "He deceived me. He was one man before we wed, and another man after. It was Cyrus. He... poisoned everything."

Ben barked a laugh. "It wasn't Cyrus driving that wagon through the river."

Ellen's cheeks colored, and her voice was softer when she spoke. "You should forget about that."

Ben sniffed. "I cannot. I don't understand why you married him."

Ellen looked toward camp. She stepped forward and with her free hand, she took his, a gesture at odds with her cool ire. She hadn't taken his hand for *him*. She'd done it for whoever was watching. "You wouldn't understand. You are a man." She smiled and stroked his cheek.

He hated how deceitful she could be, cutting him low at the same moment as she touched him with such intimacy. Nevertheless, her touch turned his voice gravelly as he said, "Perhaps you too changed after marriage. Perhaps you were not the only one deceived."

Ellen's eyes narrowed and she moved to step away, her chicken following, but Ben caught her waist. "Who is watching?"

Ellen twisted her head away and glanced toward camp. "I cannot tell, but they are acting as though this is a theater and we are the actors."

Ben gave her a wolfish smile. "Are we not?" He slid his hand up her neck and hooked a thumb under her chin, tilting her face toward him. Her pulse thrummed under his fingertips, warm and quick. Her nostrils flared in anger, but she didn't move to escape, devoted to the charade.

She watched him and, unlike the first time he'd kissed her, her eyes weren't full of fear. Neither were they full of longing.

Ben twisted so he stood between Ellen and the camp. He dipped his head, giving the appearance of a kiss. Instead of pressing his mouth to her lips, he pressed his cheekbone to hers. "We should be more loving with one another."

He released her and she caught his lapels and drew a shuddering breath. Ben smiled; he'd affected her. It hadn't been fear in her eyes when she thought he might kiss her again. It had been challenge, and he was more than up for it.

CHAPTER 17

*E*llen gripped his jacket and sucked in a breath. Somehow, anticipation had stolen her breath, and she tried to find it while she clung to his coat. Anger and desire crackled within her. Impossible to tell which emotion dominated the other. She hated that.

She gave him a fake smile and roughly took his arm. "I can be loving." She sneered and took a purposeful step toward camp. He followed easily. Ellen pouted. Could she cause him any discomfort? If she picked up Goldie and ran, Ben would match her pace. When she mocked him, he gave it right back. He didn't even anger, not the way Titus did. When she tried her best to anger him, she'd succeeded only in angering herself.

"Is this loving?" He jangled their arms, hers gripping his like it was a rope stretched across a swollen river.

She released him, but he wrapped an arm around her shoulders. His jacket shifted, sending the scent of him her way—spice and smoke and leather.

"You smell." She pressed at him, but he held her close.

"I'll bathe tonight."

Ellen almost felt guilty. The icy water made bathing an uncomfortable chore, and truly he didn't smell bad in the least. In fact, the thought of him bathing had Ellen wondering what he would smell like without a day's work on his skin.

She shook it away and since her left side was pressed against his ribs, she felt his laugh rumble through her.

His arm tightened. "Are you thinking of me taking a bath?"

"No." Ellen pushed at him again, but he refused to give her any space. It almost felt good to push a man and know she wouldn't suffer for it. She settled in closer than before and breathed deep. This wasn't real, but it could teach her a bit about what to seek in her next marriage. A man who didn't budge, who was solid like a tree with roots just as deep.

The chickens seemed to understand their direction and moved easily with them. After a few more steps, she risked speaking her mind. "You'll do well, taking care of your family." His hold loosened the slightest bit and Ellen found herself leaning in to make up the difference. "They all look up to you, even Will."

"Our pa was big on that. We were all responsible for the younger ones."

"And you're the oldest. Big responsibility for a young boy."

Ben was silent and Ellen could picture him younger, face like Chet's, thinner with less hair darkening his jaw.

"Good thing I'm not a young boy."

"Good thing." Ellen sent a gentle elbow into his ribs.

"We haven't had any trouble from Cyrus."

Ellen frowned. "I know." The unexpected peace was somehow unsettling.

"It feels wrong."

"Yes." Ellen breathed the word, surprised at the way he unknowingly agreed with her. "Like he gave up too easily."

Ben must have shortened his stride because their steps synced. What would it be like to live under the protection of this man's wing? To walk at his side? To discuss how to protect his family?

When they reached camp, the figure who'd been watching them strode closer.

Ben released his hold of Ellen and reached out to shake hands with the man. "Fox, good to see you."

Fox nodded and glanced at Ellen. His face was familiar, and Ellen tried not to stare as she attempted to place where she'd seen him. He seemed to be more familiar than the rest of the folks she'd met along the trail.

"D'you have a minute?" Fox's eyes shifted.

"Sure." Ben gestured toward their wagons.

Fox glanced over but shook his head. "Alone." He nodded once toward Ellen. "She should come too."

That piqued Ellen's interest, so she slung an arm around Ben's waist and gripped his jacket with the other, signaling that she wasn't going to be sent away. Out of their entire company, she might be the most desperate to leave Independence.

Ben nodded. "Let me put these chickens in the pen." Ellen scooped Goldie into her arms. Ben tussled a bit with Elf, but not nearly as much as Ellen had when tying that bit of twine around her foot.

They moved quickly, placing the chickens in the wagon and tying the bonnet smaller before Ben draped his arm around Ellen's shoulders once more and turned to lead her and Fox back the way they came.

Ellen stood between the men, her chest swelling with the privilege of being part of whatever was about to transpire.

Titus would have sent her away, told her this wasn't a woman's place. Ben held her tight, making her feel like she didn't just belong here—she was wanted.

They stopped walking and Fox crossed his arms, his stance wide. "You won't find a guide."

Ellen gaped at how easily Fox had dropped the guillotine on their hopes. How could he be sure enough to claim this?

"No?" Ben said simply.

Ellen glanced up. Did men possess a language of their own, with several meanings hidden within each word?

"Cyrus Moren has paid your guide not to take this company west."

Ellen felt like she'd been struck, the wind stolen from her chest. "Cyrus?" she whispered with what little remaining breath she possessed.

"No guide will cross him. He's vital to every company that leaves this town. The only reason he didn't stop your company before is because he supplied everyone before your marriage happened."

Ben glanced at Ellen and pulled her closer.

Her throat grew thick at his false show of solidarity. Surely, he wanted to shove her away, to curse her for her recklessness in involving his family with someone as powerful as Cyrus.

"Will you take us?" Ben asked.

Ellen glanced sharply up at her fake husband. What qualified Fox to take them west? Folks paid for experience. If they followed this young man, they'd all die before they reached Colorado.

"I'll take you, but you need to know something first."

Ben stiffened under Ellen's hold. She brushed a hand over his chest, hoping to settle whatever rose within him.

"There's a reason I ain't taking folks across anymore."

Ben waited and Ellen recognized the tactic. He'd done this when he asked about her husbands, waited until she gave him the answers he sought.

Fox's words came slowly. "I took a company a few years back. We left too late, got caught in the mountains. We lost too many."

With the obvious pain in Fox's voice, Ellen expected Ben to soothe the man's insecurities, to tell him that didn't matter so long as Fox got their party across the plains.

Instead, Ben said, "Why'd you leave so late?"

Ellen started at the cruel question and Ben's grip on her tightened.

Fox toed the ground, the setting sun cast shadows across his face that lent a sadness she hadn't seen before. "I was proud. Thought I had experience those others didn't."

"Did you?"

Fox sighed. "Maybe."

"Well, we aren't too late. Not yet."

Fox's gaze shifted to the camp. "If we hit a trail calamity, we can't turn back. We have to go forward at my say so."

"You're our only option. Folks will have to agree."

Fox sighed and nodded, not at all pleased.

"How soon can you leave?"

Fox's gaze slowly lifted and met Ben's. "I could pull up stakes tomorrow, but we ought to give everyone else at least two days."

Excitement hummed through Ben, or perhaps it was Ellen. Their bodies were close enough to feel as though they were one.

"We'll be ready." Ben's voice rumbled against Ellen, and she couldn't stop herself from leaning into him.

They'd passed three days without Cyrus giving them any grief. Hopefully, he'd leave them alone for another two.

Ellen's hopes were granted, and before the sun rose on the second day, their company started for Oregon. Fox insisted Ben's family lead the train of wagons, followed by Fox's responsibilities, the brides. Fox rode his mule down the line and spoke with folks throughout the day. Sometimes he rode alone and Ellen watched, wondering what he was thinking. Did he still blame himself for the death of those lost over those mountains? What would happen if circumstances slowed their company and they too were forced to traverse snowy mountains?

The going was slow, making it easy to carry on a conversation. Ben walked to the side of the oxen, tapping their rumps with a stick every so often. The rumble of wheels covered conversation and Ellen found herself speaking easily with Ben.

"You did well, convincing Fox to take us."

Ben shook his head. "We needed a guide, but he needed a company to get those women west. Safety in numbers."

"Whatever it was, I am glad. What would we have done, pretending to be wed for another year?"

Ben huffed a laugh. She enjoyed how easy he was to speak with while he was tending the oxen and watching the western horizon. If she didn't know better, she might think it was she who tongue-tied him. Or maybe it was merely the east and with every step he took to his new life, his tongue loosened.

By the time they circled the wagons for the night, Ellen was ready to collapse into her bed, but she groaned in frustration. She would have to feign sleeping in Ben's tent first. He was still tending stock when her chores were done, so she climbed into his tent.

The air was cold on her skin and without an idea for how long she would have to wait, she tucked herself between his quilts and closed her eyes.

The scent of him was strongest here. She'd gotten tastes of it when they were playing their respective roles. But now there was less chance for them to act, and the farther they got from Independence, the more likely it was Ben would call an end to their ruse.

She gave a disappointed exhale, not understanding her feelings. When they revealed the truth, Ellen might become a pariah among the company. Ben had said it before—they might have played their parts a bit too well. Now folks would think her a wanton woman. But out west that didn't matter. Men married painted ladies without thought. Ellen would be no different.

All she had to do was endure. She'd built a genuine friendship with Fenna and Molly, the only women who knew the truth. Surely, they would support Ellen if the company turned against her.

With her head on his pillow, she fought within herself, listing concerns and then convincing herself not to worry, until sleep fell upon her and she dreamed of Ben's arms around her, safe and strong.

She woke with a start and listened for the usual cacophony of the company. During the day there was nary a silent moment. The creak of wagons, the calls of the men pushing the oxen to keep going, children crying for any number of reasons. But now all was silent. She twisted, groping in the dark, and her icy hands brushed against something warm.

She buried her fingers into it before she understood what it was. She gasped and ripped her hands away, buried them against her stomach. "Ben?"

"What?" he groaned.

"What are you doing?" Ellen pushed at him. "Are you *asleep?*"

"I *was.*" He shifted, as though she was a mere fly to be swatted away from his face.

"Why did you let me sleep?"

Ben groaned and turned over, away from Ellen. She reached out again and touched her icy fingers to his neck. He grunted and caught her hand. She tried to tug free, but he rolled toward her again and groped his way up her arm. He pressed his hand to her neck, but instead of returning the chill she'd given him, his hands were warm.

"How are you so hot?"

He flipped his fingers, as though searching for a cold spot, and when he earned no response, he pulled away. Ellen leveraged his hold on her and scooted closer to him, whispering, "How long has the camp been asleep?"

Ben yawned. "Don't know."

"Can you sneak me to Molly's tent?" It was next to theirs, and Ellen shouldn't be afraid of the dark, but she wanted Ben to watch her go just in case. If the big bad wolf really did exist, this prairie would most certainly be his home.

Ben fell silent for a moment. Had he fallen asleep? She pressed on his chest, and he sucked in a breath. *Asleep.*

"Huh?" he mumbled.

"Help me get to Molly's tent." Ellen tried to keep the irritation out of her voice.

"Can't."

"What?" Ellen started to untangle herself, exposing herself to the frigid night air. The degree of cold told her it was late, much later than the time she usually switched tents.

Ben brushed a hand down his face, the stubble scratching his palm. "A fellow was watching me today. Sam said he's been watching me since yesterday."

Ellen kept her hands on his chest, enjoying his warmth, and hoped he was too sleepy to notice. "Watching you?"

"Watching us."

Ellen pulled her hands away, no longer worried about a chill when they might be discovered. Only a day outside Independence. Cyrus could make that ride in a few hours. "Who is it?"

"Don't know, but you should stay in here."

Staying here wasn't a risk. Propriety only had her sleeping in Molly's tent. That and the idea that there was safety in numbers and Molly would otherwise be alone. Maybe once they told the truth to everyone, Ellen could continue to share a tent with Molly.

For now though, Ben was right. She tucked her feet back into the quilts and burrowed deep. Her corset pinched, but she wasn't about to dress down. She'd slept this long; surely, she could sleep the rest of the night.

As she settled the blankets around her, she squinted at Ben in the dark, trying to see what he was covered with. "Do you have quilts?"

Ellen reached out and grabbed the blanket covering him. She tried to count but could only find one layer.

Ben brushed her hands away. "I'm fine."

Ellen's heart sank. "I'm not taking all your quilts. Where did you even get that one? Is one of your brothers sleeping with less tonight?"

They used all the quilts. The summer would warm and as they went along the need for heavy bedding would lessen, but for now each one of them used every quilt in their stores.

But Ben was sleeping with one and Ellen knew well that wasn't enough. She and Molly shared a bed, shared warmth and quilts, and on some nights that still wasn't enough.

She sat up, the blankets falling and exposing her clothes

to the cold, which took no time crawling through her layers and chasing off any bit of remaining sleepiness.

The inside of the tent was nearly pitch black. There were no lanterns lit outside, no fires to lend their light.

"What are you doing?" Ben sounded annoyed, and Ellen hoped that was just sleepiness talking.

"I'm going to make us a bed." She chewed her lip. "Give me your blanket."

"No." His tone was hard. He rolled away. Ellen gripped the fabric near his feet and tried to pull, but his frame flexed, and the quilt refused to give.

She went down on her knees and groped in the dark until she found his shoulders. She crawled closer and leaned in to whisper in his ear, "I'm going to make us a bed that will keep you warm all night."

"I'm warm."

Ellen froze. Blinked. He *was* warm. His hands had been warmer than hers. "How?"

"Go to bed."

She didn't want to argue, but she wasn't sure how much of the night was left and she was already up. She leaned in again. "We may as well make sure both of us stay warm for the rest of the night. One blanket won't keep you warm for several hours."

He huffed and released the quilt, flinging it at her so it covered her face. He let out a chuckle that was muffled by the fabric over her head. She tugged it off and didn't waste time. She set to work folding his quilt into a long barrier and laying it along the length of where she'd slept. She pushed it closer, knowing she would be on the coldest part, against the canvas wall, but hoping to give Ben ample space to sleep.

Then she gathered the quilts she'd been using and laid them out flat, spanning the distance on both sides of her makeshift divider.

She nodded, content. "Okay, you climb in first."

Ben did so without a word, and Ellen wondered if he possessed the ability to sleep sitting up. With the help of spirits, her pa had done so plenty of times throughout her childhood. Perhaps it was a skill men were born with, along with snoring too loud and angering too quickly.

He took up his same spot on the ground, but Ellen walked around and pushed at his side. "You're too far from the barrier."

"The what?" He sounded tired, and Ellen chewed her lip, feeling bad that she wasn't allowing him to sleep. She buoyed herself up with the hope that a bit of work now would mean a decent night's sleep later.

She pushed on him and this time he obliged, scooting closer, closer until she felt he'd gone far enough. She covered him with the quilts and even tucked the fabric around his chin, preening like a bird who is content with her ability to build a nest.

She wasted no time in climbing into her side of the bed, which was admittedly tighter than she'd imagined. She tucked the quilts against the canvas side, hoping it would provide insulation against the chill night air.

"You're too close," Ben mumbled.

Ellen continued tucking herself in, then balled her icy hands together and pressed them into her chest. "It's fine."

And it was. Unlike her time spent with any other man, Ellen didn't doubt Ben's honor. She felt safer here, tucked into a bed at his side, than she'd felt with most men standing in a crowd in broad daylight.

He didn't argue, and soon he breathed deeply. She listened to it, letting it lull her to sleep. After the day she'd had and the warmth that Ben lent to her little cocoon, it wasn't difficult to fall asleep.

But when she did, she dreamed of being in Ben's arms, of

both of them holding one another in bed the way he'd held her while they'd talked with Fox. Of him pressing her face up to his, only to refuse to kiss her with an angry face.

She dreamed she was a dry, cracked prairie in want of a hard rain.

CHAPTER 18

*E*llen woke and in a moment her face warmed as she remembered where she was and what lustful thoughts had accompanied her dreams. She was curled around her makeshift barrier like a miner clinging to his bottle of spirits.

She gulped and pressed up to sit. Ben was gone, but the quilts were folded over one another on top of her, providing Ellen with additional layers. Her body was still so warm that the chill morning air didn't even bite at her the way it had done last night. She only hoped that same warmth had comforted Ben when he woke.

Ellen set to work, tidying and packing their tent. She brought her first bundle to the wagon and Ben was there, greasing the axles. He barely looked at her before resuming his work.

That brief look wasn't enough. It was never enough with him, not before and certainly not after her dreams. Her throat grew thick and she watched his back. How could she teach herself that he wasn't for her? How could she sync her logical mind with her emotions, the part of her that controlled her dreams?

Besides, she should wish for invisibility. It was preferable. But in the sanctuary of her own mind she didn't have to feign modesty. She wasn't the prettiest of women, but she'd often drawn the gaze of a man. Once she made it west, where women were scarce, invisibility would be impossible.

When she finished packing her and Ben's tent and belongings into the wagon, she found Fenna and a pot of mush for breakfast. She made two bowls and went off in search of Ben, finding him hitching oxen to her wagon.

Ellen passed him his bowl and ran a hand along the bony animal. "You take good care of them."

Ben nodded, his mouth already full as though he were starving. He pointed his spoon at her. "You should drive them today."

Ellen's eyes bulged. "Me?"

"It's not driving them on the seat the way your husband was."

Ellen stepped closer. "Husband?" she challenged, eyebrows raised.

Ben's eyes cut around them, but in a camp like this, simply seeing nobody didn't mean there wasn't a body around the corner of the wagon. Privacy was like fairies. She could choose to believe in it if it made her feel better. That belief, however, didn't make it true.

"Titus. He didn't have to drive them like they were a team of horses."

"He didn't know much about going west." Ellen thought of the family who had owned this wagon before them. No doubt when they heard what happened to the company, they would be glad misfortune took one future and replaced it with another.

She'd grieved to take everything from them, but just now

she couldn't feel bad for it. Was it vile that she was grateful Titus had taken her west, had taken their wagon and died? It surely was. She gulped, looking at Ben. Did he guess how awful of a person she was?

"Can't say many of us know what we're doing. That's why we listen to those in charge."

Ellen lifted her eyes and spotted Fox on his mule, with another one trailing behind him covered in packs. "Who takes care of the women while he goes off and scouts the next section of the trail?"

"An older couple are traveling close. They'll help where needed."

"He travels light enough." Fox was different from their last guide in the way he insisted on eating with a different wagon every night. Said it helped him get to know folks and also ensure they were eating properly. Not too much, but also not too little.

Ben followed her gaze. "He isn't planning to set up when he arrives. He has no need of anything but shelter."

Ellen smiled to think of traveling so light. She knew better than most that a single person was easier to care for than any other number. "Your lives are quite different."

Ben sniffed.

"Do you wish yours was more like his?"

Ben drew a deep breath, his shoulders lifting and falling. He passed her his empty bowl and patted an ox on the rump. "I would never wish to be without my family."

Ellen nodded. Such a foreign concept. In her family, the older ones left as soon as they could. They checked in from time to time to make sure the littlest ones had what they needed, maybe spoiling them with a candy or a rag doll. But they didn't look out for one another the way these Bridgers did.

Soon the company was off. Ben and Ellen had taken their

turn being the first wagon. Today Fox had selected someone else to be the first. This position was the most desirable because it meant walking in fresh air instead of the dust from other wagons. Though they'd lost around thirty folks to death or abandonment, their company was still near one hundred souls and they kicked up enough dust to fill every crevice. Ellen couldn't imagine how bad it would be to walk at the very back. But she would find out soon enough.

They'd been walking for what she figured was an hour when Ben passed her the long stick. Ellen gulped, looking at the thing. She'd watched him all the day before. He'd used it as a walking stick until it was time to prod the oxen along, at which time he'd tapped at the spot just below their tails to urge them to keep moving.

She took it from his hand and looked up at him.

He smiled, his eyes softening toward her for the first time. "You'll do just fine."

"Will you stay with me? What if they decide to run off?"

Ben laughed. "That's the beauty of oxen. They're too dumb to bolt."

Ellen nodded and drew a bolstering breath.

Ben moved around her so she was nearest the oxen. He pointed toward the animals. "Don't tangle their legs. Just hit them there, between their tails and the hardware."

Ellen did it, the stick bounding off their muscled flanks. And that was it. She shrugged. "Simple enough."

Ben smiled again, transforming his face. Two in one day. How many more surprises would this trail bring her?

Again, the noise of animals and people and wagons drowned out their conversation and Ellen spoke without the fear of being overheard. "Did you sleep well last night?"

The lines of his face turned hard. "Well enough."

She swallowed her disappointment at losing his smile, though she shouldn't be shocked. She'd never been able to make Titus happy. Why should she think she could do so for Ben? "You weren't happy with me changing up our sleeping arrangement."

"It was fine."

"You are grumpy when you're woken up."

He sniffed a laugh. "You can tell your friends that. It's something only a wife would know."

Ellen didn't have friends. The folks who spoke to her were acquaintances. If they came back, she might have answers for them, but perhaps they would ask different questions and Ellen would have to lie to them some more. "Tell me about Jane."

She felt rather than saw him freeze. He didn't stop walking, but it was as though his other movements halted. His swinging arms, his breathing, even the wind that fluttered the short hairs sticking out from his hat.

"Fenna told me she was very beautiful."

Fenna had said a lot of other things, but for some reason this was the thing Ellen's mind snagged on. How beautiful? Ben was a handsome figure himself, and Ellen wouldn't have expected him to settle for anyone who was less than him, but Ellen vainly wondered if Jane was prettier than she was.

There was no looking glass in any of their wagons; not even Molly had one. Ellen was certain she wasn't as put together as this girl who had held Ben's heart for an undetermined amount of time.

"How long were you two…" She searched for the word. "Friendly?"

Ben sucked in a breath, his face pulled down in a scowl. He didn't like this topic, but Ellen was determined to get at least a few answers before he changed the subject.

"Can't rightly say. We grew up around one another and over time it grew."

"Did you love her?"

He lowered his brows, but instead of looking harsh, he appeared thoughtful. "Can't rightly say."

A band around Ellen's chest loosened a fraction. "Why didn't she come west?"

"Didn't want to."

"Why did she end the courtship?"

Ben's throat bobbed. Ellen recalled pressing her cold fingers to that throat last night. Recalled the warmth that seemed to emanate from his every part. How could a woman part with a man like him? Why would she?

"Her family didn't approve of my family. Of me."

"Those are two different things."

"Maybe. They wanted me to sign up with the confederates, to fight for the rebel cause."

Ellen already knew the Bridgers didn't agree with their neighbors. "And when you wouldn't…"

"She said that was the only way to show her family my commitment to her."

Ellen snorted. "You were more likely to get killed. If she wanted a husband, she would have done better to keep you close."

Ben fell quiet. Ellen searched his face for a mournful expression, grief over the loss of his woman. But all she saw was hard determination.

"Keep them moving." He gestured to the oxen that had fallen back a bit from the wagon ahead.

Ellen jumped to comply, whacking the oxen with a little too much force and bringing them much closer to the wagon in front. She laid the stick over her shoulder like a young child heading out to a pool to fish.

She stared ahead, afraid to look at Ben while she said what was on her mind. "You deserve a woman who doesn't care what her parents think. You deserve a woman who wants just you and nothing else. She wasn't good enough for you."

"She was too good." His words were delivered quickly, like it was the one thing Ben was sure about. His tone brooked no argument.

Ellen had to bite her tongue. Worthiness wasn't something to be told—it had to be felt. She hated this Jane for preventing Ben from understanding his value. Any woman, married or not, would appreciate the type of husband Ben would be. What were the women in North Carolina drinking that none of the Bridger men could find themselves a bride?

"She's a fool," Ellen said, quietly enough that perhaps Ben hadn't heard. But she hoped he did.

CHAPTER 19

Ben had to get away from Ellen. She'd spread over him like ivy on a brick house, her tendrils crawling into every crevice, rooting out the soft places and filling them with her endless questions.

He left to check on his brothers, doing his best to ignore the expression of fear on Ellen's face when he left her to drive the oxen alone.

Molly intercepted him. She gripped his arm. "Ellen never joined me last night."

"I told you she wouldn't."

Molly scoffed. "I didn't believe she would agree to it." Molly released her grip and stared at the wide valley before them. "I'm not sure how you two are going to unravel the knot you've tied."

"Me neither," Ben mumbled. He continued walking at her side, content with any excuse to be away from Ellen.

"You don't have to, you know. I saw that kiss."

Ben's eyes cut to Molly, his suspicion all but confirmed. "You *called* for the kiss."

Molly grinned. "You're welcome."

Ben shook his head, but he couldn't stop the smile. Somehow, this distant cousin he barely knew carried a piece of his mother. That realization softened the ache that weighed heavy in his chest. His mother was gone, but he would still find her in places. He hoped that would stay true for the rest of his life. And Molly was with them, an addition his mother had approved, and she was his responsibility now.

He surveyed her profile. "What of you? Is there a man you'll be kissing any time soon?"

Molly scoffed. "Sorry to say, but I don't plan to marry."

She was a pretty woman, but Will had already informed him she'd refused several offers of marriage. "I wonder if you'll be given a choice."

Molly glared up at him. "Will you be selling me off?"

Ben shook his head. "The way I hear it, women are scarce. Those men will be on their best behavior for you."

"I'm sure they will, but I doubt there will be a man past the Rockies who could tempt me."

Ben thought of Fox. "There's a man up there whose job it is to get us that far. Don't let him hear you saying there are no good folks out there."

"I didn't say that."

Ben was through with this conversation. She might be under his protection, but she was just as haughty as when they were children. Too prissy to get a little dirt on her shiny boots.

"Just watch your words." He dropped back to find Sam.

Since Ben was helping Ellen with her wagon, Sam had been left in charge of the wagon he and Ben had shared before the twister. He was old enough, but somehow Ben had yet to truly see Sam as a man and not a boy.

"How's it going?"

Sam smirked. "Heard you spent the night with your wife."

Ben leveled him with a stare. "Don't jest." He glanced

around. "Have you seen that fellow today, the one who was watching us?"

"He was watching *you*, not us. Or perhaps he's eyeing the woman you're pretending is your wife. Plenty of men are mourning the lost opportunity."

"Good. Hopefully they'll be glad to take up the mantle when we tell them the truth."

Sam tapped the oxen's hindquarters and gestured toward the front of the train. "Better go see if your wife needs help."

Ben lifted his gaze to see Ellen and her wagon veering outside the line of wheels. She was jogging far away from the oxen's heads and waving her stick in the air like a wizard trying to cast a spell.

Ben grit his teeth and jogged to her.

She saw him, her eyes wild. "Ben! They won't get back in line."

He marched closer, and though his body told him to comfort her, he only took the stick from her hands. "You pushed them too close to the wagon in front. They had nowhere else to go but to the side."

"I didn't mean to." Her voice still sounded anxious, even though he had taken control of the stick.

Ben spread his arms wide on the outside of the oxen and walked like a shepherd gathering his flock. Ever so slowly, the oxen moved back into the line of wagons.

When they were where they needed to be, he relaxed and faced Ellen again. "You need to keep them on the trail, else we'll break a wheel on a hidden rock."

"I didn't mean to." Her voice was pained, apologetic. Then her eyes flashed to him and she pointed at his chest. "You had no business leaving me like that."

"Maybe if you didn't push so hard, there wouldn't have been an issue."

"Are you talking about me pushing the oxen or you?"

Ben's gaze flashed to hers. Her jaw was set and her brows clashed together.

He jerked his head toward the back. "Why don't you walk with Molly for a bit?"

"Happy to." She crossed her arms and planted her feet. The train continued and, like a rock on the side of a river, everything flowed past her stiff form.

Ben turned away and stared at the wide expanse of land ahead of them. She was right; he'd left her alone too soon. It wasn't ridiculous for someone learning how to drive oxen to get the pressure wrong, to get off the path. She'd done nothing wrong, except for the way she had drawn out his darkest thoughts.

He hadn't been good enough for Jane. If this life gave him a few years, he would have a farm and livestock. He would have a house built and a decent place for a woman to make into a home. Not Jane, but someone.

He pictured the scene laid out on this prairie. As much as he tried to envision deeper the greens and richer earth promised in Oregon, all he saw was the yellows and browns that swathed everything from the canvas on Ellen's wagon to the dust on his boots.

Ellen did not join him again until they stopped that evening. What was more unnerving than being around her was that he'd finally identified the man who'd been watching him. His face wasn't familiar as part of their first company, but they'd gained a few new travelers in their days in Independence. It was impossible to tell if he was a new member or just unknown to Ben.

The man was careful to never meet Ben's eyes, but he lurked nearby, setting up his camp near the center where he could easily spy on the Bridgers. Ben saw no wagon and figured the man must be one of the single men traveling with mules, like Fox.

Ellen walked by, her head high and arrogant. Ben reached out and caught her hand. She tore it away, but when her gaze met Ben's, her glare faltered as she read his expression.

Her eyes cut to the side, and she stepped forward with a jerky breath, as though merely pretending not to hate him was a challenge. She wasn't even pretending well.

Her bonnet was off, hanging by its strings on her back. He ran a hand over her hair and cupped her face. "I'm sorry." She had a smudge of dirt on her cheek and Ben slid the pad of his thumb over it, lightening the mark but not wiping it away entirely.

Ellen narrowed her eyes, not fooled for one moment. This apology wasn't real. It was merely a show, its falsity proved by the way he touched her, caressed her even. He nearly laughed. He'd not touched Jane this way when he'd proposed. Yet here he was, play-acting like holding Ellen in his arms was the most natural thing in the world.

"Don't be angry with me."

Her throat bobbed as she smoothed the lapels of his coat.

Ben didn't dare look up to see if their guard still played audience. He slid his hand down Ellen's arm and lifted the bucket from her hands. It was filled with utensils the women would use for making dinner. She allowed him to take it and they walked by one another's side around the corner of the camp and out of sight… unless the man was devoted enough to lie on his belly and watch their legs.

With a stubborn set to her mouth, Ellen took the bucket back, though it was only a few more steps to where Fenna and Molly were stoking a fire. "What was that about?"

"That man Sam mentioned. I saw him. I want to show him to you, see if you recognize him as a friend of Cyrus."

Ellen set the pail down. Ben stayed at her side. "Fenna, can you spare Ellen for a bit? We need to do something."

Fenna nodded and Ben gripped Ellen's arm.

She pulled it free and glared at him. "Fenna is tired. We all are. I'm not leaving her to make the food by herself."

"I need you to see this man."

Ellen planted her feet. "It doesn't matter. If he's here as Cyrus' eyes and ears, he'll have nothing to report. In a few days, it won't matter anyhow."

Ben wanted to toss her over his shoulder. He stepped close enough that her skirts brushed the toes of his boots. "A wife doesn't act this way, stomping past her husband with her head held high, ignoring his requests, scowling at him all day."

"Everyone saw the way you left me with the oxen today, the way you chastised me afterward. I assure you, if that's how you act as a husband, then I am acting exactly as a wife would."

Ben growled and raised his hands, balling them into fists and letting her see just what she was doing to him.

She glanced at his fists, but with an unexpected expression. If he had to label it, he would have called it curious. "I'm not afraid of you." Her tone wasn't the haughty one that should have accompanied those words. Instead, it was almost incredulous. She twirled and marched around the wagon again. If that man was still there, Ben couldn't go after her.

A chuckle came from the fire. Fenna.

"I'd say you've met your match, Ben Bridger."

Ben lowered his brows. "What'd you go telling her about Jane for?"

Fenna shrugged. "She was asking, and she needs to know at least a little. You aren't giving her much."

He gestured in the direction Ellen had gone. "She doesn't stick around long enough to listen."

Fenna smiled at him in a way that was so like his mama, it took the anger right out of him.

He left the warmth of the fire to go find Sam and see if

caring for the animals could take his mind off this cantankerous woman he'd foolishly agreed to help.

The next morning, Ellen woke before Ben. They set up their bed the same way as before, with the divider between them. Once again, in her sleep, Ellen had scooted as close to the barrier as possible. She no longer dreamt of Ben. She didn't dream of anything. So tired was she after the day spent walking, that when she woke before the sun, it felt as though she'd just fallen asleep.

She pushed out of the covers, careful to place them over Ben again before tugging loose the ties on their canvas tent.

When she stepped into the dewy morning, she thought she might still be dreaming, or rather, caught in a nightmare.

"Good morning," Cyrus drawled. He rose from the three-legged stool he was sitting on.

Ellen tried to speak, to say his name, to reply in any form, but her throat was too dry, her mouth tacky from sleep. She coughed and backed up into the tent. She scrambled toward Ben and shook him awake.

"Ben, it's Cyrus." Her whisper worked, and Ben was up and looking around dazedly.

"Cyrus is here," she repeated. "Outside our tent."

She stared at the opening, waiting for him to climb in. Fear lodged in her chest, ballooning bigger until she gripped at her collar, sure it was going to burst.

Ben crouched, being too tall to stand upright in the tent. He strode through the opening, feet bare but fully clothed. Ellen winced to think Cyrus might take the clothes as a sign that they had yet to consummate the marriage. She hoped the chill air would be a good enough reason to wear clothes.

"What are you doing here?" Ben's voice was firm and held no note of sleep.

Ellen crawled out behind him and stepped to the side, glaring at Cyrus.

Cyrus leered at both of them. "Came to travel the day with you. I don't want to miss seeing my brother's grave."

Ellen's blood turned as cold as the springs that bubbled from the earth. "Titus' grave?"

Cyrus' leer faded, and his eyes turned to ice as they pinned Ellen. "I ain't letting him stay buried in some unmarked grave. He'll go in the family plot."

Ben stepped between the two, breaking the connection. "I'll show you to his grave. We can ride ahead today."

Ben's shirt was untucked, and it billowed in the wind like a sail pulling him away from her. Ellen grabbed it, leaning in so her chin brushed against his shoulder. "You cannot go with him. He'll kill you."

Cyrus chuckled. "I'll travel with the company. There are a few more folks with me that have the same intention."

Ellen scanned the camp, but all she saw was pitched tents and wagons. If there were other folks who had joined their company last night, they were still asleep.

"I suggest you rejoin your party and keep to the back of the train."

"Or what?" Cyrus stepped forward.

Ben matched his step, and Ellen bolted between them, placing a hand on each man's chest. "That's enough." She turned to Ben and placed both hands on his chest. Rather than the soft warmth he emanated when he slept, touching him now was like pressing her hands onto a boulder. His clothing was chilled and his cheeks red. "Darling." She tried to break the cloud of anger that stormed in Ben's eyes.

As angry as she'd ever made him, it was nothing compared to what he was feeling now. His gaze flicked down to her, softening. He wrapped an arm around her, placing it between her shoulder blades and pressing her closer.

Though she knew it was for show, she couldn't help but compare Ben to Titus. Titus had never been kinder to her when Cyrus was near. If anything, he often took out his anger with Cyrus on her. But one look at her and Ben's anger had abated, something Ellen had prayed for time and again to happen with Titus. For her presence to be enough for him.

It never had been.

Ellen twisted to face Cyrus, sure to stay between Ben's arms. "He should be buried with the family. We'll be glad to show you to his grave."

Molly's head poked out of her tent, scowling as she always did in the morning.

Ellen turned to Ben, but spoke loud enough that Cyrus could hear. "I need to get started on breakfast."

Ben nodded and guided her with his hands until she was behind him. That was one thing Ben and Titus shared—the desire to stay between Ellen and Cyrus. Just as she'd been before, Ellen was grateful for it.

As afraid as she'd been before, she was more afraid now. The way Cyrus had looked at her was less enamored and more obsessed. He wasn't grieving Titus' loss any longer. He was angry, as though he'd gambled and lost his best horse. Except, unlike a mustang, Ellen was ill-equipped to run away and live alone in the wild.

CHAPTER 20

The day dragged endlessly but also sped by too quickly. Ellen's stomach churned to know Cyrus was among them. When she saw the area where the twister had hit their party, her stomach finally overcame her willpower, and she stumbled farther into the grass and fell to her knees, emptying her stomach of its scant remnants.

When she lifted her head to wipe her mouth, Ben was there with a hanky in hand. She took it, her hand shaking.

Ben placed a heavy hand on her back. "I'll show Cyrus. No widow should watch her husband be unburied."

Ellen shook her head. "It's not that." She looked up into his blue eyes. "Do you think he'll unwrap him?" Their first trail guide had warned them all about injuries from guns. She'd never thought of the party blaming her for Titus' death. But did Cyrus understand that risk? Now certainly wasn't the time to explain it.

"I thought about it. Wondered if we should tell him how Titus died and risk whatever he assumes, or wait and hope he doesn't have the stomach to check the body."

Ellen's insides turned again, and she coughed, but nothing

came out. There was little to be done. Only time would tell what Cyrus discovered.

Ben helped her to her feet and she kept his handkerchief, tucking it into her belt to wash later. He plucked the stick from the grass where he'd abandoned it.

She looked at her wagon, still in formation. He was right. The oxen didn't need much prodding to keep going. It was too much prodding that was the problem.

"I'm sorry I pressed you about Jane."

"You were right to wonder. I guess it's all still a bit raw."

"You still love her?"

Ben surveyed the land before them with a quizzical brow. "No. But I worry about what my mama wants, and getting hitched ain't so easy as finding a wife. I'm not equipped to care for a woman."

Ellen had never felt so cared for in her entire life. "You're doing a fine job with me."

Ben huffed. "I didn't have much choice."

Ellen tried not to let the comment sting. "I'm saying when you find the woman you want to marry, you'll figure out how to care for her."

The company reached the space where their dead were buried. Though they could have continued for the day, Fox was content to stop. He said it was rare that family was able to visit a trail grave. Usually the only visitors were new pioneers or wolves.

Since there was daylight left, Ellen and Ben showed Cyrus the grave and left him with it. As they readied camp, Ellen couldn't stop her eyes from wandering to the activity around Titus' grave. When Cyrus pulled his body out, Ellen stopped all pretense and crawled under a wagon, lying on her belly to watch.

She'd sewn Titus into a sheet before they'd buried him. She watched with relief as Cyrus and another fellow loaded his body into a wagon. Cyrus leaned heavily on the side of the wagon, his head hanging low. Eventually, he straightened and helped a few others load their dead into that same wagon, the bodies being placed shoulder to shoulder in the bed.

Something kicked her foot and she twisted to see Molly with a plate of dinner.

Ellen sighed. "I'm sorry." She crawled out from under the wagon, but Molly sat on the ground, crossing her legs and passing the plate over to Ellen.

"We have plenty of time tonight." She nodded toward the darkened earth of the unburied graves. "How are you?"

Ellen chose to stare at her plate. "My husband isn't a man I mourn." She jerked her gaze to Molly. "Have you visited your aunt and uncle's graves?"

Molly shook her head.

Ellen's chest tightened with guilt. She'd been so absorbed in her own fears, she hadn't even thought that this family who had so generously assisted her were orphans and became such on this very swath of earth.

"I'll go with you."

Ellen stood, her dinner in one hand, and offered the other hand to Molly. The pair weaved through camp, coming up on the other side. The Bridgers had been near the front of the company when the twister had hit.

She glanced at Molly, the tiniest bit jealous that this woman had so much family willing to care for her, love her, protect her. This fidelity required nothing from Molly. Nobody questioned, nobody demanded a ruse. She could just…be.

Ellen cleared her throat. "I'm sorry, I don't know where…"

Molly lifted a finger, and Ellen followed her gaze.

Ben knelt near a grave, one hand pressed to the dirt and the other pressed to his forehead. It was a position of such grief Ellen wanted to look away, but she could not. Instead, her feet moved toward him, carrying her to a sadness she had never known.

When Harry had died, Ellen had been somber, but she'd also been worried and even angry. He'd taken her away from every safety she'd had, then died and left her to fend for herself. Sure, she'd missed him, his easy laugh and his smile. But there had been little time for grief when the money was running out and their plans were shattered. She'd needed to find work and, in the long term, a husband. Grief had to wait.

Ellen reached Ben and placed a hand on his shoulder, squeezing it. If she'd been big and strong like him, she might have done more. Might have lifted him into her arms and held him the way he needed. But she was not. She had to wait for him to take what he wanted. Wasn't that true in all areas of her life? Small and insignificant, forced to use feminine wiles to try for what she wanted—what she needed.

Ben rose off his haunches and stood. Ellen kept her hand on his shoulder, and as he twisted, her arm wrapped around him. Though there was nobody to witness their show of affection save Molly, she held him close, pressing her face to his chest.

His hands hung lifeless at his sides, but slowly they came up and circled her ribs. He breathed in, squeezing her tighter, and for the smallest moment Ellen knew she finally had something to offer him. He'd done so much and she'd only taken, but in this instant she was giving what he needed.

He relaxed his hold but kept his arms around her as he turned to face the grave.

"Is that one your mama's?"

Ben nodded, his scratchy chin catching in her hair and pulling a few wisps free from her bun.

"I'm sorry for your loss." The words were so often said,

but what else was there to say? She didn't know the woman. Didn't know how Ben was feeling.

His arms tightened slightly and loosened again, more like a flinch than an embrace, but Ellen wouldn't complain. He released her and stepped back, scrubbing his face with his hand.

Ellen cleared her throat, a bit embarrassed at her display. She turned to find Molly, whose face was crumpled with the pain of her loss, her arms wrapped around herself like armor. Ellen caught Ben's hand and led him to his cousin. He slipped an easy arm around Molly's shoulders and his cousin leaned into him, a whimper escaping her mouth.

Ellen left them to grieve with one another. She didn't look back as she returned to camp to help clean up the meal.

She went to her wagon to gather the buckets they used for washing and found a young man leaning against it. He pressed away and approached Ellen. She watched him with a jolt of fear rolling through her limbs.

"Ellen," the boy said, his face darting to either side. She couldn't see his eyes under the shade of his hat, but something felt off.

"Sir, I don't know—"

The boy removed his hat and a tumble of blonde hair cascaded onto his shoulder. No, not *his*. Ellen blinked. "Petra?"

Petra glanced over her shoulder. Ellen followed her gaze and saw Demi's head peeking out from the bonnet of Ellen's wagon.

"Demi? What are you two doing here?" Ellen surveyed Petra's disguise once again. "Your parents. They must be worried sick."

Petra drew near and took Ellen's hands. "Can we hide out in your wagon? Just for a few days?"

Ellen glanced at Demi, already inside. "I—"

"You said you had extra food. We've brought our own clothes and extra boots."

Demi jangled a pair of boots by their laces out of the wagon.

Ellen huffed. She had offered Demi to accompany her. She focused on Petra again. "Your wedding?"

Petra shook her head. "I cannot go through with it."

Ellen glanced at Demi. She forever lived in Petra's shadow and had been, no doubt, lassoed into Petra's attempt to run away from a match Demi would have died for.

Demi met her gaze. "We want to go west."

Ellen stepped around Petra and approached the wagon. When she stood before Demi, she asked, "*You* want to go west?"

Petra had always been able to talk Demi into anything, but this adventure included the chance Demi could lose her life. This wasn't a path to take to please somebody else.

"There's no future for me back there." She jutted her chin east, toward Independence.

"You might die." Ellen turned to Petra. "Both of you could die. I could die."

Petra straightened. "We want to go west. Are you saying there is no longer room and food with your wagon?"

Ellen cocked her head and met Petra's haughty look. "There's room." After all, her wagon was originally outfitted for a family of six. "I just... I'm traveling with a party now."

Petra stepped closer. "Nobody can know. Not yet."

Ellen sighed. She was only just about to escape one web of lies and now she would be stepping into another. But perhaps that was the answer. In just a few days, she would no longer be Ben's problem, so there was no need to tell him about this development.

She closed her eyes and pinched the bridge of her nose. "Stay out of sight and don't eat anything. All food must be rationed. You'll be fed with us, as well as hungry just like all of us."

Petra nodded vigorously, but it was Demi Ellen watched. Her friend showed no sign of backing down. No sign of crawling from the wagon and hightailing it home.

A pot clanged in the distance. "I need to go help clear up dinner. Have you two eaten yet today?"

Petra worried her lip with a sheepish expression.

"You've already helped yourself to my food?" Ellen calmed her irritation. "I'll come back tonight, if I can. But Cyrus is here and I'm not through with this ruse of being Ben's bride. You'll have to take care of yourself for a bit longer. And stop eating my food. I'll be sure to make extra and bring some to you at mealtimes."

She moved to leave, but stopped and turned back. "I'll also bring you dishes and laundry to be cleaned. This isn't a hotel."

Petra and Demi nodded vigorously.

Ellen left, praying she hadn't made a mistake inviting Demi to come along back in Independence. She was glad she'd come, taken a chance at life beyond her parents' reach. But Petra... She must have eavesdropped on the whole conversation, taken the offer as her own.

Ellen rounded a corner and found Fenna talking softly to Will. Ellen shifted into a shadow and watched them for a moment. Newly married with so much life ahead of them. They'd beat the odds already. Something in her heart told her they would do it again. They'd make it to Oregon and create that life Ben had described.

She stepped out of her hiding spot and gathered a few dishes. She should take them to Demi and Petra, but they wouldn't know where to get water or where to put the dishes when they were cleaned.

She took out her frustration on the pots, scrubbing away

the crusted potatoes with vigor that would have impressed even her pa.

She tried her best not to think how she was going to hide this from Ben. He might not be sleeping in her wagon, but he would be driving it during the day. Would the oxen need more food since they were carrying a greater load? Would Ben be able to tell they wanted more? Or was she going to have to sneak food to the oxen as well as to the Anderson sisters?

CHAPTER 21

*B*en stood at his parents' graves with his arm around his cousin. His mind was elsewhere, replaying the way he'd fairly clung to Ellen when she'd come to him. She was the one woman in their party who didn't remind him of his mother, and yet when he'd been crushed by the weight of losing his parents, it had been the press of her forehead to his chest that had allowed him to draw a real breath.

He slipped his arm off Molly's shoulders. "Should we head back?"

Molly nodded.

Ben tried to shorten his strides enough to accompany Molly back, but he found himself constantly having to mindfully slow down. His legs seemed intent on taking him all the way to Ellen as quickly as possible. Spending the night with her by his side wasn't enough. He wanted more.

Ellen met him just as he and Molly entered camp. She pressed a bowl of dinner into his hands and leaned close. "We need to talk."

Ben nodded. He wanted to talk to her, but what would he

say? That he wanted to court her for real? To tell the company of their lie and sleep separately again so he might act as a proper beau and win her heart? But Cyrus was here, and though he'd behaved so far, Ben was waiting for him to play his last card.

"I have to tend to the oxen. Would you like to come?"

Ellen nodded, and he looped her arm through his as they made their way to where the oxen were hobbled.

Out of the crush of wagons, it was easy to be certain nobody lurked out of sight to overhear them. Ben turned and nudged Ellen to do the same. The few people who had come to collect their dead were in a line, heading back east. There still remained a few hours of daylight left for them to make decent progress. A tall figure caught Ben's eye, and he leaned closer to Ellen. "Do you see Cyrus?"

"Yes." Ellen spoke quickly as though these words had been on the edge of her lips all this time. "How much longer must we pretend?"

Ben blinked. He'd been so caught up in what he wanted to say, he hadn't given thought to what she wanted to talk about. "I think it's a bit soon to stop now." Their original plan had been four days onto the trail, but now that Cyrus was here, would they need another four days?

"How long do you think? I mean, he could turn back and be here in the morning."

"Are you saying you'd like to pretend for another four days?"

She chewed her cheek. "I don't know. Maybe just two more would be necessary."

Ben nodded. "I can do two." Strangely, his heart fluttered at the prospect. He couldn't decide if he would rather pretend to be married or truly be courting. He couldn't help but recall their kiss or the way he was allowed to embrace her. That would all stop the moment they revealed the truth.

What would be left would be real, but it would somehow be less.

His feet shuffled, begging to take him closer. Instead, he turned and scooped feed from the barrel and sprinkled it over the prairie grass. The stiff blades would make up most of the animals' diet these months on the trail, but he knew adding nutrient-rich feed would make their oxen last longer. Possibly long enough to be of use to him when they reached Oregon.

He turned to Ellen. "Thank you. For today."

She tore her gaze from Cyrus' retreating form, confusion rippling across her brow. Her actions at his parents' graves hadn't meant anything to her, but it had meant everything to him. He nodded and started back to camp. She might be in dire straits, but she wasn't interested in him as a real husband. If she were, it would surely only be for convenience's sake, not because she wanted a life with him in Oregon.

She had her own wagon and a life to build. She wouldn't need him when they arrived. Perhaps if he played nice along the way, she would consider him then. He would know it was a true desire and not one borne out of a woman's desperation.

When they reached camp, Ben walked toward her wagon, intending to pull the tent down from the hooks on the side.

Ellen rushed ahead of him. "What are you doing?"

He pointed to the tent. "Getting the tent out."

"I'll get it. After all, it's my tent and my wagon. I should learn how to do everything for myself if I'll be on my own soon."

Ben lowered his brows. Her request was reasonable, yet there was something to the way she spoke that made him narrow his eyes. "Of course."

She stepped forward and lifted onto her toes to untie the bundle from the wagon.

He doubted she'd be able to set up the tent alone. Even he preferred help. If someone was nearby, he always asked for assistance holding the post while one of them placed the stakes. He had never planned to abandon her completely. Was that what she'd thought of him?

But he had taught her to drive her wagon, and she was right. She ought to learn how to set up her own camp too, however much it pained him to think of her completely alone.

He made his way to the fire, his empty bowl of dinner still in his hand. He hadn't even noticed eating it. She was so quick to offer bits of herself, but she took them away faster than he had time to appreciate what she'd given.

Ellen watched Ben walk away. Did she imagine the droop to his shoulders? She rushed to untie the tent from the hooks on the side of her wagon. She didn't dare speak to the sisters hiding on the other side of the bonnet. It was a miracle nobody had spotted her speaking to them earlier, and she was unwilling to test fate.

She unrolled the tent, certain it would be just fine to set up on her own. After all, most mornings she was the one to take it down. Reversing her steps couldn't be that difficult.

But after half an hour wrestling with the post, only for it to fall the moment she tried to pin a stake to the ground, she stomped her foot in frustration. She twisted to survey camp. Who was available to help her? Ben stood, leaning against one of his brothers' wagons, and even from this distance she could see the smirk on his face.

"Need a bit of help?" he called. Ellen huffed, ready to

reject his offer out of stubborn pride. But he pushed away and came toward her. "I can't usually do it on my own either. When I do, I dig the post into the ground with a spade."

Ellen glanced at the heap of canvas and could imagine how a set post would make all the difference.

She crawled in once more and set the post to standing. From the outside, she could just make out Ben's silhouette as he plucked the mallet from the ground, pulled one corner of the tent tight, and pounded the stake into the ground. "You know, I never planned to leave you on your own."

He stood and walked to another corner, pulling it tight as well. The post wobbled, but Ellen gripped it tighter and put her body weight into holding it firm. She'd never helped with this, always busy with some other chore when the tents were set up.

Once again, she thought of Molly, whose tent was set up daily without any effort on her part. Rather than feeling jealous, she felt hope. For the first time in her life, Ellen glimpsed the life she could have, the family she could create. These brief days spent with Bridgers had taught her more about family than her entire twenty years.

When Ben was pounding in the last stake, Ellen rushed to her wagon and pulled her trunk from inside. She grabbed a lantern for good measure, hoping she would leave Ben with zero reason to enter or approach her wagon all night.

She stopped at the exit to the wagon. "You two have enough to stay warm tonight?"

They nodded with eyes wide as an owl's and Ellen turned to go. If she was to keep their secret, she would need to quit worrying about them and act as naturally as possible. Ben might already be suspicious of her behavior. Demi and Petra had made it here on their own. Surely, they would manage a few more days.

Then what? Ellen would drive her wagon away from

these folks she'd grown so attached to? Or she would tell Ben that she'd been lying to him these past few days? Or perhaps she could tell a new lie. Say they showed up the very day she had to tell him.

When they crawled into bed that night, Ben watched her. She tried to continue as normally as possible, but finally she couldn't take it. "What are you looking at?"

Ben flinched as though she'd struck him, and she instantly regretted the venom in her voice.

She pressed her fingertips into her temple. "I'm sorry. Today has been terrible."

Ben fussed with the quilts, straightening each corner. "Cyrus is gone."

It was true, they'd watched him drive away. But she hadn't exactly felt relief when she'd watched him go. Whatever she felt was too slippery for her to identify. A mixture of foreboding and hope, two things that would never settle well together. "How can we be sure nobody stayed behind?"

Ben shook his head. "I spoke to Fox myself. Anyone who joins will have to pay their fee and nobody has done so."

Ellen's blood cooled. The fee. Did Petra and Demi have any money? Ellen surely didn't. She had provisions but nothing else. Perhaps Fox would trade a few good meals. It might mean the three women would have to go without food for some days to keep the rations at a safe level. She sighed, angry with Petra for taking too long to convince Demi to come west. Angry with her for inviting herself to come along. And angry that though Ben was in this tent beside her, she felt as alone as ever.

Once they were bedded down, their usual wad of blankets between them, Ben spoke. "Do you plan to separate from our group once we tell the truth?"

Ellen turned to face him, fear lodging in her throat. "Do you want me to?"

"No. I just wondered. Earlier today I told you I planned to continue helping, but you didn't seem too keen on the idea."

Ellen recalled. She'd been so caught up with trying to get back to her wagon, she had barely registered his words. "Distracted, I guess."

"So?"

"So, what?"

Ben shifted, his gentle whisper now held an edge. "So are you going to leave as soon as you no longer need me?"

If she wasn't mistaken, that was pain in his voice. "I didn't think...do you want me to stay?"

He cleared his throat. "We're in the same company. We may as well stay together. You and Fenna have a good routine for meals and such."

He made it sound terribly practical. It would be if she didn't have two stowaways in her wagon just now, neither of which would have the skills to match Fenna's in cooking over an open fire. If she distanced herself from the Bridgers, she would be doing most of the work alone until Demi and Petra learned how to be helpful.

"I dearly enjoy Fenna and Molly. Your entire family is quite wonderful."

"You'll stay?"

"I don't know. What about the rest of the company? What will they think? They know we've been sharing this tent. When we tell them the truth, they'll hardly believe I wasn't tainted in the process. If we stay together, it will only solidify their imaginings."

"Is there a man in the company whose opinion you hold in high esteem?"

Ellen blinked at the question. "No."

"Once you get west, nobody will care about rumors."

"Yes, I've heard it all before. They're desperate and they'll take any body so long as she is a female." She hated the undercurrent of those remarks. It made her feel like a piece of livestock, her flanks checked and found acceptable for the job.

She sought Ben's profile in the dark. The familiar planes of his forehead, nose, and lips. Did he find her acceptable? She brushed away the vain notion. All that mattered was that he found her worthy of helping. "Thank you for all of this. You've endured much more than I expected when I made this arrangement."

The corner of his mouth lifted.

That slight smile had her leaning closer. "I'll stay. I will be your personal maid for the rest of this journey. Laundry, mending, food prepared and cleared. Anything you need, I'll do it with my sincerest gratitude."

Ben turned to face her, pressing down the barrier so she could see his eyes. "Anyone would have done what I did." He hummed a laugh. "Sam would have done it, had he thought of it."

"Are you saying this was your idea and not mine?"

His eyes crinkled and danced. "I take no issue with you claiming all the blame for this foolhardy situation."

Ellen smiled. "It was foolish, wasn't it. How naïve we were."

"I have a feeling we're going to be saying that about ourselves when we look back at this very moment. When we try to tell the truth and it ends up being every bit as difficult as it's been to live this lie."

"Folks are nosier than I expected them to be." She remembered the wedding night, how she and Ben were shown to their tent, a few shameless souls even lingering to listen.

"Your new friend Molly is among the worst of them."

Ellen laughed. "She was your cousin before she was my friend." Then she tilted her head. "How do you mean?"

"It was her who called for us to kiss."

"No!" Ellen gasped, scandalized.

"She's not as innocent as she claims to be."

"I cannot believe it." Though it really wasn't incredible. Molly was a meddler if ever Ellen knew one. "Are you certain?"

Ben shrugged. "Ask her."

Ellen blushed. Did that whole incident make Ben heat the way it did her? The mention of it was embarrassing enough. She could never ask Molly outright.

"How soon will you marry once you reach Oregon?"

Something in Ellen's mind perked at his query. First, he'd asked if a man in their company had her eye. Now he wanted to know *when* she planned to marry. Could he be... jealous? She almost laughed out loud. More than once, Fenna had remarked on how practical Ben was. Surely, he merely wished to ensure Ellen was planning her life.

"I don't know. I guess it depends on my situation when I arrive. If I have enough to set myself up, I might wait a bit. With all those men, there is surely work doing laundry, mending, cooking."

Ben chuckled. "Is that all you think you are good for?"

She frowned, thinking of the other things men wanted from her. "It's what I am willing to give."

He gave an audible gulp and Ellen's cheeks heated again. She could barely speak of kissing the man, yet she shamelessly referenced marital relations.

She sucked in a breath, her mind racing to recover from her bold topic. "And you? I've heard Sam speak of your mother's wish. Is he taking it more seriously than you?"

Ben's brows lowered. "I would think you would appreciate my willingness to let that promise lie. I can't very well have two wives, even if one of them is pretend."

"I do appreciate it. I just wonder if you too have your eye

on a woman in the company. One who might help you fulfill that promise."

She waited with bated breath. There were plenty of women for him to choose from. Young ones who were heading west with their parents. Older ones, like her, who were widowed. Even spinsters like Molly. Any of them would look fine at Ben's side.

"I want to get set up first. My mother was not in her right mind when she demanded that vow. I will marry one day. She never needed to worry about that. And I've got Molly to care for. If my mother feared my turning into a heathen, Molly is sure to do a fine job preventing that."

"She is quite pretty, even with her spectacles. I never saw a woman so pretty and unmarried at her age."

"I wonder if I will wish my mother hadn't allowed Molly to come. She's not nearly as helpful as you."

Ellen warmed at the veiled compliment. "She'll get better. She's got a kind enough heart." Molly was often in a book, but the rare times she joined the living for long enough to notice a need, Molly had proved quick to help.

Had that been her intention when she'd called for Ben and Ellen to kiss? Helping? Ellen sunk deeper into her covers as a smile stretched across her face. If that truly was Molly, Ellen was grateful to her friend.

After spending so much time with Ben, it would have been a shame to part ways without her ever knowing the press of his lips. Strange how a touch she'd experienced so often before could still cause sudsy bubbles to burst in her belly.

She closed her eyes, picturing all the women in their company, trying to imagine how she would feel to see Ben's arm around another, to see him lifting another's trunk into their shared wagon, to see him tuck into his tent with her.

In that moment, she could not pretend that she had no

feelings toward this man. No mortal woman could resist. Not while he cared for her, not while watching him interact with his family, and especially not after he had kissed her. She hoped, with overwhelming desperation, that he kept his commitment not to marry soon. If she was lucky, she'd be far away from him when that day came.

CHAPTER 22

*E*llen had insisted on driving the oxen herself today, and as the sun progressed across the sky, Ben found himself with nothing to do. He saddled one of their family's mounts and rode to the front to Fox's side.

The man was an admirable fellow, mild tempered and quiet, but he held an air of command that made Ben wonder if he'd ever served in the army.

Fox didn't turn when Ben reached his side. "It'll be a longer day today. We'll camp at the river's edge and cross in the morning."

Ben glanced west to the wide Platte River they'd been following all day. "How many times will we cross it?"

Fox's shoulders heaved a sigh. "Three, maybe four, depending. The more times we cross, the better time we're making, but if the water is too high…"

Ben remembered the reason Fox stopped guiding folks west. "Don't doubt yourself. We all make mistakes." Though Ben knew next to nothing about crossing rivers, he trusted this man implicitly. If anything, the fact that he'd failed in the past meant he would be more careful this time around.

"Cyrus left you two alone."

Ben huffed a laugh. "About time."

"Are you surprised it took so long?" He shook his head. "I'm surprised he gave up at all. He's not the type of man to let anything go. Everyone knew he had a hankering for Ellen Moren."

Rage ballooned in Ben's chest. "No wonder Titus tried to get her out of town." Silence fell between them while Ben tried to calm the anger roiling inside him.

By afternoon, Fox asked for Ben to assist in informing the company that it would be a while yet before they stopped. Both men rode down the long line of wagons, spreading the news. Some folks groaned, but most knew there was nothing to be done and merely nodded when Ben went on.

He found Ellen at the side of her oxen. Rather than a look of relief when he approached, her mouth turned down and she glanced toward her wagon.

Ben reined in his mount. "You doin' alright?" He cast a critical eye over the wagon. It was in line and everything appeared to be working properly.

She smiled, but it didn't reach her eyes. "Just great. I heard there will be a delay."

Ben huffed a laugh. Word of mouth was faster than even his mount.

"Past nightfall. It's going to be tiresome. I'd like to help." He nodded at her long stick.

She lifted it, draping it across her shoulders and hanging her wrists over it, looking like she'd driven oxen all her life. "No. I'll be just fine."

He held her gaze for a beat, unconvinced. "I'll come by later to check on you."

She huffed and turned forward. He continued down the line, frustrated by her refusal to allow him to help, but equally frustrated trying to understand the mystery of why he cared so much.

What he'd said yesterday was true; he wouldn't feel right marrying a woman before he could provide for her. A man could sleep under the stars, but a woman, she needed floors and a stove.

It was one thing to live like this on the trail west. It was another thing entirely to do so for a prolonged period of time. He had too much pride to force anyone into such a living when he could give her something far better if he only had the chance to work his way into it.

Ellen had denied his help another two times before they reached the river. Will and Fenna were tending to a mother who'd been laboring all day, so each of Ben's remaining brothers was driving a wagon.

Ben ferried folks as well as stubborn mules across. By the time Sam's wagon reached the front of the line, Ben's nerves were frayed.

He rode his horse across the water to meet Sam. "Here, let me drive it. You ride Red."

Sam chuckled. "No, you don't. I'll do just fine." Sam waved him away.

Ben climbed down, his boots splashing into the river. "Sam," he warned.

Sam jerked his head toward the back. "Chet will need your help. I surely don't."

Ben stood there for another moment, but Sam was right. It wasn't fair to hold up the entire company so Ben could personally drive every one of their family's wagons across the river.

"Not too slow," he warned.

"And not too fast. I got it. I've had as much experience crossing rivers as you have."

The truth of his pointed words stung, but Ben abandoned the argument and walked Red down to the next wagon.

He held Red's reins out to Chet. "You ride across. I'll drive the wagon."

Chet's eyes were wide as saucers, but he shook his head. "I can do it."

"I know you can, but Ellen needs a ride across too, and she ain't gonna be comfortable in that saddle with a man as big as myself."

Chet chewed his lip, then nodded, smiling. He took the reins, placing his driving stick in Ben's hands.

Chet climbed onto the horse with ease. Legs that were long and spindly a few months ago were now thicker and commanding as he kicked the horse forward. By the time they reached Oregon, there wouldn't be a speck of boyhood left in him.

Ben climbed into the wagon seat, the stick in his hands. He watched with trepidation as Sam took the first Bridger wagon across. Breath exploded out of him the moment Sam's wagon reached the far bank.

Just as quickly, Ben sucked in a new breath and held it while he urged the oxen along. He could feel the pressure of the current against the wheels and tapped the oxen's hindquarters harder, encouraging them to keep their pace steady, to not stop and risk the wagon being swept away.

When he was partway through the river, Chet rode by with a woman on Red's back, but she didn't possess Ellen's familiar honey-hued hair. He squinted, trying to make out who it was Chet had deemed more important than obeying Ben's orders, but the woman didn't look familiar in the least.

When Chet dropped her at the far bank and turned to ride back through, Ben tried to catch Chet's attention, but the boy focused on the water. Ben forced his mind to his own task.

He was just making it up the bank with his wagon and team when Chet appeared again with another woman who wasn't Ellen on the back of his horse. He let her off, and she left for the camp. Ben climbed down, his blood thrumming in his ears.

"What are you doing?" He stared at the second woman's back. Did he know her? He couldn't be sure. Then he focused on Chet once more. "I told you to take Ellen across, not every girl in the company."

Chet tried to argue, but Ben took the reins from his brother's hands and motioned for him to get off.

"I thought you said Ellen wouldn't be comfortable—"

"She'll have to deal." Ben huffed, turning the horse back to the river. "Take the wagon to camp."

He found Ellen's wagon just behind the rest of his family's wagons. He stopped at the twins' wagon. "Will one of you drive Ellen's wagon across?"

Alex nodded and stepped away from Nate, following Ben down to Ellen's wagon.

She looked up innocently when he approached. Her expression held none of the stubborn refusal for help she'd shown earlier. Suddenly an idea occurred to him. "Did you refuse Chet's help?" She'd been doing so all day. He shouldn't have been surprised that she'd kept it up.

"I already told you; I don't need any help."

Ben narrowed his eyes. "You're going to drive this wagon and team across that river?" He pointed to the muddy water, his brows raised as he dared her hold her bluff.

Her throat bobbed.

Ben smirked. "That's what I thought."

He gestured for Alex to take his position. Ellen gave Alex the stick as he climbed onto the bench seat.

Ben urged his mount closer and slipped his boot from the

stirrup. Ellen turned and surveyed the horse and rider before her.

Ben offered a hand, and she slipped her foot into the stirrup before Ben hoisted her onto his lap. With both her legs on one side he felt every bit the chivalrous knight. Only he doubted the princesses in the stories drove their heroes into such irritation.

He kept one arm wrapped around her waist. It was difficult to remain angry with her while he savored the feel of her pressed so close to him. While he acknowledged just how fleeting this contact was going to be.

With a nod to Alex, Ben turned Red around and urged the horse back into the cold waters. The deeper the horse went, the higher the water became, until Ellen was leaning into Ben, her knees in her chest as she tried to keep her boots dry.

Red came out on the other side, and though Ben could have stopped there, he maintained his hold on Ellen's waist, unwilling to separate from her.

This river crossing was the end of their ruse. Cyrus wouldn't risk his life crossing this river for a woman who didn't want to marry him. He had a burial to attend to. He was long gone, and there was no longer a good reason for Ben to be holding onto Ellen.

Yet he kept his horse walking, kept her close to him.

Until she twisted. "Where are we going?"

The words were there. *Let's keep pretending.* He'd be thrilled to pretend all the way to Oregon and find a preacher who would speak true words. Instead, something caught his eye. Ellen's wagon, with its familiar orange spade, was parked on the edge of the company and two women were standing at the back. One of them climbed up and disappeared inside.

"Your wagon!" Ben kicked the horse faster, holding tight

to Ellen not for his sake, but so she didn't fall off with the movement.

"What?" she cried, but he didn't answer. He pulled to a stop at her wagon and practically heaved Ellen to the ground, following quickly himself. He took several long strides to the opening where two women had disappeared and hefted himself up on the edge.

"What are you doing?" he demanded. The women stood among the goods. They didn't seem to be stealing anything, yet what could their intentions be? "Did you know on the trail thievery is punishable by death?"

Their eyes widened with such fear, his chivalry begged him to apologize and leave them alone. He ignored it. If he was going to end his ruse with Ellen, she couldn't seem like an easy target. Otherwise, all her goods would be gone within a week.

Ellen stood on the ground next to him and tugged at his sleeve. He turned, irritated with her interruption.

"Ben, leave them be. They're my friends."

Ben's brows clashed together. He looked between Ellen and the two women who were admittedly familiar, though he couldn't place them. "Your friends?"

He'd never seen her with anyone in the company except his family. When did she make friends? "Why are they in your wagon?"

"Ben, please come down from there."

He stepped down slowly, the wagon frame blocking his view of the terrified women.

He turned to Ellen, silent with expectation.

"They're my friends from home, remember?"

Once she said it, it was easy to place them on that porch across from Cyrus' shop.

Ellen cleared her throat. "They're"—she licked her lips,

her eyes pleading for something he didn't understand—"coming in my wagon. Sharing my rations."

Ben raised his brows. "Your rations?"

Ellen's throat bobbed and she nodded.

His mind whirled. He'd been in her wagon countless times. "How long have you been hiding them?"

What he didn't say was "how long have you been hiding them *from me?*" His personal affront was nothing compared to the danger of eating through her rations before they arrived in Oregon. Sure, she had more than she needed, but that didn't mean she wouldn't open a barrel to find it infested with weevils or rotten from getting wet.

"Just since yesterday. They came with Cyrus."

Ben's ears grew hot. "They're his friends, and you have allowed them into our lives?"

"No." Her voice was firm. "They are *my* friends. They only came with the party Cyrus led. They stayed here when everyone else left back home."

The danger of Cyrus disappeared, but Ben's pulse thrummed in his ears. "Why did you hide them?"

Ellen chewed her lip. "Their parents might come for them."

Ben tossed his hands. "Ellen, we are less than a week outside Independence. Of course, their parents will come for them. And likely bring Cyrus too." He spun and stalked a few steps away. Just when he thought himself rid of that man, she dashed that hope to pieces.

"We can still tell everyone the truth about us. End our agreement." Her eyes pleaded with him to understand.

Ben turned. "What about when he returns? Will you go with him?"

Ellen flinched. "Of course not."

"I'm beginning to wonder if leaving you with him would have been better all around."

Her face fell, and he closed his eyes against the hastily spoken words. Of course, he would not have left her there. But why hadn't she come to him, confided in him? Apparently, the closeness he thought they'd gained was one-sided.

He glanced at the wagon. Both women had poked their faces over the wooden side. "You two need to pay Fox your dues."

"Ben—"

He cut Ellen a look, silencing whatever argument had been on her lips.

"You cannot ask him to take folks across for free. This is his livelihood. You might be intent on squandering yours, but I assure you Fox is not taking this job lightly."

"Of course," Ellen said, as if the words were as painful as feigning love for him had been. Torture.

One of the women stood up. "We have money. We can pay him whatever he needs. And we can buy Ellen more food too."

Ben wanted to spit. He spread his arms wide. "Do you see a trading post?" He shook his head. He wanted to say so much more, but Ellen's face was still somber and, as angry as he was, he couldn't bring himself to be any crueler.

Instead, he turned and stalked away, matching his steps to his beating heart.

CHAPTER 23

Ben was right. If the worst happened and Mr. Anderson came after his daughters, Cyrus would be part of the rescue party and she would have to see him once more.

She wouldn't ask Ben to interfere on their behalf, not again. She would need to find her own way this time.

As she worked alongside the others to set up camp in the fading daylight, she searched for Ben to no avail. What she did see was the many faces that had become familiar to her these past days on the trail and weeks camping outside Independence.

Maybe it wouldn't matter if Cyrus came again. Maybe those who knew Cyrus were far enough away from him that they wouldn't feel obliged to support him if he attempted to force Ellen back home. The rest of these folks had no reason to be loyal to a town bully they never knew. Perhaps Ellen had more than just the Bridger family to support her.

So why was Ben's approval the only one that mattered?

Camp was set up and dinner cleaned before Ben appeared, glaring and dusty.

"Where've you been?" Sam asked what Ellen could not.

Ben spared Sam a glance before continuing to the fire, where he stuck his hands out to the warmth. "With the livestock."

Ellen retrieved the bowl of beans she'd saved from dinner and passed it to him.

He took it with a dull *thank you*, but he looked at her a moment too long, far longer than he'd given Sam.

Ellen swallowed, more than curious about what was in that head of his. She glanced at Sam, who nodded and walked in the direction of the tents.

"I'm sorry you're cross with me," she said. "I've been thinking—"

"Cross with you?" Ben gave a hard laugh. "I have no reason to be. As you said, it's your wagon. You can do what you please."

Ellen winced, her words sounding sharper in his deep and ornery baritone. A thought occurred to her. Had Ben been relying on her supplies for his own family? They had never discussed payment of any sort for his assistance. "You can have anything you want from my wagon. If it weren't for you, it would still be at Cyrus' shop."

Ben ate the beans slowly, his brow as low as it had been when he arrived in camp.

Ellen sighed. There was no use waiting. "We can reveal the truth. Tell everyone. I won't sleep in your tent tonight."

Ben's stare at the fire didn't waver. She waited long enough that she couldn't tell whether he had forgotten what she suggested, or if he hadn't heard it at all.

She inched toward him. "I'll see if Molly wants a companion again."

Again, he said nothing. His gaze didn't shift.

"Good night, Ben Bridger," she said, but it felt like goodbye.

Ellen walked away, her heart heavier than before. She thought he'd be thrilled at the prospect of ending their charade, severing their ties to one another. He should have been. But his slumped shoulders, tight jaw, and stretched silence said exactly how unhappy he was, how much she'd hurt him when she'd hidden the Anderson sisters from him.

Ellen made her way to Molly's tent. When she arrived, it was clear Molly was inside. A lantern was lit, as it was most every night, and Ellen could see Molly's silhouette inside, her head bowed over what was most assuredly a book.

"May I come in?" Ellen spoke at the tent's entrance. Without a door post to knock, it was the best form of etiquette they had.

An easy "come in" sounded from inside.

Ellen poked her head through the flaps to find Molly with a quilt draped over her shoulders and a book resting in her lap.

No use in waiting. "Can I sleep here tonight?"

Concern rippled across Molly's brow. "Everything okay?"

Ellen nodded. An unexplained knot rose in her throat, and she tried to swallow it down.

"Of course, you can sleep in here. Did you and Ben argue?"

Ellen shook her head, though it was true. "We're just ready to tell everyone the truth. It doesn't matter if folks see me here with you all night."

Molly smiled. "I've never been anyone's shameful secret before. Too bad it was so short-lived."

Ellen couldn't help but grin in return. "I'm ready to be honest again. It was awful having to pretend to love a—"

"Handsome man whom every single woman in this camp would fall to her knees for?"

Ellen reared. Though Molly's words were light, her tone was anything but. "Are you angry with me?"

Molly huffed, her shoulders sinking lower. "No. I just don't understand you two. You're good for one another. Why are you denying it?"

It was Ellen's turn to don the quizzical brow. "Good for him? I'm the one who needs him, not the other way around."

"He is rather useful to your situation, but I think there's more to his bluff. Don't think that just because he's good, that he's not also doing this because he wants it. Wants you. If I were you, I'd take it. There aren't many men here to match him, save perhaps Will and that guide."

"Fox?"

Molly nodded, growing animated. "He knows so much, more than my books—at least the books regarding the trail." She chewed her lip, contemplating something internally. "He still couldn't beat me in a match of wits."

Ellen couldn't confirm or deny Molly's estimation of the man. Ben held him in high regard, but she'd only spoken with him a few times. One thing she did know—Molly had more wits than any one person should possess. "I doubt anyone could match you at wits. I'm still unsure how you convinced your folks to let you come west."

Molly snickered. "That was only on the promise of grandchildren. They'd all but given up hope of that in Virginia."

Ellen cocked an eyebrow. "I'm sure men were falling at your feet."

Molly gave a wistful sigh. "There was a time that was true. But I'm twenty-five now and haven't yet found a man I prefer to my books."

Ellen did her best to imagine a life where she enjoyed the luxury of rejecting eligible men as a leisure activity.

The crunch of boots outside the tent whipped both women's heads in the same direction—towards Ben's tent.

Ellen couldn't suppress a sigh, and Molly didn't miss it.

Molly lifted her brow in a look so smug Ellen knew Ben was right. It *had* been Molly who'd called for the kiss. She'd had good intentions, but she was mistaken. Ben and Ellen weren't good for one another. They were convenient for a time, but that moment was fast drawing to a close, if it hadn't disappeared already.

The endless days blended together until they were four days west of the graves. Ellen had kept close to her wagon, not because the Anderson sisters were there, but because word had finally spread that she and Ben weren't married. As she feared, folks looked at her with a mix of intrigue and disdain. She couldn't decide which was worse, the fact that they knew, or that not one soul had bothered to ask her directly if the rumor was true.

The Anderson sisters deemed it time to escape their wagon cage, and Ellen nervously led them to the Bridger camp to be introduced.

Most everyone was gathered around the fire with supper in their hands. Ellen had been careful to make extra portions that sat in the pot, waiting to be served to Demi and Petra once they were revealed to the group.

"Chet, you remember my two friends you helped across the river?"

Chet nodded, lifting a spoon in greeting as his mouth was full of food.

"I'd like the rest of you to meet them. This is Demi and Petra Anderson. They are my dear friends from home, and they will be traveling the rest of the way with my wagon."

Fenna's smile faltered at the last words, but she quickly replaced her mask. "Pleased to meet you both."

Chet wasn't so muted. "Where's *their* wagon?"

Ellen drew in a breath. She hated to reveal her lie, but she wasn't about to spin it even larger.

Just as she was about to speak a voice came from the shadows of a wagon. "They ain't got a wagon. Just bodies in need of food and shelter." *Ben.*

"Which I have plenty of." Ellen threw a sharp glance at Ben. "My wagon was originally outfitted for six. Three of us will do just fine."

She turned to Demi and Petra. "Let me introduce you."

Ellen went through the family. Meeting them all at once meant neither sister was going to remember much. "You'll learn their names," she assured them.

"Will you still be part of our group?" Chet's tone held a hope that Ellen found extremely comforting. At least one Bridger didn't hate her.

But Ben spoke first, stepping out of the dark. "She's not our responsibility anymore. She can go where she pleases."

Sam jerked his attention away from the beautiful Petra. "They're still only three women. They should be under our protection."

"I didn't say they couldn't. Just that there's no requirement anymore."

"We may be just women, but we found our way here just fine." Petra's voice was haughty, and Ellen winced.

"I didn't mean any offense, ma'am. Just that there's been some talk. Men taking privileges and such." Sam ducked his head under the guise of taking a bite of dinner, but Ellen had seen Petra's words cut a man and she knew the look.

She spread her hands out as though diffusing a field fire. "We will stay with the group. We will eat from my rations alone, but we will be nearby."

"Have they been sleeping in your wagon?" Molly's voice was curious more than accusatory.

"Yes," Ellen answered, wondering how much the woman had already deduced.

Molly shrugged. "There's little room in there for you. You're welcome to continue sharing my tent."

Ellen smiled. "Thank you." She stepped near the dinner pot. "Has everyone had their share?"

She'd covertly added more food to the dinner preparations, but now she realized her sneakiness had been a mistake. She'd just promised not to eat their rations and now she was about to serve her friends from the family's pot.

"I must have mis-measured. We made too much." Fenna nodded, but her smile was still dim.

Ellen pulled a face. "I added a bit from my stores in anticipation of Demi and Petra joining us."

Fenna stepped forward and grasped the ladle. "I'm sure you ladies are starved." She scooped and passed bowls to Ellen, who passed it along until all three of them were served.

Ellen itched to bring a bowl to Ben, a peace offering. But he wouldn't accept. Not the offering anyhow. He seemed incapable of refusing food. He'd kept his distance all day, speaking to her only when necessary or if he was offering to relieve her of her duties driving the oxen.

He came to the pot and served himself a portion. "Word is out like a wildfire. The entire camp knows you're a single woman again. I suggest you stay close to camp tonight if you don't want to be interrogated all evening."

Ellen almost smiled at the image his words conjured. No doubt he'd already suffered a similar interrogation. That was likely what had kept him away from camp.

"They'll be mighty glad to have another Bridger man on the market." Ellen scanned the brothers. "I must admit being close to you Bridgers has given me a slice of popularity I will sorely miss."

"But you're staying close." Fenna's words were slow and measured.

"Yes."

Fenna gave a single nod, as though Ellen's words were just the assurance she was hoping for.

The rest of the evening passed with more conversation than usual, as everyone was quite curious about Demi and Petra's lives in Independence. The two women skirted questions about their parents allowing them to go. Unmarried women without their parents on the trail was an anomaly, but the Bridger family took it for granted because of Molly's unique situation.

Ellen noted any other single women in camp. There were several, but none of them traveled alone. It was as everyone said; single women didn't have a place out west. Burden or bride—those seemed the only classifications of the westering women.

Demi and Petra were deep in conversation with Fenna and Will when Ben sidled up to Ellen.

Ben's eyes darted to the pair of sisters. "I'll not have you bring more trouble to our door."

Ellen flinched and turned, her shoulder brushing his chest. He was closer than he should have been. She placed a hand on his chest and stepped back.

He watched as her hand slipped away. "If their father comes for them, I'll not stand in his way."

"They're old enough to know their own minds."

Ben's gaze clashed with her own. "If that's true, they're old enough to stay without our interference."

Ellen swallowed, hating that *our* no longer included her. She hated that he felt the need to clarify, to come to her away from everyone and have a conversation in hushed tones about how he was no longer beholden to her and her problems.

Hurt and anger swirled, making her heart beat in her ears. "I see you are thrilled to be free of me. I cannot believe I ever thought pretending to be married to you was going to be anything other than misery."

Ben huffed a hard laugh. "And yet you found me night after night."

Ellen reared in surprise.

"I had to give you the divider to snuggle, or else I'd wake up daily with your limbs curled around mine."

Ellen's cheeks flamed and she glared, but she didn't have the confidence to contradict him. She recalled more than once waking up twisted around the divider. "At least now the divide is finally great enough for the both of us."

Ben straightened, turning his serious face away from her.

She'd rarely had the last word with a man, but now she'd tasted the experience, she found it wasn't to her liking. She wanted him to retort, to prove he was cruel and she was better off away from him.

Instead, his gaze softened. "What happened to her face?"

The kindness in his voice dashed Ellen's fury like snow kicked over a flame.

She didn't need to follow his gaze to know he spoke of Demi and her scars. "A fire when she was young. Her arm has it too."

"Must have hurt a great deal."

Ellen turned so her shoulders matched the angle of Ben's. "I'm sure it did. It happened before I knew her. But scars like that, they hurt long after the pain has gone."

She felt Ben's eyes on her, but she kept her focus on Demi, on her sweet smile and the way she preened under the attention of the Bridger twins. The pair had joined the conversation and were listening to Demi with rapt attention.

"She doesn't usually get much attention..." Ellen turned

but Ben wasn't there. She spun, but he had disappeared like smoke in the night.

"I like him." Petra's voice startled her.

Ellen pressed a hand to her chest. "Gracious, Petra. You're likely to give a girl a fainting spell." Ellen followed Petra's gaze to where the twins sat with Demi.

"Which one?" Ellen eyed the twins. She knew them the least, as they stuck close to one another. She smiled to think of these sisters marrying twins and staying close.

"Your man. Ben."

Ellen glanced backward, a strange fear rolling through her that Ben remained close enough to hear. Even a man as grumbly as Ben would have his eye caught by a woman with Petra's beauty.

Ellen turned back. "You like Ben?"

"I like him for you." She nudged Ellen.

Ellen reared. "I don't... he isn't."

"I know it wasn't real. But maybe it could be."

Ellen shook her head.

"I've seen plenty these last few days."

"He's ornery."

"But he's fair."

Ellen's brows drew tight.

Petra huffed, her gaze turning distant. "It's the charming ones you need to look out for."

Ellen remained silent. If she could have described Petra's fiancé with one word, *charming* might be just the one.

"There's something raw and honest about a man who doesn't care what others think. They're the same in public as they are behind closed doors. You know just what you're getting." There was a depth to the way her eyes reflected the firelight. A knowing.

Ellen leaned against Petra's arm. "Every one of his brothers is easier to get along with than he is."

Ellen should have been celebrating all her options for husbands now that everyone in camp could know the truth. Instead, it seemed her best option had gone, disappeared as swiftly as Ben had left her side.

CHAPTER 24

Now that he wasn't connected to Ellen, Ben discovered spare time he hadn't even known he'd given up. He walked at Molly's side, listening to her read aloud from a small book she carried. Some nonsense about how a woman's humors were created by God to balance a man's humors and one never understood what balance felt like until they'd experienced marriage for themselves.

Fox came up on his mule and Molly stopped, removing her glasses and lifting her eyes to their guide.

"Fair weather today," Fox remarked.

"It is *spring*," Molly countered, like Fox was a fool for his gratitude.

Fox only dipped his head in acknowledgement.

Though the weather here was different than North Carolina, Ben read something in the set of Fox's shoulders. "You think it's the calm before the storm?"

Fox bobbed his head. "Could be."

Molly took Ben's arm. "Storm?"

Ben nodded, consumed with a childish fear of what could

come. Would it be another tornado? Would more of his family be lost?

"Any way to tell what type?"

Fox scanned the sky, as though reading something that could never be written in one of Molly's novels. "Rain." He pressed his lips. "Can't tell how much."

"My book says a good guide can tell the weather."

Fox cut a glance to Molly. "No man can tell God's plans."

"Not if He's going to change them, but once they're decided, I think an experienced man can figure them out."

Ben cut his cousin a look. Did she have no manners?

Fox only laughed. "I'll do my best, Widow Bridger."

He kicked his horse and returned to the front.

Ben turned to his cousin, ready to chastise her for her rudeness, but she spoke first. "Widow? Who does he think I am? I'm not old enough to be a widow."

"Ellen is a widow twice over."

"Yes, well, she's... different."

Molly rarely stalled her speech, and this lapse in wit intrigued him. "Different?"

Molly clicked her tongue. "I only mean she got married young and out of necessity. I'm sure women like that often botch the job the first time around and marry the type to die early."

"So she's lucky to have had another chance?" Ben's words were meant to be in jest, but he remembered who her second husband had been. Who his brother had been.

Molly winced. "She did a rather poor job the second time too."

He felt the strangest need to correct Molly. Not because Ellen needed protecting, but because Molly needed correcting. "Not everyone has the luxury of becoming spinsters."

"I know." Molly turned to him as though he'd merely confirmed her earlier words. "It's a pity, really. Ellen could have found a nice boring banker who would have showered her with gifts and affection all her days." She cocked her head in a jaunty way. "Although, from what I hear, her last marriage wasn't short on affection." She gave Ben a coy look. "Two brothers obsessed with the same woman. It could have been written by Shakespeare."

Ben glanced at the book in her hands. "How many of those did you bring?"

"Books?" Molly sighed. "Not nearly enough. Though, I admit, I had thought to read more on the trail. I never thought I would be too tired to read, but even with my new tent-mate, I find myself drifting off after only a couple pages."

"A shame," Ben deadpanned.

"It is." Molly nodded.

When Ben left her, he felt strangely like their encounter had brought them closer, even though they hadn't agreed on a single subject.

He had taken over for Sam, driving the oxen pulling their parents' wagon, when Billy Pratt, a young man who was on the trail with his family, approached him.

"Heya, Ben."

"Hello," Ben replied, noting the sweat on the boy's brow. Even with the calm Fox had spoken of, the heat wasn't enough to draw a sweat unless this boy had been running.

"I wanted to ask you about Ellen Moren."

Ben's hands tightened around the driving stick. "Yes?"

"Well, I wondered if you're the man I need to speak with. About permission to court her and such."

Ben's eyes almost rolled to the back of his skull. He had no authority over the men Ellen allowed to court her. But Billy Pratt was nowhere near the type of man she'd consider. He was too young and—Ben squinted at the boy—possibly shorter than her. Plus, he was the youngest in his family.

Surely his older brothers should be the ones asking to spend time with Ellen.

"You asking for yourself?"

Billy nodded vigorously, his small chin nearly disappearing into his neck.

Ben almost feigned authority and refused Billy's request, but a sinister idea surfaced instead. "You're a bit young."

"I know." Billy attempted to kick a rock, but missed and stepped on it instead, rolling his ankle and recovering with practiced precision.

"It won't be easy winning her over."

Billy's eyes brightened as they turned fully to Ben.

"I know a fair bit about her."

Billy nodded. He hadn't taken his eyes off Ben the entire time.

Ben jerked his chin toward the front. "Eyes forward or you'll break your ankle."

Billy did so and dropped back a bit so he could still watch Ben while looking where he was going.

"First, she needs her oxen brushed down every night."

"I can do that." Billy's enthusiasm almost dimmed Ben's heart, but the idea of giving Ellen more help than she knew what to do with was too great a temptation.

"Her wagon is the one with the orange spade. Her tent should be set up before dinner is through."

Billy nodded again. "What else?"

"I'll have to think on it. Come see me tomorrow."

Billy skipped off, and Ben watched him go with a smile.

Fox pushed the company to continue later than normal. When they finally stopped, the guide took his time walking through camp and letting everyone know the news—rain was coming, and if it was still raining in the morning, the company wouldn't move on right away. The bugle would tell them when it was time.

Ben had hardly finished unhitching the animals before he caught sight of Billy with Ellen's tent in hand. Compared to the pranks he and his brothers used to pull on one another, this was nothing.

He glanced at the sky, feeling the balminess that had thickened the air throughout the day. If he had to guess, it would be heavy rain tonight. He glanced at the wagons, wondering if they wouldn't be a better spot to sleep, but there wasn't enough room for everyone to sleep inside one. They couldn't risk unpacking items and leaving them to the elements.

Tonight, Ellen would regret giving up her wagon to her friends. If the rain was hard enough, not even the tents would keep them dry.

Will strode over. "Fox says to expect a storm."

Ben nodded. "Rain, I think. Hopefully that's all."

"Rain can do plenty of damage."

"You and Fenna should make room in a wagon. I'll try and do the same for Molly."

Will departed with a nod, and Ben tried to squelch the desire to clear a space for Ellen too. She wasn't his responsibility. Not anymore. She had her friends, and she still had a community among his family. He didn't need to ensure she rested comfortably.

After some work, Ben had been able to clear a narrow space for Molly to sleep. It was too narrow for any of his brothers, and he wondered how Will was faring, trying to find space for himself and Fenna. It was good Ellen wasn't his responsibility because he wouldn't have been able to make any additional space anyway. Not in this wagon with Molly anyhow.

Since they hadn't stopped until dark, every one of the usual tasks took longer. By the time Ben was finished, the camp had gone to sleep. He passed Will's wagon and heard soft conversation. He smiled, but something lingered in his chest long after he was tucked into his own tent. He lay on his back, eyes open, trying to name the emotion. It wasn't jealousy, nor was it bitterness. It tasted a lot like longing. When he closed his eyes, Ellen's face filled his vision, and he was too tired to drive her away.

CHAPTER 25

*E*llen opened her eyes, wondering why she was awake. It was impossible to tell the time without a clock. All she knew was that it was still dark and she was cold. She rolled onto her side, her hips digging into the ground beneath her. When the quilts moved, she felt a whole new cold. Not that of the air inside her covers shifting, but a wet cold.

She sat up with a start and patted her hands around the dark floor. Each one sounded with a splat. Wet.

The rain pounding on the tent had been a lovely lullaby while she'd slept. Now it served to drown out her words as she called to Molly.

Ellen had to shake her friend awake. "There's water in the tent."

Molly sat up slowly. "What?"

"Water." Ellen stood and gathered her quilts up around her like a too-full skirt, hoping at least a few of them were still dry.

Molly leaned back down on her elbow but shot up again. "It's wet in here."

Ellen huffed. "Gather your things. I think we'll need to make do somewhere else."

But where? Their best chance would be to take refuge under a wagon and hope the rain wasn't powerful enough to flood that dry area too.

Once Molly had her things, they crowded to the edge of the tent. Ellen did her best to ignore the way her stockings sucked water from the ground and chilled her legs. Donning her boots would require setting her blankets on the ground; she needed dry quilts more than she needed dry feet.

"My wagon is the biggest. We can sleep under there."

Molly bumped Ellen with her own pile of bedding. "Ben cleared space in the wagon for me."

Ellen turned sharply to Molly. "What?"

Molly huffed. "He knew the rain would be bad. He told me to sleep in the wagon."

"Why didn't you?" Ellen knew this was a silly conversation to have just now. With every moment they waited, their feet got wetter. Ellen hoped she'd left her boots standing upright and not on their sides, filling with water. She wouldn't know the answer until morning.

But she could get an answer to this right now. "Molly, why did you sleep in the tent?"

"I didn't want to leave you alone all night. It wasn't fair that he didn't make space for you too."

Somehow Molly's anger on Ellen's behalf soothed her own hurt at being disregarded. *"You* are his ward, not I."

Nevertheless, a crowded wagon was still a better option than a wet tent. "Which wagon?"

"Aunt and Uncle's."

Though their parents had both passed, no brother had taken over full responsibility for the wagon. They all just shared the load of driving it and greasing the axles and all the other small tasks. A bit like they'd done with her and her wagon at the beginning, before Ben had taken charge. She tried to ignore the bite in her belly at remembering how she too had once been under Ben's care and protection. Obviously, that was completely gone now.

Ellen tried to envision where that wagon was parked. As soon as they stepped into the rain, they could run without wasting time deciding on a direction.

"I'll go first. Once I'm inside, you can come next."

Molly nodded and, before she lost her nerve, Ellen darted between the flaps of the tent. She whipped her head around, determining where exactly the wagon was. In the dark with rain pelting her face, she couldn't rightly see.

She came to a stop, turning and wishing she'd had the forethought to leave the blankets. But a memory came of Ben climbing out of his parents' wagon. It must have been when he was clearing the space for Molly.

She turned and spotted the white bonnet in the dark. She ran frantically for it, the sleeves of her dress soaked through and her skin prickling with cold. When she reached the tail she gathered her blankets, tossing them over the edge and then hauling herself up next. She threw one leg over the tailgate and stepped right on the blankets with her muddy stocking. It didn't matter. The way the rain stopped so suddenly the moment she was under the bonnet told her the vehicle was parked at the right angle to keep them dry. The rain lashed at the sides instead of either end. They would be dry in here for the rest of the night.

She allowed herself to stand and shiver for a moment before lifting her blankets up in preparation for Molly throwing herself over the tailgate.

It was then that Ellen saw there was but a narrow alley of space cleared. Ben truly hadn't bothered to make any more space for another body. She stared at the strip of space, her body convulsing with cold.

She couldn't wallow for long. Molly slammed into the gate and Ellen twisted, grabbing the quilts from her friend's hands and stepping back to allow Molly space to enter.

Molly gasped, clutching a crate near her head. "I think the Lord is pouring a bucket. Surely this cannot last much longer."

But weather knew no laws.

"Molly, there isn't much space. I'll help you get set up, then I'll go to my wagon."

Molly turned to Ellen. "Your friends are in there."

"I know, but there will be more room than in here."

There wasn't. But Molly had already proved that she would suffer in loyalty, and Ellen couldn't submit her friend to such an awful night. Only one of them needed to suffer. Besides, she might be able to claim the only spot of dry land in their tent. There had to be *something* left.

The two women worked together, using their sense of touch to see which blankets were the most damp and laying those on the bottom to be used as insulation from the cold.

Once they'd made Molly's bed, Ellen swallowed, readying herself to step into the drenching rain once more. She ought to go to her wagon anyway to get dry clothes. There was no salvaging what she wore. As it was, Molly might be better off sleeping nude if her trunk of clothing wasn't already in this wagon.

"I'll be back for my blankets once I've found my spot."

Molly was already removing her skirt. "If you aren't back soon enough, I shall search for you."

Ellen laughed, knowing full well that as spoiled as Molly might be, she wasn't one to cower in the face of a challenge. As promised, she would crawl from her warm bed to seek Ellen. Ellen crawled back into the pounding rain. At least she hadn't lost Molly when she'd lost Ben.

Ellen reached her wagon and hauled herself in, her numb

toes slipping on the tongue and causing her to hit her chin, but she made it inside. Her wagon wasn't facing the same direction as the Bridgers' and the floor inside was damp.

She removed her stockings, unwilling to allow any more water to seep inside. She cast around for something to soak up the pool already forming. And another thing to cover the hole.

What she found instead was an empty wagon.

She turned, as though the Anderson sisters had merely played a trick on her and hidden. But no, the wagon was empty.

"Demi? Petra?" Ellen whispered, as though there was anyone to be mindful of.

Nothing. She blinked. Where could they have gone? She supposed the Bridgers did have a few extra tents. They might have lent one. And it had been a good idea, since her wagon interior wasn't half as dry as Molly's.

She sighed, pushing worries about Demi and Petra from her mind. She needed a warm place to sleep. She needed dry clothes. She felt her way around the stacked crates and barrels to find her crate. She opened it and fingered the dry clothes with a sigh.

Blankets first, then dry clothes.

She assessed the floor of her wagon. It had twice as much space as Molly's had. Still tight for two women, but Demi and Petra were used to sharing a bed, and it wasn't as though they'd had much choice in the amount of space they were given. Wagons were meant to haul supplies. It wasn't a traveling inn, though she supposed someone like Fox might be able to make a living bringing such a thing across the plains.

Confident that this was where she would be sleeping for whatever remained of this night, Ellen ventured back out into the pouring rain. Her bare feet squelched in the mud as she passed the group of tents to reach Molly.

Molly was sitting up when Ellen entered. "My wagon is empty."

"Oh?"

"They must have used the tent tonight." Though Ellen seriously doubted their ability to set the tent up, even with two of them. Surely their beds were wet. It was only a matter of time before they came to the wagon for shelter.

"Will you be okay alone?" Molly's voice held a tremor.

"No folks are out in this." Ellen wrung a bit of wet from her hair for emphasis.

"Of course," Molly said. Ellen wished she could see her friend's expression, to really know if Molly would feel safe. She could always invite her to share the bed in her wagon. It might be warmer to have two anyway. But Molly's legs were already tucked into the bed she'd arranged.

One last dash back to her wagon and Ellen reached her sanctuary once more. She threw the blankets in as far as they would go and hoped there weren't any pools of water yet undiscovered.

She removed her skirt and tucked it into the criss-cross of ropes that stretched the bonnet over the wagon's ribs. The water would still drench her skirt, but if she placed something on the floor underneath, whatever dripped would be caught, and hopefully the rest of the wagon bed would remain dry until morning.

With shaking limbs, she set up her little apartment, draping her soaked blouse over a barrel, knowing full well it wouldn't be dry by morning. With the privacy allowed her by her hanging skirt, she stripped down and redressed in dry clothes. Then she laid the blankets into a cozy bed and burrowed in.

Her teeth chattered, but eventually sleep overcame her and, uncomfortable as she was, she slept.

CHAPTER 26

*B*en woke with a start. He brought his fingers to the back of his head, prodding the hair there, which was cold and wet to the touch. He snapped up and scurried out of his bed, pressing his hands all around the ground, seeking the water he knew must be pooling on his waxed canvas. He found none, but to be sure, he used his flint to light the lantern. For one moment, he expected its glow to catch on the planes of Ellen's sleeping face, but of course she wasn't there. She wouldn't ever be again, not after the way he'd spoken to her at the fire tonight.

He glanced toward his tent opening. If his tent was leaking water, he might not be the only one. He had set up a tent for Ellen's two friends and he hoped he'd done a good enough job of it that they hadn't piled themselves in with Molly and Ellen.

A strong gust of wind hit the walls of Ben's tent and the wet canvas bumped and bellowed. He was reminded of the winds of the tornado that took his parents. The idea only compounded his fears, and he abandoned any care he had for the inside of his tent.

He stuck the lantern and his head out of the tent, trying to see if there were any other lights on, any other folks about. As he scanned the points of each of his family's tents, his gaze snagged on one. Molly's tent. He knew full well she should have been inside. The problem was the tent was no longer standing. It was lying in a crumpled heap; the poles must have given out in the wind.

Ben placed the lantern on the ground and launched himself from his tent. He reached Molly's tent in a panic. He'd heard of folks being smothered in a collapsed tent. Wet fabric would only do a more thorough job. He tried to find the opening and gave up, settling for crawling along the whole of the tent and assuring himself there were no bodies inside.

"Molly?" he called into the driving rain. "Ellen?"

Perhaps Molly had led them to the wagon. He stood and collected the lantern, a strange desperation pounding in his chest. What if Cyrus came for Ellen? There wasn't a better night for it. He could have sent his brother's body on home and stayed behind to torment Ellen.

He shook his head, trying to fling off the wild thoughts circling like the swirling rain. Reaching the wagon, he climbed up inside. "Molly?" he whispered. "Ellen?"

A mumble came from the blankets and Molly's head peeked out from the cocoon. "Ben?"

"Is Ellen in here with you?"

Molly stifled a yawn. "She's in her wagon."

Ben sighed. This was too much like a game of musical chairs. He didn't have the patience for it, but Molly's account of Ellen's location wasn't enough.

He climbed back out as another strong gust came, causing him to stumble sideways as he sought his own answer.

He reached Ellen's wagon and hung the lantern on one of the many hooks while he hauled himself up, balancing on the tongue before ducking inside the bonnet and out of the rain. A gust came, rocking the wagon, and Ben fell against the stack of crates inside.

"Who's there?" a panicked voice wavered from deeper in the wagon. He could tell from her voice that she was frightened of him. He could also tell she was standing, not asleep as Molly had been.

"Ellen, it's me, Ben."

Another gust rocked the wagon and he cursed the maker of this wagon, finer than his family's wagons and with a better suspension system that made it the most unstable just now.

A thump told him Ellen caught herself on the crates as he had done.

"What are you doing here?" Her words held a tremor.

He stepped closer, squinting until he could make out the planes of her face and the variation in colors from the layers of clothing she wore.

"I came to see if you were safe."

Another gust came, but instead of rocking the wagon, it snapped the loose canvas in the bonnet, causing it to moan and creak with the movement. Ben tried to keep his mind present and not allow it to wander to the tornado. To what had happened the last time he'd experienced strong winds on this prairie. Near this very spot.

He felt around the crates, ensuring they were all tied down. The last thing Ellen needed was to be crushed in the night by her own possessions.

As he neared her, Ellen pushed at his arm. "Why are you here?"

"I'm just making sure—"

She pushed again. "I'm not your ward. You don't need to look out for me." Another gust came, and he braced himself on both sides of her makeshift bed.

A small cry escaped her lips and his heart tore down the middle. She'd been so brave facing Cyrus, knowing what her life might have been and yet taking what she needed to get away from him. He didn't resent her for all the trouble she'd brought upon him and his family. He would tell anyone to do the same. After all, weren't the strong supposed to lift the weak? Yet Ellen had never been weak.

She moved to push him again and must have misjudged his position, because she fell into him, her shoulder pressing into his chest. She quickly recovered, placing both hands on his torso and pressing away. "You're all wet! Get out of here."

Ben resisted catching her against him, knowing she was right. "My dry clothes are in here."

"Ugh!" Ellen groaned and stepped away from him. She pointed at him. "Step off my bedding, if you will."

Ben thought of his own bedding, abandoned in search of Ellen and Molly. He'd have to take shelter with one of his brothers tonight. They wouldn't thank him for it. He shrugged out of his coat, the wettest of his clothing.

Ellen climbed onto a crate and dug around in an upper section of her storage. During their travels, she'd been doing his washing and had a better idea of where everything was. In the days since they'd called off their ruse, he hadn't yet claimed his things.

She climbed back down and pressed a ball of fabric into his hands. Then she shrugged out of her coat and held it out. He eyed the material in her hands. "I'm not going to take your jacket."

She jangled it at him. "It's yours."

Ben eyed the item with new understanding. Then he looked again at her whole ensemble. "Is that my shirt, too?"

Ellen huffed and let her head fall to one side.

The longer he looked the more he recognized. She wore

his shirt, which came nearly to her knees. Her bloomers stuck out the bottom and... were those his wool socks?

He smiled, strangely pleased to see her clothed in his garb.

"I'll give it all back." She turned to climb back up the crates, but Ben stepped forward and caught her waist.

"Ellen, I don't mind."

She lowered and he found he couldn't step away.

Another gust of wind rocked the wagon, and Ellen's breath hitched as she gripped the ropes holding the crates in place.

Ben slid his hand up her back, rubbing circles between her shoulder blades. "It's not as bad. It's a regular storm. There are just no buildings to block the wind."

Ellen shrugged him off. "I know." But as soon as she released her hold, the wagon shifted again and she fell into him, the ball of clothes pressed between them.

As much as she had cared before, she didn't resent his damp proximity any longer. He wrapped his arm around her and tried his best to stop her shaking.

She straightened and wiped at her nose. "Do you know where Demi and Petra are?"

Ben smiled. "Billy Pratt set your tent up. I saw them making their bed inside."

"Billy Pratt?"

"He wanted to be helpful to the newly single Ellen Moren."

She scoffed and pressed away from him. "I'm fine. You can go."

Strangely, he knew she would be fine. That being afraid wasn't the same as being in danger. Yet he could not leave her.

"I have nowhere to sleep."

Ellen froze and glanced up at him. He longed for the

lantern he'd left on the tail of the wagon, though no doubt the flame had died in the rain by now. He wanted to see her face, to know if she would take pity on him.

"Your tent?"

"My bed is wet."

Ellen huffed a sigh. "Ours too." She gestured to the blankets on the floor. "All of it is wet somewhere."

"If I get into dry clothes, can I stay here?" Normally it would be too bold an ask, but they'd shared space enough times. Surely by now Ellen trusted him.

Ellen's mouth opened, but she hesitated. Finally, she said, "Of course." Her tone spoke to the practical necessity of it, but his heart wanted the impossible. It wanted her to ask him to stay, to beg him. To tell him she still needed him, wanted him, longed for him.

She picked up the clothes that had fallen to the floor. "Get changed and I'll fix the bed."

He took the clothes but passed the jacket back. It wasn't until she'd slid it back on that he turned away and undid the top button of his shirt. There were no nightclothes on the trail. He usually wore his underclothes, or when Ellen had shared his tent, his cleanest clothes which he would then wear the next day.

He pulled his shirt off and reached to feel in the pile for a dry shirt. He vaguely wondered if Ellen had turned away, granting him privacy, and if she hadn't, how much she was seeing just now. Funny how the lines of propriety were blurred between them. He'd known her for such a short time, yet he'd kissed her. He'd lied for her. When fear had overcome him over the tent being smashed, it wasn't his cousin, his own blood, who had consumed his thoughts.

Under the scant cover of his long shirt, he removed his pants and stepped into the dry ones Ellen had found for him. He draped his wet clothes over the tailgate, careful not to let the wet skirt hanging there dampen these new clothes. Then he turned and found her sitting up in a pile of quilts.

She lifted one off the floor and offered it to him.

Ben draped it over his shoulders, catching it in the front. He drew a deep inhale of her scent. A scent he hadn't realized he'd missed these last two days without her in his tent.

She gestured him closer. "Come this way. It's driest over here."

Crates were stacked against the opening on the other side, and if rain was getting in, the storage had stopped it reaching Ellen's makeshift bed.

He stepped closer and she caught the end of his blanket, pulling him down on his knees in front of her.

The rain outside came harder, a wave of noise so loud they would have had to yell to be heard above the din. Along with it came another gust of wind, but Ellen was already making his heart pound as much as was possible.

She didn't cry out as she'd done before. Was she feeling whatever he felt? Did she truly feel safer with him here, as though he could control the weather the way he controlled her oxen?

Ellen scooted back toward the head of her bed and tucked her legs under the covers. "It's tight, but we've slept close before."

Ben recalled the way she'd held him in the night when she didn't even realize it. She knew it now. He'd bungled the way he'd shared that information. What else would he bungle before their journey was through?

As he moved to sit at the head, it was obvious they wouldn't fit shoulder to shoulder. "Ellen, it's too tight."

Ellen shifted to the side and tugged at Ben, who obliged and shifted so his back was against the wall. Ellen adjusted the blankets around his legs and middle. He allowed her, curious what she had in mind. "Now scoot down until you're lying on your back."

"Ellen." There wouldn't be room no matter which position he lay. But being this close to her again filled him with such joy, he didn't dare risk arguing.

Once he was situated on his back, his one side pressed tightly to the crates, Ellen scooted in on her side, stopping so her head was near his shoulder. She adjusted the quilts.

"Ellen, you cannot balance on your side all night."

She stopped fussing with the blankets and patted his chest lightly. "Unlike you, I have something to lean against."

She finished with the quilts and lay down, her face pressed between the wall and his arm.

He shifted. "That cannot be comfortable."

"It's fine," she said, her words muffled by the fabric of his shirt.

He laughed out loud and sat up. Ellen sat up too. In the tight space, every move had to be in sync.

"Ben." She groaned. She was obviously frustrated with him ruining all her adjustments, but the familiar way she said his name chased away the last of the night's chill.

He lay back down, shifting slightly so his elbow pressed against her wall. "Lie down."

She did and his arm acted like a pillow under her head.

"Better?"

She shifted around. "Your arm is going to be numb." She moved a bit more and rested one hand on his chest. Only the tips of her fingers poked out of the cuff of her jacket. His jacket. His arm tightened involuntarily around her, savoring the press of her body against his.

This woman was totally encased in him. A possessive emotion rolled through him. "Are you wearing my socks?"

A beat of silence had him smiling.

"Yes." Her tone was quiet, bashful.

Ben snickered.

She lifted her hand and gave his chest a sound thump. "Mine were soaked."

He laughed louder. "I wore my boots in. I'm afraid to see the state of this wagon come morning."

Ellen tugged the quilts higher, using her free hand to tuck them around his shoulder and under his chin. She then did the same to herself and rested her hand on his chest again.

"Thank you."

Ben grunted. "For what, taking up most of your sleeping space?"

"For telling Billy to set up my tent. For looking after me after I'd hurt you."

Ben's chest felt too tight to reply, so he lay there while the rain continued to pound outside. The wagon even shifted a few more times, but as low as they were, the movement wasn't as dramatic. Or perhaps with Ellen in his arms, he didn't care. Just like when she'd proposed a fake marriage. Then his mind had been so consumed with her, all other thoughts had leached away. In this case, the fear dissipated. Though holding her guaranteed nothing, he was content to lie here with her in his arms, and he didn't much care what went on outside.

CHAPTER 27

*E*llen blinked awake, warm and dry and curiously relaxed by the soft pitter of light rain outside. Nothing like the storm that had raged in the night. The interior of the wagon was still dark, though some light streamed in on either side of her skirt, hanging to block the bonnet's opening.

She turned her head and discovered the source of her warmth.

Ben.

She was curled against him, sharing his body heat. She wanted to burrow closer, to partake of the blaze that always emanated from him while he slept. But she could not ignore her bladder.

She softly crawled out from the covers, sucking in a sharp breath as the chill air soaked through her clothes and kissed her skin. Her gaze scanned the wagon's interior for a moment before she remembered her boots were still inside her collapsed tent. She would have to go barefoot.

She dug in the Anderson women's crates and located a skirt, which she pulled on and tied over top the billowy ends of

Ben's shirt. It gaped at the neck, too large for a woman, but she worked the buttons on his jacket and covered the shirt entirely.

As she was about to exit, the morning light caught on a mess of mud. Ben's boots. She glanced back at him, his breathing slow and deep. He wouldn't miss them any time soon. She stepped in, his bulky stockings doing nothing to fill the cavernous insides, and as she crawled from the wagon, they threatened to slip with each step. Perhaps she would have been better off bare-footed. She spotted a lantern hanging on the edge, snuffed and abandoned. Ben must have brought it last night when he'd been searching for her.

She smiled as she stepped off the wagon, the boots squelching into the mud. The rain may have eased, but the ground had not yet absorbed all the water that had dumped from the sky.

She looked at the too-large boots on her feet. He'd searched for her. He hadn't needed to. There was no commitment between them, not anymore. Yet he'd cared.

The thought made her wiggle her toes. She smiled as she made her way to a bush to relieve herself. She tried to step on tufts of spiky prairie grass, but these boots were going to be a mess no matter what she did.

Once she'd finished her business, she righted her clothing and retraced her steps back to camp. So focused was she on avoiding the muddiest parts of her route, that she was nearly toe to toe with someone before she bothered looking up to see who it was.

Tall, broad, and mean.

Cyrus.

He wore a cruel smirk.

She stared at him, disbelief freezing her throat.

"I didn't think you'd come right to me," he said, his tone teasing.

Ellen mustered all the bravado and did her best to keep her voice from shaking. "Ben is close. You better leave before he comes—"

A slap to her face cut her off. Her knees buckled and she fell to the ground, only to be hauled up again by her arm. Something cold pressed to her neck. "Scream and I'll slit your throat."

With both hands, Ellen gripped the arm holding the knife, but Cyrus was a laborer and she wasn't strong enough to fight him off. Any movement she could force would likely result in her demise.

He pressed his mouth to her ear. "I took care of your dear husband." The warmth of his breath on her ear was like the mud they stood in. Thick, cold, and filthy.

His words stole her exhale, and images of Cyrus' blade slicing across sleeping Ben's neck felt like a knife to her own gut. With each new image, Ellen's spine grew weak as she considered what their ruse had cost Ben.

Cyrus dragged her away. She hardly cared to fight him. She should have known she couldn't escape him. That all the distance in the world would not prevent him from getting what he wanted. That convincing someone to help her would only result in more pain.

She had to curl her toes to keep Ben's boots from sliding off as Cyrus dragged her through the mud, pulling her past the company's hobbled animals. Soon they stopped and Ellen was able to get her feet under her once again.

"Stay quiet." His icy tone turned her stomach, and her lips pressed tight as he removed his hand from her mouth and pressed her back against something warm. It knickered in response and Ellen glanced to the side, barely noticing the horse she leaned against. Cyrus pulled her hands together and tied them with a strip of cloth.

When he was done tying her hands, Cyrus fumbled with something near her waist, then said, "Alright, climb up."

He twisted her and held the stirrup, waiting for her to place her foot inside. A tiny part of her pleaded to resist, begged her to heave herself at him and run back to camp. But they were too far, and he was too fast, and she would trip over these boots. And Ben was dead.

"Cyrus—"

He slapped her, a sharp blow to her face. Her knees gave way, but Cyrus caught the waist of her skirt and pushed her toward the horse. "Up."

She lifted a shaking leg and Cyrus caught her foot with the stirrup. He boosted her onto the saddle. For a moment, her instinct flashed, and she imagined herself flying across the prairie on Cyrus' horse. She kicked the sides of the horse, but the beast only shifted from one hip to the other.

Cyrus walked to the front and untied the reins from a heavy branch on the ground. Ellen glared at the traitorous wood and stiffened as Cyrus climbed up behind her. "Didn't think I'd let you take off without me, did you?"

Ellen rolled her shoulders, trying to push him away, but he wrapped one arm around her waist, angling the knife on the saddle horn so it was pointing at her belly. If this horse caught its foot and stumbled, Ellen would be gutted. Was that what Cyrus had already done to Ben? How could he have done it so quickly, in only the time it took to relieve herself? But Ben had been sleeping so peacefully. With Cyrus pressed against her back and his plans yet unrevealed, death could very well be a gift.

Ellen turned to view the camp. Farther away than she expected.

Cyrus shifted and brought the blade back to her throat. "Don't even think about it."

Ellen gulped but did as he bid and faced forward again.

There was no point in escape. Whoever helped her would only suffer Ben's fate.

Cyrus' hands appeared and he pressed fabric across her eyes, tying it in the back.

The loss of her vision made her heart thump harder. "Where are we going?" Ellen whispered, though her cheek still burned from the last time she'd spoken.

Cyrus was silent behind her, his breathing even, as though hauling her from camp had been as simple as carrying a parcel under one arm.

As they moved across the wide earth, Ellen couldn't tell how much time had passed. But her face and neck felt as stiff and cold as an iron chain by the time the sun grew bright enough to light the edges of her blindfold.

Cyrus stopped the horse and climbed off. Ellen used her shoulder to lift the blindfold. Before her was the outline of a wagon and as her vision cleared, Ellen saw a pair of boots hanging out the back. Familiar boots. Titus' boots. They were no longer wrapped in a sheet.

"Titus," she whispered.

Cyrus pulled her roughly off the horse and pinned her to his side.

Without a word, he walked her to the wagon, revealing the rest of Titus' body in the bed of the wagon. She gulped. The sheet she'd wrapped him in lay open like a bread cloth, revealing its unbaked contents.

Cyrus pressed the blade to her back. "Get in."

Ellen turned, horrified.

He only nodded toward Titus. "You did this. Now go lie by your husband."

Cyrus pushed her forward, but the opening of the wagon was at her ribs. There was no way she could climb in without her hands. What was more, her entire body shook, and it wasn't with cold.

"Cyrus, I didn't do this."

"I know you didn't. But that bastard has paid, and now you will too."

Cyrus scooped her up and hefted her into the wagon, dropping her painfully onto the plank bed. One of Ben's boots slid down her foot and thumped to the ground.

He pointed with the knife that still held a stain of blood. "Lie by your husband."

She met his eyes, searching for some of that affection she'd been so afraid of during her marriage to Titus. She found the absence of it even more terrifying.

She scooted back so her legs were completely inside the wagon.

Cyrus' gaze fell on her shoeless foot, then dropped to the ground. His eyes narrowed and he gripped the boot she still wore, yanking it off and tossing it near the other one.

"Lie down." Cyrus spoke between clenched teeth.

Ellen couldn't. She could barely stand the cold touch of Titus' leg against hers. "Cyrus, I can't." Her voice broke, hot tears warming her cheeks as fear gripped her in its harsh claws.

He stepped closer and pressed against the foot of the wagon. "Did you plan for it? Did you ask that man to shoot Titus?"

"Titus shot himself!" Ellen blurted before Cyrus could interrupt her again.

Shock registered on Cyrus' face, but it cleared too quickly. "How dare you." He gripped her foot and dragged her to the edge, then gripped both her arms. His hands pinched her skin through Ben's jacket. His eyes searched hers for a moment, and though she did her best to read his thoughts, it was impossible to tell whether he desired or hated her.

He leaned close, his breath reeking in her face. "My brother would never—"

"It was an accident."

Cyrus waited, his focus shifting between her eyes in search of the truth.

"It was during the storm. You know how he loved that rifle. He was desperate to save it. He didn't want it to get carried away."

Ellen gulped, afraid of saying too much and just as terrified of not saying enough. Titus had held that rifle in such reverence because Cyrus had gotten the wheelwright shop. Would bringing that up make Cyrus softer or harder? She didn't know. What little she understood about this man was gone. He was a stranger and more dangerous than ever before.

"He only wanted to preserve his inheritance," she dared to say, her voice just above a whisper.

Cyrus held her stare, and she could almost see belief in his eyes before he wiped it away and pressed her backward. She brought her knees up, but it turned out he didn't want to hurt her. He only wanted her on her back by her husband. He pressed her stockinged feet together and tied them the same as her hands.

Ellen blinked up at the rain that peppered her face. Still a constant drizzle from the night before. The sky was lighter at the edge of her vision. Toward the center she could still see stars, and in every constellation, she saw Ben's face.

"You killed Ben?" He'd told her so, and yet, she refused to believe it.

Cyrus gave a hard laugh and cinched the binding tighter around her ankles. "Don't pretend like you care." He finished, climbing into the wagon and stepping near Ellen's face as he walked to the head. "You didn't care when Titus died. I saw it in the way you threw yourself at me."

Denial reared, then died on her lips. She wasn't going to get anywhere by contradicting him. She waited, letting her heart resume a reasonable tempo. "Titus hid me from you." She repeated Cyrus' words. Words that had once frightened her and now might just be her salvation if she could remind him of the loving feelings he'd once had.

He gripped her under both arms and dragged her higher in the wagon until her hips were level with Titus' hips. He set her down gently, a contrast to the way he'd tied her feet just moments before. It gave her hope.

But every time she dared hope, she thought of Ben, dead in her wagon. In the bed they'd shared for the first time not out of commitment, but out of comfort and need for one another.

Cyrus sat on his haunches, inches from her head. His face hovered above her, blocking out the rain. "He knew I would have had you myself."

Ellen gulped at the disconnected terms, like she was a possession and not a person. If she was going to save herself, she had to draw him out, make him forget about Titus.

"You were the elder brother. More capable, more established. Every girl in town was hoping for your attention." But as she spoke, she thought not of Cyrus, but of Ben. The way his family relied on him. What they'd already lost. How they would mourn when they discovered his body.

Cyrus' eyes narrowed, drawing her attention back to the danger at hand. Had she gone too far? But it was true. Many women hoped for his affection. That wasn't to say their fathers didn't know him well enough to keep their daughters away.

"They would speak to me of it because you and I were so close. They thought I could... connect you to them."

Cyrus' eyes remained tight.

"Petra hoped for a chance, before her engagement." It was

a lie, but Petra was the prettiest woman she knew and living so close meant she'd had interactions with Cyrus.

Cyrus scoffed. "Petra hated me, always thought she was too good."

"It was an act." Ellen boldly raised her tied hands to touch Cyrus' chin. "Don't tell me you never teased a girl you were sweet on."

Cyrus moved away from her touch, but his mouth twisted in what could be contemplation.

"You know her parents. She could never have been so forward to tell you how she felt. But she told me."

Cyrus jerked his chin and stood, climbing out of the wagon.

"Cyrus!" Ellen shouted, desperation clawing the word up her throat. She didn't know if anything she said was making any difference, but if he left he took her chances with him.

He weaved his head over the side of the wagon and back into sight. "You didn't want me. You could have chosen me, but instead you chose *him*." Cyrus didn't nod toward Titus, but west, toward camp.

He might have forgiven her for marrying Titus, but he would never forgive her for marrying Ben.

He disappeared from her sight, and she called after him, shouting his name. He didn't answer. Soon the wagon jostled with movement and Ellen did her best to keep away from Titus' rotting body. She shouted at Cyrus until her voice cracked and her throat burned.

Even still she tried, though the rain soaked Ben's jacket and she couldn't stop herself from imagining him as cold as Titus.

CHAPTER 28

A shout drew him from his sleep and Ben jolted awake, his hands hovering as he took in his surroundings. Ellen's wagon. He let out a sigh.

But... she was gone. Perhaps she'd left for Molly's tent, just like the last time they'd shared a bed.

"Ben!" A shout came from outside.

"In here!" Ben replied, untangling from the quilts.

He stood, searching the ground for his boots. They were gone, along with Ellen.

He tugged the wool socks from his feet and climbed from the wagon, his bare feet hitting the muddy earth.

Fenna caught his arms. "It's Sam. He's been stabbed."

The news washed over him like a bucket of water, clearing away any sleepiness. "Stabbed?"

Fenna ignored his query and turned, rushing away.

Ben followed on her heels until he reached Will's medical tent, larger than all the others to contain a cot for patients as needed.

Ben pushed through to find Sam on Will's cot, his clothes pushed aside to expose a bloody wound. "Who did this?"

Will barely spared Ben a glance. "I need clean water. Get a fire going."

Fenna turned to Ben. "Chet is checking on everyone else. Making sure all are safe."

Ben knew who was capable of this, but Cyrus was gone, and he had never shown issue with any of Ben's brothers. If it were Cyrus, he would have attacked Ben or Ellen. Not Sam.

"Press here," Will demanded.

Ben stepped forward automatically to press the wound.

Will turned and rummaged in his bag, returning with bandages. "They missed the liver." Will met Ben's gaze. "He's lucky. But we need him to wake up."

Ben assisted Will for another half hour before Will sent him out to check on the others. Chet sat on a three-legged stool outside the tent. Ben approached and clapped him on the shoulder. "How is everyone else?" He looked toward Ellen's wagon, anxious to find his boots.

Chet looked up with puffy eyes. "Molly is in her tent. Alex and Nate are tending the stock."

Ben glanced back at the tent containing the rest of his family. Yet he couldn't feel relief, not with Sam still unconscious. He looked out at the damp earth. The rain had stopped and the sky was mostly white with small patches of pale blue.

"And Ellen?"

Chet gave Ben a confused look. "I thought you said she wasn't our responsibility any longer."

Ben sighed. So he had. "You're right." He tousled Chet's hair and moved toward the wagon. He climbed up, sticking his head through the bonnet's opening. "Ellen?" He checked the floor a second time, ensuring his boots really were gone. He turned, glancing at his tent but certain he had worn them here last night. "Ellen?"

Nothing. He climbed inside, but everything looked the same as when he'd left it that morning.

He climbed back out and found Fenna and Molly at the fire. It had been used to boil water for Sam's wound and now they had a bit of hash in a pan.

"Where's Ellen? She has my boots."

Molly looked at Fenna. "Must still be asleep."

Uncertainty gargled in his stomach. "You haven't seen her all morning?"

Molly shook her head. "Not since last night. She slept in her wagon."

Fenna had watched him climb from Ellen's wagon that morning. She raised her brows at Ben, but he didn't have time for propriety. "She was gone before I woke up."

Fenna straightened her back. "We'll spread out. Find her." She set the spatula down and swung the pan out of the coals. "I'll check with the sisters."

Ben's hands started to shake as he stomped barefoot through camp, searching every face for her. But with the violence that had been done to Sam, a bowl-sized ball of lead sank deep in Ben's gut. The longer he searched, the more certain he was that something had happened to her. Soon that small ball of lead had grown and sat heavy in his middle.

He made his way back to camp and when he met Fenna's worried look, he knew they'd had little luck too. He started for Will's tent. Hopefully Sam had made progress.

"Here." Molly thrust a bundle at him, her chin wobbling with an emotion Ben didn't have the capacity to try and interpret.

Ben glanced down at the bundle and back at Molly. "It's her boots."

Ben swallowed, his mouth as dry as a boulder in the sun. He didn't understand anything. Only that everything in him was chanting *wrong*.

He ducked into the tent with Sam and looked at Will. "Has he woken?"

Will shook his head.

"Ellen's missing."

Will's discouraged face lit in shock. "Ellen?"

"I don't know how long. It must have been Cyrus. Maybe he thought Sam was me, maybe he thought to hurt me in another way." Ben shook his head at his lack of answers. "He's taken Ellen."

Will's mouth was grim as he nodded, and Ben bolted to the livestock. When he reached Red, he realized he still had Ellen's boots in his hands. He stuffed them into his saddle bag and saddled Red. If Cyrus had taken her in the night, he would only have a few hours' head start.

Ben was tightening the girth on Red's saddle when Fenna ran over. She passed him a satchel and an oiled slicker.

Helping him into it, she said, "You know where he's going. Keep your head and be smart." She draped the satchel over his head so it hung near his hip. He kissed the top of her head and climbed into the saddle.

He wanted to say something about seeing them soon, but the words died in his throat. "Don't wait for me."

He turned and dug bare heels into Red's flanks. The beast shot off, willing to run after so many days plodding along the trail. Ben hoped the beast had plenty of strength stored; he would need it.

CHAPTER 29

*E*llen's voice was gone. She'd screamed herself so hoarse that her cries were as soft as the mewl of a newborn kitten. If Cyrus heard her, he ignored it.

The sun was higher in the sky, and she estimated it to be about ten in the morning. Chores at camp would be long finished and the company would be on the trail. Everything she'd grown to hold dear, moving farther out of her reach. She shifted her fingers, wincing at the pain in her wrists. She'd struggled against her restraints and now she was paying for it.

If she arched her back and looked up, she could see Cyrus driving the wagon. "Cyrus." She tried with her weakened voice.

A crack split the air and Cyrus turned.

"Cyrus," she tried again, grateful for whatever had happened to the wagon to cause Cyrus to turn. Maybe the wheels were breaking. But Cyrus was a wheelwright and he'd have it fixed too quickly. She hoped it was the axle.

Another crack came and Ellen closed her eyes, content with whatever was going wrong in Cyrus' plan.

But then a gunshot sounded, and Ellen's ears rang. Her eyes flew open to see Cyrus above her, pointing a long-barreled rifle at something behind them.

Ellen lifted her head, tucking her chin into her chest to rake the landscape. The wheels hit a bump, and Ellen's head cracked against the floor of the wagon. Spots appeared in her vision. As soon as they cleared, she raised her head again, trying to catch sight of whatever Cyrus was shooting at.

Cyrus released another volley of bullets and the wagon hit another rut. The ride became so bumpy that Ellen was sure the horses had been frightened off the path. With each jostle, Titus' body shifted closer to Ellen. She tried to push at him, but she was too weak and her position too awkward.

A streak of dark caught her eye and she froze, trying to make out what it was. A rider. Had one of the Bridger brothers come for her? Her heart leapt at the same moment it sank.

"Cyrus!" she tried to scream, but she didn't stand a chance of being heard. Their quiet pace was no longer. The horses pulling the wagon were running and shots were volleying back and forth. Cyrus roared in pain and a dark spot appeared near his waist, growing as the blood seeped through his clothing. He muttered curses as he tried to get a bead on his target rather than staunch the flow of blood.

They hit a bump so great, Ellen's entire body lifted from the bed of the wagon. Unfortunately, so did Titus' and he landed even closer to her side. Ellen came down partially on top of him.

Though shots were still being fired, Ellen couldn't stop herself from crying out and scrambling to a sitting position, crowding into the corner of the wagon. With her head above the sides, she could see the rider. He was a ways off, but she was certain he was atop Fenna's horse Red. It also looked like he wore Ben's hat.

Ellen ducked her head, sinking into herself, wondering which brother had taken it and, along with it, claimed Ben's promise to protect her. Or perhaps they'd only come to avenge their brother. If that was the case, they should be equally angry with Ellen for bringing this cruel man to their doorstep.

Guilt surged within her. She was the reason Ben was dead, the reason one of his own was here now, facing Cyrus' gunfire. The least she could do was repay Ben for his sacrifice.

Ellen sat up again and shifted until her bound feet were underneath her. She waited, unsure whether to wait until after Cyrus' next missed shot, or to go now and risk being shot by either party.

A bullet screamed from Cyrus' gun, and Ellen had her answer. She leaped up and twisted in the air, reaching her tied hands out at Cyrus. She hit his gun but was falling before she knew what good she'd done. She hit the hard earth with a thud that stole her breath. Her head spun with the sudden lack of movement. No more bumping along the road, no more galloping hooves.

She rolled to her side, her mouth working like a fish. Had her body forgotten how to draw a breath? In an instant it was there. She gasped the air, sucking it in like she'd come up from a dive in the lake.

Still coughing, she looked around and spotted Cyrus, speeding away.

Thundering hooves came toward her from the opposite side, and she instinctively curled into a ball, groaning. The slightest movement played pain up and down her ribs. A spray of dirt and small rocks peppered her as the galloping stopped.

She'd not been trampled. Thank the Lord. Ellen opened her eyes and saw legs and, oddly enough, bare feet rushing toward her. The owner leaped over her as more shots were fired. She winced, anticipating the burn of a bullet wound. But the Bridger brother was putting himself between her and Cyrus' shots.

She twisted and crawled on her stomach to latch onto his legs. "Get behind me!" she tried to scream, but he brushed her off. Had he even heard her, or was he merely rejecting her plea? She stayed curled around his legs, one of them kneeling on the ground and the other up. He leaned into it every time he fired a shot. With every shot, tears leaked from Ellen's eyes. Cyrus had killed Ben. What might he still do to this brother?

Eventually, the shots ceased and the brother muttered a curse. He pulled Ellen's tied hands from where they clasped his pant leg.

"Are you alright?"

Her vision blurry, she nodded. Not only did this brother look like Ben, but with her eyes closed he even sounded like Ben. She had never noticed that before. How much the brothers sounded alike. There was so much she hadn't learned about Ben and now he was gone.

Her restraints tightened, but then the binding fell away.

She nodded at her legs. "My feet too."

"Gracious, Ellen. What were you thinking, jumping from a wagon without arms or legs to catch you?"

Even his tone was Ben's. Hope flickered to life and Ellen wiped at her eyes, blinking at the figure above her. "Ben?"

He cut the ties that bound her ankles and clicked his tongue. "I have your shoes in my saddlebag. I passed my own boots discarded on the trail. We'll pick them up on the way back."

Ellen reached up and touched his chin. He flinched away, but she was too unnerved to be shy. She chased him and held his face in her hands, staring into his eyes. "You're alive."

"What?" he said, louder, as though she was the one who hadn't heard.

"You're alive." She strained her voice, attempting to give him more volume.

"Yeah," he said, as though it were the most obvious thing in the world.

"Cyrus said..."

But Ben was up and glaring into the distance. Ellen's ribs cried out as she pressed to sitting, then standing.

Cyrus' wagon was visible only by the dust it made on the road. Ben leaned closer, like he was itching to chase him down.

She touched his sleeve. "You aren't going after him, are you?"

He turned his sharp gaze on her. "If I had two horses, you can be certain I would."

Ellen touched his arm, his shoulder. She couldn't stop herself making sure he was really there. "I thought you were dead."

Ben strode away, out of her reach, and she followed painfully. When she arrived at the horse, Ben was eying her with concern. "Can you ride?"

What other choice was there? "Yes."

He held the stirrup in place, and she gripped the saddle and lifted her leg, but pain streaked across her torso like lightning and she cried out.

Ben pressed a hand into her back. "What is it?"

"My ribs." Ellen wanted to sink down and hide in the grass until her ribs were healed. She wanted Ben to stay with her. They could make a home right here of rocks and dirt.

He caught her face and surveyed it with such fear, Ellen's mind emptied of all words. "Can you breathe alright?"

Ellen sucked in a breath. It hurt, but her body seemed to be holding the air properly. She nodded.

"I'll get up first and pull you on." He caught her gaze. "It's not going to feel good."

If it hurt to breathe, she didn't doubt his words.

Ben climbed on, then Ellen forced herself to turn around while Ben stuck his hands under her arms and hauled her up. She wanted to cry out, but her lungs must have been busy, and her voice didn't have a mind to lend a hand either.

He set her on the saddle in front of him. "You'll need to swing your leg over."

Ellen slumped against his chest and shook her head. It hurt too bad to attempt anything else.

"Okay," he said into her hair, his words heating her scalp and healing her heart.

Ben turned the horse away from Cyrus, and Ellen got a crawly feeling. She didn't want to have her back to that man. "How do you know he won't come for us?"

"He tried to murder my brother. If I see him again, I'll kill him."

Ellen thought of the blood that had colored Cyrus' shirt. "You hit him. He's injured."

"If he has any brains, he won't come after me while he's wounded."

Ellen blinked, Ben's earlier words registering. "Wait. Who did he try to murder?"

The horse started walking and Ellen had to focus on breathing through the pain that hit her with every step. But with that concentration came realization. Cyrus hadn't killed Ben, but he'd harmed one of his brothers.

Through gritted teeth she asked, "Who?"

There was a moment's pause, then Ben said, "Sam."

Ellen sucked in a breath, holding tight to the pain as she imagined Sam's suffering. It wasn't until that moment that she realized, besides Ben, Sam was her favorite. That she would have felt awful to hear of any brother being harmed. But Sam... "I'm so sorry."

"You have nothing to apologize for. I believe Cyrus thought he was me."

"You two are the most similar." Sam was a younger, blue-eyed, carefree version of Ben.

Silence fell and, after a time, the night's events caught up to her. Though her side was still pulsing with pain, she was safe in Ben's arms, so she drifted into a dreamless sleep.

When she woke, she was somehow more fatigued. "Do we have to go all the way to Oregon?"

Ben laughed and rested his chin on her head. "You can stop whenever you'd like."

"I'd like to stop now," she said, though she knew he meant stopping her wagon and setting up her life.

Ben slowed the horse to a halt. "Do you need a break?"

Ellen sighed at the cessation of movement on her pained ribs. She reached a hand and gingerly fingered her ribs, finding the two that felt the worst. They needed to continue, to catch the company, but she wanted nothing more than to be still. "Just a little one."

She drew a deep inhale and regretted it immediately. Closing her eyes, she basked in the stillness, only for her mind to take in just how unstill she really was. Her own ribs moved with each shallow breath she took, but at her back, Ben's chest rose and fell with his breathing. Then, under her legs, which were still to one side, the horse breathed.

If she listened, she could also hear the prairie breathing beneath all of them, drawing in the water that had fallen last night and leaving some of it in pools to share with the flora and fauna. The air was still heavy with the dew the morning sun hadn't yet burned away.

Ben's arms loosened as he relaxed his hold on the reins. Where they no longer touched, her skin chilled in an instant.

Her clothing was damp from the rain and the sudden iciness made her shudder.

"I'm cold without you," she whispered, not because her voice wouldn't allow it, but because she'd used all her courage just saying the words at all.

Ben moved farther away, taking away her backrest. She opened her mouth to protest, but he was removing his slicker.

He tried to drape it over her shoulders, but there wasn't enough room. So he slid off the horse and, with his boots on the ground, arranged it around her shoulders. "Without me so close, can you swing your other leg? I can help."

His words were so tender, such a contrast to how he usually spoke to her. She couldn't stop the smile that lifted the side of her mouth. If she'd known he was just a knight who wanted to save a princess, she might have gotten herself burned by the dragon long ago.

Her smile fell as Ben moved closer, intent on correcting her seat on the horse. With one hand supporting her neck and shoulders, his other hand on her foot, they managed to center her on the saddle. Though the effort pained her, once it was done, her muscles sang at the new, easier position.

"I can walk for a bit if you'd rather have the seat to yourself for a while." He adjusted the slicker around both her legs. It was made of oiled leather and was meant more for shelter from the rain than for warmth, but the gesture remained. He still wanted to care for her. She couldn't help but wonder just how long he would offer this protection to her.

Ellen reached out a hand to him. "I need your support."

He sighed and climbed onto the horse. It was impossible to tell if his exhale was one of frustration or relief.

If she chose to go all the way to Oregon and park her wagon on his plot of land, would he sigh and let her? If she made herself at home in his kitchen once it was built, would he nod and thank her for the grub? If she put herself to bed on his mattress, would he bother with a divider?

She turned her head to press her ear against the bare skin above his collar. She closed her eyes, thankful for the warmth he shared now and content not to press for more.

Not yet.

CHAPTER 30

Ben tightened his hold on the reins as he felt the cold of her ear press into the hollow at the base of his neck. He wanted to pull her closer, but he feared hurting her. He wanted to beg her to stay with him, but just as he couldn't provide warmth for her now, the fact remained that he had nothing to offer her once they reached Oregon.

They rode until nightfall, but Ben wondered if Ellen would be able to sleep with how much she'd slept throughout the day. He cherished those minutes when her exhales grew heavy and she sank deeper into him. But then her head lolled and she woke, straightening and moving away, just slightly, her message clear. She couldn't relax around him, not the way he wanted her to.

They reached a stream, and Ben stopped to water Red. He climbed off, stretching his back. With Ellen leaning against him all day, his muscles were working harder than usual.

Ellen started to climb down, wincing with the movement, but she needed to stretch just as badly as he did. He stepped close and helped her, careful to avoid all her ribs, the very place he wanted to touch her most.

"Do you want to stop for the night?" He set her down on the prairie grass. They really should keep going. If they stopped, it would only take them longer to join the company and the safety numbers offered. But Ellen was injured, and he'd already pushed her to her limit by putting her on a horse all day.

"Does the horse need a break?" she croaked, her voice barely above a whisper.

Ben patted Red on the rump. "He's doing just fine."

Ellen reached her hand and twirled a bit of Red's mane. "Can Will fix my ribs?"

Ben swallowed, grief for her pain swirling within him and clogging his throat. Mixed in was worry over Sam. What would they find when they returned? Was his brother alive?

"He'll be able to help." Even if it was just offering a tonic to soothe the pain.

"Then let's keep going."

Ben adjusted the blanket on Red's back. "If you stop before Oregon, where do you want to make your life?"

Ellen was silent for a long moment. He listened to her breathing, a noise he was growing quite familiar with. She was considering his question. He cursed himself for not speaking the words he should have said. They repeated in his head: *I'll stop wherever you stop.* But she felt indebted to him, and he wouldn't ask her to pay any more than she was willing to give.

Yet selfishness rose inside him, a diamondback serpent weaving its way through the grass and threatening to strike any threat. Ellen telling him she was leaving him forever was the most frightening threat of all.

"Don't leave me."

"I want to stay with your family."

They spoke at the same time, and Ellen stopped, twisting to look up, then wincing at the movement.

Ben's heart thumped against his ribs, chastising him for his moment of bravery.

"You"—Ellen cleared her hoarse throat—"want me to stay?"

"I don't want you to leave." He said it as though the two things weren't the same, and Ellen's face fell. He stepped closer, anxious to calm her worries. Likely the same worries that Jane had felt, that Ben didn't truly love her. He would not allow Ellen to feel the same—she meant too much to him.

"I know I don't have much. I'm not asking you to commit to me, forever or anything. I just... if it would make you happy, I'd love for you to stay near my family." He swallowed. "And myself."

Ellen stepped closer and took his face in her hands with the same strength she'd shown when he'd first found her on the ground and she'd been unsure if the man protecting her was really him. "Do you want me to stay with you?"

"Of course." He considered glossing over his wants, pretending that it was for his family's sake. But he couldn't lie to her, not after the way he'd rode Red so hard trying to find her. If she hadn't been too injured to stand, he would have swept her into his arms right then.

She squinted at him, as if he were one of Molly's books and she needed to reread a passage. "Do you love me, Benjamin Bridger?"

He let out a shaky laugh. There was that bold woman again. The woman he thought was a burr in his boot, but here she was, using her bare feet to trample his defenses, and he couldn't be more grateful. "I do."

She didn't smile, but continued to look at him with a wariness that frustrated him. Were words not enough for her? He knocked her hands away and caught the back of her head in his palm. He stepped closer, snaking one arm low on her hips, giving her pained ribs ample space.

She let her head rest in his hand and submitted easily when he angled her chin up toward his. He lowered his mouth to hers, feeling the warmth of her breath tickle his lips as he spoke. "Do you think I am pretending?" He made a show of looking around them. "There is nobody to pretend for, my dear."

She smiled at the oft-used term of endearment. Her gaze flicked to his lips and he felt a surge of joy. She wanted him. But he'd been wanted before. A moment wasn't enough. He wanted forever. "Will you be my wife by law? Share my tent for love? Let me drive your oxen?"

She barked a laugh, then whimpered, gripping her side. She lifted her eyes to meet his gaze once more and nodded.

"Is that a yes?"

"Say you love me, Benjamin Bridger, and I will say yes."

"I love you." He pressed his mouth to hers. At first, the swiftness brought with it the memory of that first kiss, the one the crowd had pressured them into. But instead of pulling away, Ellen leaned closer, her breath coming out in a soft sigh.

Ben submitted himself to the warmth of her lips. How many times had he imagined this, how many mornings had he woken up with her body pressed against his, her eyes still closed in something that looked like surrender? But now she was awake and allowing him to consume her. He realized his imagination was as weak as Molly's stew. It had no depth, it was nothing compared to what simmered inside him now.

Her lips moved against his, exploring with a familiarity that didn't belong to a first real kiss. A familiarity that belonged to both something new and something forever. It was a kiss that called every bluff, every ruse, and every denial.

"I love you," he said again, against her lips.

"Yes." She finally gave her answer, and he covered her mouth with his once more.

EPILOGUE

*E*llen placed one hand in Ben's and rested the other on his shoulder. They danced in slow circles, much like they'd done during their fake wedding celebration. But, this time, there was no music and they were alone. Ben had rented them a room from a soldier at Fort Kearney and, for the first time in months, Ellen slept with walls around her and a roof overhead.

She was still in her dress, lent to her by Molly for the ceremony. She lifted a suspicious eye to Ben. "Was the preacher drunk?"

"I sobered him up the best I could."

Ellen laughed. Everything was different on the trail. How much more had yet to change with each turn of their wagon wheels? Could it have been just over a month ago that she'd sworn another husband would only bring her grief?

She laid her head on his shoulder, breathing deep. Her ribs were healed, and Sam was up and about once more. For a time, Petra had been his unwilling companion in the sick wagon, and though Ellen should be glad that he had someone to change his dressings, she didn't like the way he stared after her, nor the way Petra ignored his attention. That woman had broken her share of hearts. Seeing Sam gray and bloody had been awful enough that Ellen wasn't inclined to see his heart bruised too.

Ellen looked up at Ben. "Who was that man with Fox?"

"Said his name was Bear." He pulled away to look her in the eyes. "Do all the mountain men have animal names? Ought I to get one myself?"

"Is he joining the company?" Heaven knew they could use a few more men who knew the trail and that man, in his rawhide garb, looked to be plenty knowledgeable.

"I didn't ask. I was preoccupied, if you didn't notice." He slid his arms tighter around her, swaying though there was no music to move them. "Now tell me, what would my animal name be?"

Ellen laughed. "Maybe Badger. Aren't they cross with trespassers?"

Ben pulled away, eying her with a half-smile. "I seem to remember allowing a certain stowaway to stick around."

Ellen sobered. "Thank you." The words would never be enough to show her true gratitude.

Ben scoffed, but Ellen took both her hands and held his face between them. "I mean it. You saved me."

"I think you would have done alright if I hadn't come around."

Ellen dropped her hands and shook her head. Ben caught her chin. It was his turn to be serious. "Ellen, you are the strongest woman I know. You have endured more than you let on, and still you are kind and thoughtful of those around you."

Ellen's throat grew thick. Not until this moment did she realize she'd tried to be all those things. Hearing him confirm that she succeeded, at least in his eyes, meant more than she could find the words for.

He lifted her face to his and dipped down, kissing her thoroughly. As his lips moved over hers, she wondered how many women there were in the world living without this. Living like she had before, with husbands that took but never gave. With that, she wondered how she'd been lucky enough to find herself one of those rare wild horses who promised to run by her side for the rest of his days.

Sam promised to find himself a wife. Petra is seeking a husband for her dear sister. Their causes would line up perfectly, if it weren't for the bet… Get your copy of *Wagering for a Wife* and see which one of them will be victorious.

ALSO BY KATE CONDIE

<u>Aster Ridge Ranch</u>

Ticket to Anywhere

A Winter's Vow

A Cowboy's Vow

A Widow's Vow

A Bandit's Vow

A Secret Brother's Vow

A Christmas Vow

A Soldier's Vow

<u>Bridger Brothers</u>

To Win His Wife

To Bluff a Bride

Wagering for a Wife

Want free content and more from Kate Condie? Sign up for her newsletter at www.subscribepage.com/katecondienewsletter or follow her on social media @authorkatecondie

AUTHOR'S NOTES

As I gathered information on the Oregon Trail, one resource has been especially beneficial: a book called *The Prairie Traveler* by Randolph B. Marcy. The book was written as an aid to those preparing for the journey west. In it, Marcy details what items a traveler would need to pack, down to the number of socks.

Marcy advises that every man should be armed, but he also highlights the dangerous truth that many of the pioneers did not understand proper gun safety. The instance I write about where Titus pulls at his rifle and accidentally discharges the weapon was actually a very likely circumstance. Marcy calls this ignorant habit of pointing the barrel at oneself a "…source of many sad and fatal accidents…"

Learning about history through fiction is one of my very favorite things. I hope you enjoyed your foray into the Oregon trail, and if you're anything like me, we can all close the book and appreciate clean hands, refrigerators and flushing toilets.

ACKNOWLEDGMENTS

Always a huge thank you to my family and especially my dear hubby who keeps the kids at bay when there is work to be done. You are the heart to my stories and living life with you grants me endless inspiration.

Thank you to Michelle, my eternal sounding board. You have prevented multiple burnouts.

And to my fabulous editors, Jo Perry, Whitney Jones, Karie Crawford and Beth Hale. You are a huge support and make my words shine.

Finally, thank *you,* dear reader, for allowing me an outlet for my stories. Thank you for loving my books, for reviewing them, for sending me the kindest messages. You make this all possible.

ABOUT THE AUTHOR

Kate Condie is a speed talker from Oregon. Reading has been part of her life since childhood, where she devoured everything from mysteries, to classics, to nonfiction—and of course, romance. At first, her writing was purely journal format as she thought writing novels was for the lucky ones. She lives in Utah and spends her days surrounded by mountains with her favorite hunk, their four children and her laptop. In her free time she reads, tries to learn a host of new instruments, binge watches anything by BBC and tries to keep up with Lafayette as she sings the Hamilton soundtrack.

Made in United States
Troutdale, OR
01/05/2025